...by a combination
...gination, meticulous concern for the
...the wit to harness the two constructively'
Interzone

...mes Lovegrove's sharply observed details have the author-
...ty of good science fiction' *Times Literary Supplement*

...ovegrove has a superb and subtle eye for character detail'
Infinity Plus

...ovegrove's style is clever and literate' *SFX*

Imagined Slights

JAMES LOVEGROVE

The right of James Lovegrove to be identified as the
author of this work has been asserted by him in accordance
with the Copyright, Designs and Patents Act 1988.

This edition first published in Great Britain in 2002 by

Gollancz
An imprint of the Orion Publishing Group
Orion House, 5 Upper St Martin's Lane
London WC2H 9EA

A CIP catalogue record for this book
is available from the British Library

ISBN 1 85798 801 9

Typeset at The Spartan Press Ltd,
Lymington, Hants

Printed in Great Britain by
The Guernsey Press Co. Ltd, Guernsey, C.I.

Contents of Imagined Slights

(expressed in the form of a pie chart)

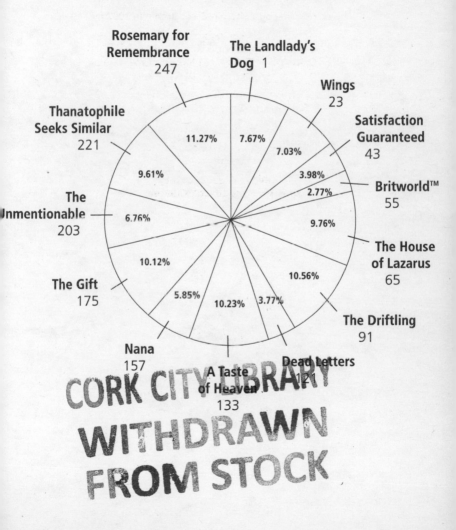

Rosemary for
Remembrance
247

The Landlady's
Dog 1

Wings
23

Satisfaction
Guaranteed
43

Thanatophile
Seeks Similar
221

Britworld™
55

The
Unmentionable
203

The House
of Lazarus
65

The Gift
175

The Driftling
91

Nana
157

Dead Letters
121

A Taste
of Heaven
133

11.27% 7.67%

7.03%

3.98%

2.77%

9.61%

9.76%

6.76%

10.12%

10.56%

5.85%

10.23% 3.77%

For P.C.

The Landlady's Dog

'What do you believe in?' she asked.

'I believe in love,' I replied, hopefully.

She rewarded me with the sweetest, most forgiving smile on Planet Earth. A smile saints would have died martyrs for. A smile to make the angels weep over their harps.

'No, but what do you *believe* in?'

'I don't know,' I said, after some thought. 'Do you mean God?'

If she meant God, we were certainly parked in the right place. The windscreen framed a view that would have persuaded a hardened atheist to reconsider the options. The sinking sun, determined not to go down without a fight, was throwing out beacons and distress flares in every direction. The sea was a vast ruby and the brisk October wind made its million facets scintillate. Along the line of the horizon a liner slid with the flat and stately grace of a tin duck in a fairground shooting gallery. On the grass nearby two seagulls were squabbling over the corpse of a baby rabbit. It was one of those scenes of grandeur and bathos that only God can pull off with such aplomb (but then He does have an unlimited budget).

'No,' she said. 'I mean, yes. Yes, that sort of thing, but not that. That doesn't count. No, what I'm trying to say is, what is your guiding principle?'

'My guiding principle,' I echoed. I had no idea where this conversation was going but I dared to hope it was heading in the direction I wanted it to. I dared to hope that Julia knew why I had been a tongue-tied geek all evening and why I had 'suddenly decided' to drive us up here rather than to the cinema as we had planned and why I was so nervous that I had slammed on the accelerator instead of the brake as we drew up to the clifftop, nearly sending my clapped-out old Ford Fiesta hurtling over the edge, and us with it. I dared to hope that her X-ray vision had penetrated my jacket pocket and found the small box nestling there, and had pierced through its inner layers of tissue paper and velvet to find the glittering prize within. I dared to hope that I wouldn't have to go through with the whole heart-stopping procedure but that she would any moment now simply say *Yes* or *I will* or *I do* and bring the agony to an end.

The trouble with Julia was that there was just no telling.

'My guiding principle,' I reiterated, wondering if I could twist this around to suit what I had to say, and deciding I couldn't. 'Help old ladies across the road, be nice to dumb animals and always wash behind my ears.' I shrugged. 'That's me, the product of a middle-class upbringing.'

Again that smile.

'Will you . . . ?' I said, then stopped. So close, so damn close, and then someone thrust an iron bar down my throat.

'Will I?'

'Explain.' There would be another chance, I was certain.

'Explain?'

'What the hell you're getting at.'

'What I'm getting at' – and she turned to face the sunset and her skin suddenly glowed mellow red – 'is that I like you, Philip. A lot. You're funny and charming and thoughtful and considerate and good-looking and you haven't got too much money and you're not a rampant egomaniac and we have a laugh together and we're friends and . . .'

For a sentence with so many *ands* in it, it carried an awful lot of *but*. I grinned anyway, slightly desperately, and said, 'I never knew that not having too much money was one of my good points.'

'Definitely. Rich men are wankers.'

'Yes, but they can afford to be.'

'I'm glad we didn't go to the film,' she said. 'I'm glad we came up here instead. I've been meaning to say this for a while but I haven't had the opportunity. I value the time we've had together.'

'Hang on, haven't you missed something out?' I said, taking a firm grip on the steering wheel.

'What?'

'Between "I haven't had the opportunity" and "I value the time we've had together".'

'I've been doing a lot of thinking lately.'

'You want to watch out for that. That's dangerous, that is.'

Rightly, she ignored me. 'There's no one else. I want to make that clear. This is all me, all my idea.'

'Well, please don't keep me in suspense any longer, Julia.'

'I'm trying to be gentle.'

'Gentle?' I could hold back the tears but I couldn't keep the damning, unmanning sob out of my voice. 'Gentle? About as gentle as a fucking crowbar!'

'Philip!'

'What about me? What about *me*?' I swear I felt the steering wheel begin to creak and bend in my hands.

'OK, I'll tell you about you. You asked me. I'll tell you. You're not a real person, Philip. You're a collection of jokes and mannerisms and one-liners, and that's all very well and fine as it goes, but there's nothing more. There's nothing inside you. You're a shell. You're hollow. There's nothing that drives you or animates you or inspires you or motivates you. You're the sum total of other people's impressions of you.' She ran a hand down the side of her face. 'I'm sorry. I never intended to say any of this.'

'Perhaps it's just as well you did.' After all, it had all the hallmarks of a deeply considered, well-rehearsed speech; it would have been a shame to let it go to waste.

'Take me home, please.'

5

I started the car and thought seriously about shifting into first instead of reverse and doing deliberately what I'd almost done accidentally before, propelling us through the flimsy fence and over the edge to plummet in a hail of broken chalk and earn us a noun-rich headline epitaph: *Young Couple In Love Pact Car Death Plunge Terror.*

But I didn't. And as we drove down the narrow, winding road, Julia staring out of the passenger-side window at the lees of the day, I found myself thanking God that I'd had the foresight not to throw away the receipt for the engagement ring.

Of course I was embarrassed and humiliated and hurt and shocked and frustrated and angry and indignant and staggered and uncomprehending and incredulous and dazed and riddled with self-doubt and all the other things a man is supposed to be when a girl gives him the elbow. Of course I was. But I was also strangely, furtively relieved. As if I had never really intended to go through with it. As if I had chosen Julia to propose to because she was the best candidate for the job, not the woman I wanted to spent the rest of my life with but the woman I thought least likely to walk out over disagreements about pay and salary and hours. Already I was planning how I would pop down to the jeweller's shop tomorrow and hand back the ring and say something self-effacing and humorous like, 'Right idea, wrong woman' and accept a credit note in lieu of a refund even if I had no idea what the hell I was going to spend it on at that tawdry junk-merchant's.

Outside her house she leaned across the handbrake and brushed her lips against my cheek.

'Just tell me there's no chance,' I said, not looking at her.

'There's no chance.'

'But say it as if you mean it.'

'There's no chance. I'm sorry. I'd like to think we could still, you know, see each other from time to time. I'd hate to think this was it.'

'That's up to you.'

6

'We could still go to the cinema together.'

'I hear they're showing *The Untouchables*.'

She drew back. 'Is that supposed to be a joke?'

'How would I know?'

She opened the door. 'I'll call you soon. I promise.'

'Great. I'll sit at home waiting. I won't eat and I won't sleep.'

She slid out. 'Goodnight, Philip.'

'Yeah. 'Night.'

It was just dark as I let myself in through the front door of the boarding house. The hallway was hung with gloom, and the mutter of televisions and radios and pianissimo strains of music drifted down the stairwell. Mercifully the door to Mrs Konwicki's flat was closed, and I tiptoed past. I had one foot on the first riser of the first flight of stairs when her dog Lech started barking. He had a deep voice and punished the air with it. I scampered to the top of the flight, and then the devil took me and I leaned down and, putting on a queer, strangulated voice, shouted, 'Shut that fucking rabid syphilitic fleabag the fuck up!' Then I fled further upstairs.

Mrs Konwicki's door opened. The hall light flicked on and she yelled up after my fleeing footsteps, 'Who's that?'

Second floor, third floor . . .

'I know who that is! Don't think I don't recognise your voice because I do.'

Fourth, fifth . . .

'I know who you are!'

I reached the door to my flat just as Mr Fleming, who lived on the second floor, came out to bawl at everyone to be quiet, shouting and running around like that, some people worked for a living, didn't you know? Someone else yelled at him to keep it down, and then Mrs Konwicki informed them both that this was a private argument between her and that idiot up there – and she knew who it was – so if they didn't mind, they could stop sticking their noses where they didn't belong.

7

Soon there were tenants out on every landing, all protesting their right to peace and quiet at the tops of their voices. The dog syncopated the whole cacophony with loud unabated rowfs.

I slipped into my flat, quietly, childishly gratified.

The next morning there was a knock at the door. I staggered blinking away from the word processor, hitting Save as I went. It was Mrs Konwicki. Lech squatted at her heels, peering up at me with a frank, unintelligible expression. He was black and bony-big and lumpish, of no discernible pedigree, a knot of sinew bound up tightly in the shape of a dog. Looking at him I felt that if I patted his head, I had an equal chance of gaining a friend or losing a hand.

I smiled, and Mrs Konwicki smiled back at me, and I smiled back harder at her and thought, *I'm in trouble, she's brought the dog, I'm in trouble.*

'May I come in?'

'It's your house, Mrs K. You can do what you like.' I stepped back and ushered her into my humble abode with a theatrical flourish.

'May Lech come in too?'

'If he likes.'

Lech liked. He pattered in after his mistress and made a quick sweep of the room, checking for strange scents, of which there were plenty, before settling down in one corner and busying his huge slow tongue in his crotch. I was reminded of a joke: why does a dog lick its balls? Because it can.

I smiled harder than ever.

'Coffee?'

'You're very kind. As black and sweet as you can make it.' She lowered herself into a chair.

'Taste of the old country, eh, Mrs K?'

'No coffee tastes like coffee from the old country.'

'Bit of a rumpus last night,' I understated as I handed her a

8

steaming cup of instant, which not only didn't taste like coffee from the old country but didn't taste like coffee from *any* country.

She sipped, squinted and sneered. 'That Mr Vowel-broke . . .'

Mrs Konwicki's accent was normally so faint it would have taken an expert to trace its origins, but when it came to English names she seemed to suffer a mental relapse and would mangle them with rich guttural abandon. (Perhaps it was her revenge for all the 'Conwikkies' that had been inflicted upon her.) Hence Mr Walbrook – who occupied the flat below mine – became Mr Vowelbroke.

'What's he done now?'

'What's he done? He started it, didn't he? Calling poor Lech those dreadful names.'

'Mr Walbrook?' Who was as quiet as a mouse, not to mention as grey and timid and innocuous.

'Well, who else could it be? It certainly wasn't you.'

'Absolutely not,' I said quickly. 'I'm very fond of Lech.'

I glanced at the dog and he looked back at me with eyes that, while doleful and wet with mucus, seemed to convey great depths of canine knowing.

'I'll see to him,' she muttered, and said no more about it.

We chatted idly for a while, and I could see her gearing herself up to say what she had really climbed five flights of stairs to say. Finally she came out with it.

'How is Jewelear?'

'Julia's fine. Why do you ask?'

'You went out with her last night. How was it?'

'OK,' I said. 'Well, not OK. She wasn't feeling very well, so I dropped her off back at her house.'

'Oh,' said Mrs Konwicki. A long, drawn-out, significant 'Oh'.

'Exactly,' I said.

'You two make such a good couple. I don't say this about just anyone, you know, but you two seem to fit together like two halves of a whole. I have hopes that she might be the girl for you, I mean *the* girl for you. Of course I'm not saying you should get married. I'm not that old-fashioned. Nowadays people live together first, don't they? It would be nice to have her living here.'

By rights, the dramatic irony should have been twisting a dagger in my heart, but I was calm, I was cool, I was fine. I used to know someone who went around pubs betting people he could stub out a cigarette on the back of his hand. He had a patch of skin at the join between thumb and forefinger which had been left numb by an accident or an operation or something. He could make anything up to twenty quid a night this way, depending on the drunkenness and gullibility of the clientele. He had to give up eventually, though, when too much scar tissue built up and it looked as if he had spotted his hand with candle-wax.

I had a numb patch in the shape of Julia and I could have stubbed cigarettes out on it all day long and never felt a thing.

'I don't think I'm quite ready,' I told her.

'No one ever is, Feelhip. I know I wasn't. I hadn't even kissed Hubert before he proposed to me. I had barely looked at him. I didn't know his name. He came up to me at a village dance and said, "Will you marry me?", and when I said no, he said, "How about a dance then?" How could I refuse? And at the end of the dance, as we tried to disentangle our hands but somehow couldn't, he asked me again and I said yes.'

If there is a household god for would-be-weds, there to ensure that embryonic proposals are not aborted, I wondered what the hell I'd done to offend the bastard.

'That's lovely,' I said.

'Lovely? I suppose so.'

'I mean, you realised then and there that this was the man for you.'

'Oh no, I didn't realise. I had a feeling, that's all, a feeling that if I didn't say yes then, I would never have another chance. You only get second chances in fairy tales.'

10

'And slushy movies.'

'It turned out to be the right decision. Hubert took me away from Poland just before the Nazis moved in. He saw it coming. He was a very . . . *aware* man, Hubert. Anyway,' she said, slapping her hands on the armrests, 'you must be busy and I can't sit here all day wasting your time. Lech!'

I nodded. I had three articles stacked like jumbo jets, circling over the deadline, gradually losing altitude. Although it's the perceived wisdom that you should throw yourself into your work when you have something to forget, I had nothing worth forgetting, so I had no more than the usual vague stirring of enthusiasm for my work. The articles would get written, but no sooner or quicker than expected.

I showed Mrs Konwicki to the door and was brave enough to run my hands along Lech's back as he padded past me after her. I don't think he noticed.

'If there's anything you want,' she said, 'anything that needs doing, you know of course that you can just ask me.' It was obvious she was talking about something more than a blocked drain or a stuck window or the hot water not coming through. I thanked her, closed the door . . .

. . . and did a little soft-shoe shuffle across the carpet and punched the air a couple of times and wondered at the miracle of plausibility that had convinced Mrs Konwicki that it was wee, sleekit, cow'rin', tim'rous Mr Walbrook who had called her dog a fucking rabid syphilitic fleabag, and not me.

Oh, I was so slippery, shit didn't stick.

The day after that, Mr Walbrook fell ill. I heard his groans coming up through the floorboards, and when I didn't receive a coherent answer to my knocking and enquiring, I called an ambulance. Mrs Konwicki supplied the master key. The ambulancemen negotiated and manhandled Mr Walbrook down four flights of stairs strapped to a stretcher. Peritonitis was the pop diagnosis.

It sent a frisson of excitement through the building. Any

event that involved suffering or sexual subterfuge did. We were that kind of building, those kind of tenants.

She tried, but Mrs Konwicki couldn't keep her nose out of my affairs. She noted the absence of Julia passing through her hallway, Julia always saying hello if the door to Mrs Konwicki's flat was open before trotting upstairs to see me. The lie about her being ill had allayed Mrs Konwicki's suspicions, but it was only a lie and lies have a very short shelf-life. A few days after Julia gave me the old heave-ho, she collared me as I was on my way out to the newspaper offices to file my three articles. I had them in a leather slipcase under my arm: one a story on the progress of the county hospital's scanner appeal, one a report on the state of sea pollution in the area, and one a film review. (At the *Weekly Herald and Advertiser* you couldn't afford to be too eclectic.) She all but dragged me into her flat. She was not a big person but her grip was extraordinarily powerful; so much strength compacted into such a slender arm.

'Sit down, Feelhip.'

'Mrs K, I'm in a bit of a hurry,' I protested, but had I really been in a hurry I would have said I was late for something. Deadline was this evening, half a day away. I sat down. Mrs Konwicki's chairs were much like the chairs in my flat – oversprung, understuffed, floral-patterned, dating from circa 1950 – but they were in better condition. Naturally everything in the room reeked of dog: dog fur, dog food, dog breath, dog. The source of the smell lay sprawled in his wicker basket, his muzzle resting on the rim, one eyebrow cocked – staring at me.

'What's happened?' she said.

'What's happened where?'

'With Jewelear. What's happened with Jewelear? Where is she? Why hasn't she been over? What have you done to her? What have you said?'

'Shouldn't you be shining a lamp in my face?'

'No jokes, Feelhip. The truth.'

Not my forte, the truth, but I did my best. 'OK. We came to a parting of the ways. One of those things. Happens to everyone. Very friendly. I'm sure we'll stay in touch. Sad.'

Mrs Konwicki mulled over this information, frowning, then said, 'That's a shame.'

'Oh yes,' I said, nodding avidly.

'Nothing you did or said? You can be very abrasive at times, Feelhip, just as you can be very charming.'

'Why does everyone automatically assume something's my fault?'

'Is it permanent, do you think?'

I took a deep breath. 'I think it is.'

'Do you have any intention of seeing her again?'

'None at all.'

'Pity.' She moved to the window, which was scrupulously net-curtained, and gazed out. I imagine she spent most of her time like this, looking out on the front porch, keeping a caring but careful eye on the comings and goings of her tenants, thinking it her right as well as her duty. Her spine was straight and her shoulders had no hunch to them and her dark hair showed only traces of white, like seams of silver in a mine. From behind, you could have lopped twenty years off her age and still felt you were doing her an injustice. But the skin beneath her eyes gave her away: it was napped and creased and a delicate shade of grey from decades of gazing. The eyes themselves had stayed bright and clear. Any fool could tell that she had been ravishingly beautiful in her youth. She still was – in a faded, wilted sort of way.

Lech gave a whistling whine and sank his head down on to his paws.

'Nothing is permanent,' said Mrs Konwicki without turning round. 'Do you love her?'

Now why hadn't I asked myself that question? 'I suppose it would be hard not to, under the circumstances.'

'None of that, Feelhip. A simple yes or no. It's very important.'

13

A long, long pause for thought. 'Yes.'

'Good. And do you want her back?'

'Why not?'

'Then I think I can help you.'

'Oh please don't try and talk to her,' I begged. 'Think how it'll look. It'll look like I asked you to be an ambassador.'

'You'll do the talking, Feelhip. First, you're going to have to invite her over to dinner.'

'That won't work. She's tasted my cooking.'

'She'll come if you ask her properly.'

'Tell her I've brought in outside caterers?'

'Be calm. Be friendly. Don't beg.'

'And she comes over and what happens?'

Now Mrs Konwicki turned. Now she fixed me with her old bright eyes, and the daylight, softened by the net curtains, glowed in a golden nimbus around her head.

'I will give you something,' she said. 'I will give you something which you will put in her food. Something that will help change her mind.'

'Like a love potion, right?'

'Yes, a little like that.'

I couldn't help myself. I snorted explosively and cried, 'Oh God!' and fired off a volley of raucous guffaws and slapped my thigh a couple of times and tried to squeeze out a few tears for good measure. 'Oh, Mrs K, be serious!'

She wasn't offended. She had been here before. 'I *am* serious, Feelhip,' she said, seriously. 'My husband, as I believe I said the other day, was a very aware man. That's to say, open-minded. He knew things. He knew things before they happened and sometimes he could influence things to happen the way he wanted. I often wonder if he didn't do this to me at the village dance. Wore a special sort of fragrance, or put something on his hands.'

'Sort of like an aphrodisiac aftershave. Jesus, why didn't he market it? He'd have made a fortune.'

'There was a woman in our village who could charm warts

away but she never took money for it. A loaf of bread, maybe, or an egg or two, but never money. It wouldn't work if she took money. That's the way of . . .' She hesitated.

'What were you going to say?'

'I was going to say magic, but it isn't magic. It used to be magic, perhaps, but now it's merely a set of rules to be followed. Like a recipe.'

'Well, frankly, Mrs K, in the opinion of this hard-nosed journalist it all sounds a bit far-fetched.' And I should know. I had made up enough far-fetched stories in my time.

'You want proof? Eh? You want proof? What about Mr Vowelbroke?'

'He's going to be discharged next week, someone told me. Mr Fleming.'

'But I said I would see to him, didn't I? And I did.'

'His appendix burst.'

She put on the sort of expression people use when they hear the authorised version of events and know better. 'I gave Mr Vowelbroke a bottle of milk. I told him the milkman had delivered one too many and I wouldn't be able to drink it before the sell-by date. He was very grateful. He didn't seem to mind that the cap had been punctured. I told him sparrows had done it.'

And all of a sudden I pictured, with awful clarity, Mr Walbrook accepting the bottle of milk, ever so humble, ever so grateful, come in handy, you're much too kind, Mrs Conwikky, and then pouring it over his corn flakes or in his tea, innocent white milk just like what the milkman delivers every day, and an hour later, hey presto, a bit of a gippy tum that develops into a nasty stomach cramp that becomes a sharp, creasing, debilitating agony, and next thing he knows he's being grappled downstairs like some awkward piece of furniture, his face slick with sweat and ghastly livid, groaning. And he didn't even know what he had done wrong. He hadn't done *anything* wrong. And there but for the grace of God . . .

It could have been me. It could have been *me*.

I hauled myself trembling out of the chair. 'Look, I've really got to go. I'm going to be late.'

'Think about what I'm offering you, Feelhip. I'm offering you a second chance. Think about it. Think about what you have to lose and what you might gain.'

I was backing out of the door, nodding madly, saying yes, saying I would, saying anything.

'Jewelear!' she said, stalking after me.

'Jewelear!' as I staggered down the hallway.

'Jewelear!' as I crashed through the front door and stumbled down the steps.

'Jewel—'

The thick door thumped shut on its spring and I was left with the cool sigh of wind and the rumble of traffic and Julia's name ringing in my ears.

I wandered like a mad and lonely cloud through town, through the straggling crowds of late-season holidaymakers grimly enjoying the last of the sunshine, through the streets of sale-shops and closing-downs, making my way down to the seafront, slithering down a set of briny concrete steps, crunching over pebbles down to the waterline, there hunkering down on my haunches and letting the waves throw themselves down at my toecaps and fall short and suck themselves back with a hiss and a seethe, regroup and hurl again. Then one particularly heavy bore came purling in and soaked my shoes even as I crabbed desperately backwards on all fours. No doubt somebody saw me and laughed.

I got to my feet and walked along the beach towards the pier. The pier had given up a long time ago. First it had been shunned by tourists, then condemned by councillors, and then a section of it had collapsed, and now it was an eyesore ignored by everyone. What remained, what teetered on rusty struts, resembled the leavings of a wedding cake after the guests have had their fill.

I stopped in its shadow and together, the pier and I, we

gazed out to sea. The seagulls wailed around us in memory of summer: *may, may, may.*

Every man is some woman's dog. I went home to Mrs Konwicki with my tail between my legs.

'You left this,' she said, handing me the leather slipcase containing my articles.

'I just want to know one thing,' I said, taking it. 'Will it work, your love potion?'

'It will work if you want it to work.'

'But will she notice? Won't it taste funny?'

'Cook something spicy like chilli con carne or a curry and she won't notice a thing. Neither will you.'

More questions, other objections, were queuing up in my head, jockeying for position, but one strand of thought held them all back: the thought of Julia, who had made life as a stringer on a no-hope local rag in a fag-end town in the arsehole of nowhere just about bearable and had made the future as a feature writer for a glamorous daily in the teeming heart of **LONDON** just about believable.

'Chilli,' I said. 'I think I can manage chilli.'

'Hello?'

'It's me.'

'Me? Philip! How are you?'

'I'm OK. Listen, I know this is short notice, but how about dinner tomorrow night?'

'Erm . . . I don't know.'

'It'd be nice to see you.'

'I'm not sure. I think I might have something on.'

'I'm cooking, but don't let that put you off.'

'*You're* cooking?'

'Yeah. Wonders will never cease.'

'Will it be just us?'

'Er, yeah. I thought we could get a vid in. But no pressure. If you don't want to, don't.'

'. . . OK. Yes. Might be fun.'

'Tomorrow. Eight. Don't be late. Or I'll get irate.'

'And in a bate.'

'And break a plate.'

'And seal your fate.'

'And your hunger I will not sate.'

'And I think we'd better stop there before the rhymes get any more contrived. See you tomorrow, Philip.'

Mrs Konwicki took me through to her kitchen and showed me shelfloads of unlabelled glass storage jars filled with powdered and preserved unnameables. Their smell painted the air pungent-sweet. No dog-smell in Mrs Konwicki's kitchen.

The dull brown powder she gave me wrapped up in a twist of paper didn't look especially potent, but according to her it could give a charging rhino a hard-on. (Actually, those are my words. Mrs Konwicki used an altogether more delicate turn of phrase.) It was made from herbs, she said, common-or-garden variety but mixed together in a certain manner which she didn't care to specify. I sniffed. The powder smelled dusty and sweet, a little like chocolate.

On one point she was quite insistent: 'You must want this, Feelhip. If there is any doubt in your heart, the smallest shred, it will not work.'

'Oh, I want it,' I said. Pretty convincingly, I might add.

'Good boy,' she said.

Thinking he was being addressed, Lech pricked up his ears.

Julia was quarter of an hour late.

I had made the chilli con carne the evening before, following the recipe in the book to the letter – with, of course, the one small addition – and had left it simmering on the Baby Belling overnight for that authentic lived-in flavour. I had tidied the flat, or at any rate broken a hole in the crust of untidiness that seemed to form over everything; I didn't want the place too clean or Julia's suspicions might be aroused. I

18

had agonised over the choice of video. Nothing mindless, nothing violent, nothing starring an actor she fancied, nothing that we had enjoyed together before, least of all anything romantic. Which didn't leave a lot.

Ah, the politics of Just Good Friends.

Her lateness, too, was political. Too early and she might have looked keen. Too late and she might have looked wary. Regardless, she looked stunning. But I didn't tell her so. Politics, again.

At first it was like boxing against an unknown opponent, a round of feinting, dancing, ducking, weaving, dodging while we sized one another up afresh. We told each other what we'd been up to this past couple of weeks, hummed a lot, agonised over awkward silences. Then WHAM! I went in with a guarded compliment about her new hairstyle. POW! She came back with how good the chilli smelled. THOK! THOK! I returned with a double jab: it was nice to see her, I was glad we were still on speaking terms. WHACK! Her remark about a good choice of video was so swift I didn't even see it coming. BIFF! I hoped she'd approve. And so on.

I suggested we eat. I opened a bottle of wine (in case we weren't punch-drunk enough already). I served the steaming chilli on mounds of basmati rice, with a bowlful of salad and thick-sliced granary bread on the side. I put on a Prodigy CD, because there was no chance we would ever have danced cheek-to-cheek to the album in the past and the tunes were too tuneless to have ever been Our Tune. We ate. We drank. We talked. The conversation slowly gathered momentum until it was flowing just like the old days.

And I watched every forkful that went into her mouth. I watched her scrape up the drips that slipped her lips. I watched her sop up the leftovers with a slice of bread. (She probably thought I had developed some weird food obsession since we split up.) And I waited. And I hoped. And I wanted. And I *believed*.

'Verdict?'

'Pretty good,' she said. 'You could be quite a chef if you put your mind to it.'

Well, what had I expected her to say? *Take me now, hot stud?*

'There was something unusual in it,' she went on. 'I'm not quite sure what it was. It was unusual.'

'Magic ingredient,' I said, tapping the side of my nose.

We watched the film sitting in separate armchairs. I didn't take any of it in. I can't remember who was in it, what they did, why they did it, who survived and who died. I know that at one point Julia started crying, and I thought, *This is it, here come the regrets and the apologies and then the reconciliation, this it it.* But it wasn't. Something sad had happened in the film. Someone had had to leave someone else, I think. Big deal. Then it was finished. THE END. Credits rolled. Julia got up and I got up and she kissed me lightly on the cheek and I expected her to step back, take a look at me and kiss me again, full on the mouth, wetly on the mouth. But she didn't.

'Thanks for a lovely evening,' was all she said.

'My pleasure,' I replied meekly.

'We'll do it again some time.'

'Yeah.'

'Fun.'

'Mm.'

She left.

I wanted to scream down the stairs after her: *I'VE CHANGED! I'M NOT HOLLOW ANY MORE! I'M FILLED WITH BELIEF! BELIEVE ME! BELIEVE ME! BELIEVE ME!*

But I didn't.

Mrs Konwicki turned up at my door bright and early and eager the following morning, Lech at her heels.

'So how did it go?'

She came all the way up five flights of stairs just to ask me that, as if she didn't know already.

'I think you could safely say that it was an utter waste of time and that your powder was about as much use as desiccated dog turd,' I replied, more in sorrow than in anger. 'Christ, Mrs K, I don't know why I believed you. No, I do. Mr Walbrook.'

'Yes, that was fortunate. The word, I think, is serendipity.'

'Seren—? Jesus . . .'

'Poor Feelhip. And you fell for it.' She leaned her head to one side and shrugged down the corners of her mouth. The shrug spread to her shoulders. 'Well, I am very plausible. But really, what *were* you hoping for? A miracle cure?'

'Would have been nice.'

'I'm afraid only God can provide those. God, and the human heart.'

'So . . .'

'Cocoa powder.'

'And . . .'

'It might have happened, you never know. It was worth a try.'

'But . . .'

'At least the two of you had an evening together. It's a start. Something to build on.' Mrs Konwicki reached out and patted my cheek. Her hand was dry as papyrus, dusty as a palm leaf awaiting monsoon. 'Mustn't hang around gossiping. Ring her, Feelhip. Keep trying. Never give up hope.'

She turned and started downstairs, but Lech stayed in the doorway for a moment longer and we stared at one another, man to man, dog to dog, and then he thumped his tail against the floor and I swear, I *swear* he was grinning.

'Lech!'

And then he leapt around and was gone, too.

Wings

The bell rang, and suddenly the corridors and shafts of the school were filled with moving bodies, and the classrooms, libraries, laboratories and gymnasia were left empty and echoing to the slamming of desk lids and doors. Dust and loose leaves of paper settled even as the teachers began to shape their lips around the words 'Class dismissed'.

Through the building the children flew with a great racketing roar, celebrating with their screams and whoops and yells the death of another school day. A dozen disparate streams of them converged in the main hallway, and when the hallway could no longer contain all these young bodies, all this enthusiasm made flesh, the main doors swung wide and spilled them out into the yard.

There the children blinked and stood dazed for a moment in the sunshine, like prisoners released from long sentences in lightless dungeons; but then, quickly adjusting to their newly regained freedom, they fell to clasping hands and exchanging grins and sharing jokes and promising to meet up later that day, or tomorrow, or whenever; and dividing into pairs and knots of three or four and the odd solemn single, up from the yard they rose on single down-thrusts of their wings and off they flew along the windy streets of Cloudcap City, satchels in hand, shirt-tails and skirt-hems fluttering, blowing like dandelion seeds to all six corners of the compass.

Amid all this fever to escape Az plodded along in his usual ungainly fashion. A few classmates patted him on the shoulder and said, 'See you' as they flew past, but Az's excruciatingly slow progress meant that no one was going to stay beside him for long. It just wasn't possible. It took Az over a minute to traverse a corridor or clamber up or down a shaft, using the metal rungs fitted into the walls especially for him, whereas it took the rest of them a handful of seconds. The other children swooped around him like swifts, like swallows, while Az was a beetle, struggling, bumbling, lumbering.

The last few children were taking off from the yard when Az finally emerged into the daylight. He watched them rise into the sky, wave to one another and flit off in different directions. He waved too, on the off-chance that one of them might happen to look back and see him and return the gesture, but it was useless; their eyes were fixed on the horizon and home.

Alone, and sunk deep in his own thoughts, Az traipsed across the yard.

Normally he would have caught the airbus and travelled home with the elders and the fledglings and all the other clipped-wings, but when he came through the school gates he found his brother Michael waiting for him on the landing platform in his Corbeau. Michael was returning the admiring glances of a pair of girls who were wafting by on the other side of the street, but catching sight of Az, he forgot about them and raised a hand and cried, 'Hey, little brother! Hop aboard!'

Az climbed into the passenger seat beside him, dumping his satchel between his feet. Michael hit a switch on the dashboard of the Corbeau, and the blades began to rotate above their heads.

Over the rising whine of the engine and the *vip-vip-vip* of chopped air he shouted, 'Good day at school?'

Az shrugged. 'So-so.'

Michael looked carefully at the little guy and saw the gloom in his face, sitting heavy there like a cumulonimbus in a blue sky. He didn't ask what the matter was. He merely said, 'I've got an idea – why don't we stop by the Ice Castle on the way home? I bet you anything there's a sundae there with your name on it.'

'Thanks. No,' said Az, buckling up his safety belt.

'OK, why don't we pop over to the Aerobowl then? I've got free passes. Come on. The Thunderhead Eagles are playing the Stratoville Shrikes.'

'Oh.'

' "Oh"? What does that mean – "Oh"? The *Shrikes*, Az. You *love* the Shrikes.'

'No. 'S all right, really. Thanks. I just want to go home.'

Michael frowned. 'Well, OK. If you say so. If you're sure.' He glanced out of the cockpit to check the street was clear, then pushed down on the joystick. The autogyro sprang from the landing platform, soaring up into the sparkling air.

The Corbeau, the latest model in the Airdyne 3-series, was *the* status-symbol two-seater of the moment – sleek, tapered, a giant's teardrop cast in bronze, every inch of the surface of its fuselage smooth and gleaming from the nose-cone with its ring of rivets to the scallop-grooved tailfins – and Michael flew it with the requisite artful recklessness, slipping and side-sliding through the air channels, descending suddenly, just as suddenly climbing, overtaking, undertaking, the aircraft responding to the tiniest nudges on the stick and pedals as though it were an extension of its pilot, a mechanical extrapolation of Michael's own abilities. And had Az been in any kind of a good mood, he would have been laughing uproariously as they nipped around the other traffic and whizzed past his schoolfellows at breakneck speed, leaving them standing just as they had left him standing earlier. But today, not even a fast ride in a classy piece of aero-engineering could lift his depression. If anything, it served to deepen it.

They whisked down Sunswept Avenue, great cubes of apartment block blurring by on either side, then took a right on to Cirrus Street, then an up on to Goshawk, and shortly after that the Corbeau was settling down on to the private landing platform that poked out like a rectangular tongue from their parents' front porch.

Az leapt out and was about to make his way up to the front

door when Michael grabbed him by the arm and turned him around with a gentle but forceful strength, bringing them face to face.

'Listen, little brother,' he said softly.

Az averted his gaze.

'I know it's not easy for you,' Michael continued, 'and I know that sometimes it must feel like the whole world's against you because of what you don't have or what you *think* you don't have. Just remember this – it doesn't matter. You're still our Az, and one lousy pair of wings isn't going to change that. If I thought it would, I'd cut mine off and give them to you right now. You understand that, don't you?'

Az nodded dumbly, not looking up.

'Good. Well, take it easy on yourself. And maybe we'll go down to the 'bowl at the weekend. How about that? Would you like that?'

Az nodded again, and Michael let him go. The whine of the autogyro rose behind him as he wandered slowly up to the porch. Michael's 'Catch you later!' was cut short by a slammed front door.

'Dear?' His mother's voice, from the kitchen. 'Azrael?' She came out into the hallway, drying her hands on a dishtowel. 'Was that Michael I heard just now? Isn't he going to stay for supper?'

Az shook his head. 'I don't know.'

'Some girl, I bet,' said his mother, indulgent wrinkles multiplying around her eyes.

'Maybe,' said Az. Then: 'I'm going up to my room.'

To reach the upper storey of the house Az had to use a contraption his father had built for him, a space-consuming succession of cantilevered wooden steps that rose diagonally through an aperture in the ceiling. A similar set of steps went from the upper storey to the rooftop conservatory. His parents used the steps whenever he was around. As a rule, they made sure to walk as much as possible when he was in the house, out of respect for his feelings.

Az's room was like any other twelve-year-old's room, save that the door went all the way down to the floor (another of his father's DIY adaptations). The carpet was strewn with clothing, books, pieces of a long-abandoned jigsaw, some small die-cast biplanes and a larger scale model of a Corbeau which Michael had given him on his last birthday, saying it would do until Az was old enough to earn his pilot's licence, at which point Michael would buy him the real thing. He dropped his satchel into the middle of all this debris and stretched out on his bed, flat on his back. Lying on his back, Az reflected, was the one thing he could do that no one else could. Some compensation. Yeah, right. What a talent. The kids at school were *forever* asking him to show them how well he could lie on his *back*.

He stared up at the ceiling for a long time, trying to think of nothing. At some point during the long slow diminuendo of the afternoon, he fell asleep.

And he dreamed.

One morning Az wakes up to find he has grown a fully fledged pair of wings. He doesn't know how they got there, he doesn't dare ask why. He simply accepts.

His parents are happy and amazed. His mother cries, his father thumbs some grit from his eye. They forgive Az. For what, they do not say, but it is enough for Az to be forgiven. He kisses them both, and prepares to fly off to school under his own steam for the first time ever.

Flying, he finds, is not so difficult. He has the instinct for it, and now he has the means. A little practice, some plummeting and frantic fluttering, and then he's on his way.

Heads turn and mouths gape in the school yard. A cry goes up. Look! Look at that! Did you ever . . . ? Who'd have thought . . . ?

Az alights in the middle of the school yard and his peers cluster round him, jabbering excitedly. They fire off a million questions at him. They ask him if they can touch his wings. He

tells them they can. They touch them with reverential awe and care. It tickles.

Word gets around, and before he knows it Az is a celebrity in school. He is clapped and cheered wherever he goes. When he glides down a shaft with his wings outstretched, every feather intricately splayed to catch the air, he descends into a hail of hurrahs. When he kites along a corridor, keeping pace with the rest of his class as they hurry from one lesson to the next, they grin and encourage him every flap of the way. During break time Az is asked to join half a dozen impromptu games of balloonball, and though he has never played before, has only ever watched from the sidelines, he soon gets the hang of it, and even scores a Horizontal Slide. The seal is put on his popularity when Mrs Ragual interrupts Phys. Ed. to ask Az for a demonstration. The class goes outside and Az soars and barrel-rolls and loops the loop for their benefit. Mrs Ragual tells him he is not just a good flyer, he is a great flyer. A natural. Then the rest of them join him in the air, and together, under Mrs Ragual's approving eye, they pass a happy, truant half-hour simply doing what they like best, wheeling and whirling and squealing and squalling like a flock of mad seagulls. All the time Az is the centre of attention, the focus of everybody's admiration. After all, anyone who can make one of Mrs Ragual's Phys. Ed. torture sessions FUN has to be some kind of a hero.

He woke up. He dared to touch his back.

Still wingless.

He rolled disconsolately over on to his side to look out of the window at Cloudcap City all laid out in neat rows and columns and tiers, up, down, left, right, reaching as high as the stratosphere and as low as the cloudtop and as far as the horizon, each block suspended by means of six-way electromagnetic positional stabilisers to form a three-dimensional latticework of buildings, between and through and around which tiny figures and aircraft of all shapes and sizes threaded their way. Most of the buildings were cubic in shape, but there were oddities. The cylinder of the Freefall Dance Palace was one, the annular Aerobowl another, the spike-spired mace-ball fantasy of the Cathedral of the Significant God a notable third.

The air being clear and his eyes being sharp, Az could make out the bird-trawlers a mile below on the cloudtop, casting their nets into the wilderness of white. He could also make out the sky-mines that ringed the city, forming a circle of stability on which the whole meniscus of floating buildings was suspended. The sky-mines looked like tulips balancing on lofty, delicately slender stems which pierced the cloudtop and went all the way down to the Ground, from where they sucked up the juices that kept the city running. Service elevators, like glass aphids, crawled up and down the stems.

He lay there watching the view for he didn't know how long. It seemed like no time and all time had passed when his mother called up from below, summoning him down for supper.

Az clumped down to the kitchen, from which emanated smells which even his gloom-ridden brain recognised as mouthwatering.

'Go and call your father,' said his mother. 'Then you can lay the table.'

Az went out into the hallway again, walked along a little way and stopped at the large trapdoor that led down to his father's workshop. He listened hard, and heard from below faint sounds of banging and tocking, clonking and clanging.

Construction.

While a working man, Az's father had spent much of his spare time dabbling in home improvements, which were usually for Az's benefit, like the steps and all the doorways in the house. When his forty-year career as a maker and mender of clocks had finally wound down, however, he had turned his hand to invention, and had begun building a series of thises

31

and thats and the others – gadgets he hoped one day to patent and sell by the million, devices intended to make everyone's lives that little bit easier. So far, not a single one had proved patent-feasible. A portable trouser-press had made its mark in all the wrong ways. A clockwork toothbrush had been a gum-bruising disaster. A pair of self-sharpening scissors had almost cost him a finger. But he went on making these things nonetheless, toiling away by the uncertain light of a low-wattage bulb, secretly, in the strictest of privacy, hope springing eternal with the completion of every new invention until that invention blew a gasket or slipped a cog or collapsed in a heap or simply failed to start. Then it was 'Oh well, back to the drawing board', with a sigh that contained neither defeat nor despair. It was almost as if Az's father wasn't really looking forward to the day one of his devices worked and was a success and made his fortune and meant that he never had to make anything else again. The old man was happy just to be in his workshop, out of harm's way, tinkering, occupying his hands and his time.

Az called down, and the sounds of construction ceased and his father's muffled voice came up.

'Yes?'

'Supper.'

'Coming.'

A moment later his father bustled up into the kitchen. 'Give me a hand here, won't you, son?' He turned his back, and Az helped him unzip and wrestle his way out of the plastic slipcovers he wore over his wings to protect them from dust and stray sparks. His father's plumage had greyed at the edges, was rough in patches like a fledgling's, and had gaps where pinfeathers had fallen out and would never grow back again; but they were fine, proud wings all the same, in excellent condition for a man his age.

'Outside, please,' said Az's mother, referring to the dusty wing covers. Her husband obediently popped them out on to the back porch. 'I shudder to think of the state of that workshop,' she went on. 'Knee-deep in shavings and scrapings and wood chips and what-have-you.'

Az's father clasped a fist to his chest. 'I would rather die than have you clean in there.'

'I wasn't offering,' his wife replied. 'I was merely remarking.'

While Az finished laying the table, his father washed his hands in the sink. Drying them on a towel, he said, quietly, as if it was no matter at all, 'Do you know, I really think I'm on to something this time.'

Az's mother, who had heard this statement or statements pretty much like it a hundred times before, said, without looking up from the stove, 'That's good, dear.'

Az said nothing.

But when his father sat down at the table, there was a gleam in his eyes Az could not remember seeing there before, a light of excitement brightening the yellowed whites. 'No, I mean it,' he said. 'I've been working on this particular project for some weeks now, and I think I'm close to cracking it.'

'Eat,' said Az's mother, placing laden plates in front of them.

They ate. His parents, reckoning Az was not in a communicative mood, left him alone and chatted between themselves, chewing over trivialities and inconsequentialities the way long-married couples do when the weighty subjects have all been thoroughly discussed and all that remains is the nitty-gritty and the fine-tuning and the splitting of hairs.

Finally Az could bear it no longer, and said, 'What?'

'*What* what?' said his father.

'What is it? The something that you're on to? What?'

The gleam re-entered the old man's eyes. 'Never you mind, Az. Wait and see.'

By this time Az's mother was intrigued too. 'Go on, Gabe,' she said. 'Give us a clue.'

'What, and ruin the suspense?'

'Is it going to make us rich?' Az asked.

33

His father made a great show of considering the question. 'Well, in one sense, yes. In another sense, no.' He grinned enigmatically. 'Wait and see.'

Az waited several days, and still did not see. Every afternoon when he came home from school he would stop quietly by the trapdoor and listen to the tink and bonk and clatter and whack-whack-whack of industry, and the tuneless humming with which his father often counterpointed the rhythm of his labours. The sounds seemed no different from the sounds his father usually made down there. They were infuriatingly ordinary.

His attempts to extract from his father even the tiniest hint as to what was taking shape in the workshop were met with gleeful stonewalling. Endless questions could be asked over the dinner table, only to be answered with a 'Maybe' or a 'Could be' or a simple 'Not saying'. Once, recalling that his father had recently bought in several sheets of copper, Az asked whether these had some bearing on the mystery, but his father pointed out, rightly, that he was constantly buying and bringing in sheets of copper. It was, he said, the most tractable and obliging metal to work with.

One evening, while flicking through a magazine, Az held up each page of advertising in turn and showed it to his father, asking, 'Is it like that?' To which, in every instance, his father replied, 'Something like that. Only completely different.' Eventually Az became so aggravated that he threw the magazine down and left the room, hearing his father chuckle merrily behind him.

There was no question of secretly investigating the workshop, violating the privacy of his father's sanctum sanctorum; so in the end there was nothing for it but to wait and wonder.

One good thing, though, came of this continuing mystery. Az was so busy thinking about what might be in the workshop that he forgot to dwell on his own problems. Teachers marked the disappearance of his depressive fits and were quietly pleased, although a tendency to daydream in class was noted in the normally diligent pupil. His classmates were for the most part indifferent to the change in his temperament, although a few of them did notice that Az no longer scowled so hard when he walked. His mind seemed to be elsewhere, on something outside himself. The more sensitive among them recognised this to be a healthy sign.

Eighteen days after his first announcement, Az's father made a second, even more impressive announcement.

It came one suppertime. Michael had dropped by on his way to pick up a girl called Raphaella and take her to a harp recital. The family were halfway through the main course when Az's father tapped his wine glass with his fork, cleared his throat and said, 'A short speech.'

Everyone groaned.

'A *very* short speech. Just to say that this Saturday will see the unveiling of a device that is going to make us the happiest family alive. I want you to be there, Michael, if you can make it.'

'This isn't another of your exploding specials, is it, Dad?' said Michael. 'Like the self-heating coffee cup?'

'It's something,' said the old man reiterated, with an extravagant display of self-restraint, 'that is going to make us the happiest family alive.'

Michael turned to Az. 'We're going to be millionaires,' he said with a confident wink.

That night Az hardly slept at all. It was ridiculous, he knew, to get all excited over a dumb invention of his father's that might not even work. But there it was. His father's enthusiasm was infectious. And so Az lay awake trying to imagine what form the device would take, what use it could be put to, how big it would be, how practical, and he ached for Saturday to come so that he could see which, if any, of his suppositions turned out to be correct.

*

The day of the unveiling arrived, and Az and his mother watched Michael and the old man haul the device up from the workshop and carry it out on to the landing platform. The device was covered by a tarpaulin, so that all anyone could say about it was that it was twelve feet long, thin at either end, bulky in the middle and angular all over. Az thought of the dinosaur skeleton in the Museum of Ancient Artefacts.

'Well?' said Az's mother, giftwrapping her impatience in a laugh.

'One moment,' said his father. 'First, a short speech.'

As before, the family groaned, as they were expected to.

Pretending not to notice, Az's father ruffled his wings and grasped his lapel like a politician. 'Once,' he began, 'long ago, we were not Airborn but Groundling, and we lived an earthbound life, circumscribed on all sides by natural boundaries – mountains, rivers, seas. Since then, the race has moved onwards and upwards, and now we live lives as close to perfection as it is possible to get. We are paragons, living embodiments of all that the Groundlings aspired to. This is our heritage and our privilege. A privilege that should not be denied to anyone. Least of all, to flesh of my flesh.' Here, he looked straight at Az, and suddenly everyone – except Az – had a pretty good idea what lay hidden beneath the tarpaulin.

There might have been more to the speech, but Az's father sensed that the game was up, and, like any good showman, he knew he should not let the audience get ahead of him, so with a grand flourish he swept back the tarpaulin, revealing his creation to the world.

Four faces were reflected in a relief mosaic of burnished copper. Three of them gawped, wide-eyed. The fourth grinned with pride.

Finally, someone spoke. It was Az's mother.

'Wings,' she exclaimed, the word tailing up into a question.

'Wings,' her husband confirmed, bringing the word back in to land.

And wings they were. Larger than lifesize, correct in every

detail, lovingly crafted in beaten copper. A pair of metal, mechanical wings.

Every feather was there, perfect down to the fine comb-teeth of its filaments and pinned into place with a free-floating bolt; every joint, too, from the ball-and-sockets at the base of the armatures to the hinges at the elbows; and a complex system of pulleys and wires connected the ensemble to a leather harness which was just the right shape and just the right size for the torso of a boy of twelve.

'Come on then,' said Az's father, taking Az by the shoulder. 'Let's try them on, shall we?'

Michael stepped forward to help, and together he and the old man loaded the wings on to Az's back and tightened the straps of the harness around his chest.

Az submitted passively to the fitting, not knowing what to think, not really thinking anything. The wings were very heavy, and when his father and Michael let go, he teetered and would have overbalanced if Michael had not caught and steadied him.

Az barely listened as his father explained how the wings worked. 'You see, they're designed to take the action of the muscles in your shoulders and translate it into wingbeats, so you'll simply be employing the natural abilities God gave you. You may have some trouble adjusting to them at first, but that's only to be expected. There's no reason why instinct shouldn't take over almost straight away. Trust me, Az. You'll be up and soaring in no time.'

Bookended by Michael and his father, Az staggered to the edge of the landing platform, the wings making a soft shimmering clatter with each step as hundreds of copper feathers shook against one another. He peered down. The rippled surface of the cloudtop was awfully far below. The bird-trawlers plying their trade down there looked as tiny as gnats.

He glanced back over his shoulder. At first he could see nothing but copper wing, but he dropped his shoulder slightly and the wing flattened out, and then he could see his mother.

There were tears in her eyes. 'Go on,' she said to him, smiling bravely. 'Don't be scared. You'll be fine.'

But he wasn't scared. He was embarrassed. The clench of his jaw wasn't one of determination but of humiliation. He felt clumsier than ever burdened by these huge metal prostheses. He felt neither Airborn nor Groundling but a horrid amalgamation of the two. A joke, a parody. What would they think of him at school when he turned up on Monday morning strapped into this ugly clattering copper contraption?

'I don't think I can go through with this,' he said.

'Nonsense,' said his father, mistaking the tremor in Az's voice for fear. 'Michael and I will make sure you're all right, won't we, Michael? Whatever happens, you won't come to any harm. Trust us.'

'Will you at least hold on to me?' Az implored.

'The only way to learn to fly is the way I learned,' said Michael. 'The way we all learn.'

'What way is that?' said Az doubtfully.

'The hard way,' said Michael, and with a grin that was devoid of malice and yet still wicked, he grabbed Az's arm. Az's father on the other side did the same, and together, chanting 'One, two, three', they heaved Az out over the edge and into space.

And let go.

There was a moment of sheer disbelief, followed by a moment of sheer terror. Then all that was lost in the sickening uprush of falling. The weight of the wings yanked Az head over heels on to his back, and down he went in a wind-shivered rattle of metal. Down he plummeted, making no attempt to right himself or flap the wings, unable even to entertain the notion of saving himself. Down in a state of dreamlike apathy, with no thought except that he was going to die. Hypnotically down, past building after building, past windows and doorways, past light aircraft and happy citizens out for a Saturday morning glide. Down, down, down, with no hope of rescue, and no desire for it either. Down without a gasp or a scream, for an elastic stretch of seconds, the landing platform above receding, the house and all the houses around it shrinking, the sky growing smaller and filling up with more and more city. Down towards the cloudtop and the Ground from where the Airborn race once sprang and which now lay forever hidden.

There was a tentative knock at the door.

'Can I come in?'

'Sure, Dad.'

Az glanced up from the book he was reading, an adventure story about sky pirates, as his father entered the room. The old man's head was contritely bowed, and his wings drooped so low their tips were almost touching the floor. The look of shame that hung on the old man's face was so comical, Az could hardly fail to smile.

His father gestured at the edge of the bed. 'May I?'

Az nodded.

The old man sat down. There was a long silence while he deliberated over his next move, then he reached out and laid one hand on Az's leg. He patted the leg, the action affectionate yet mechanical. It was clear that he had several things to say but no idea in what order to say them.

Az helped him out. 'I'm sorry if I hurt your feelings.'

'My feelings?'

'By not trying.'

'Oh. Well, I wouldn't say my feelings were *hurt*, exactly. I was a little . . . disappointed? No, not even that. I did hope . . . Well, it doesn't matter now. How *I* feel doesn't matter. It's how *you* feel that matters.'

'I feel fine. Honestly.'

'The doctor said there may be some delayed shock.'

'I feel absolutely fine, Dad. Guilty, though.'

'Guilty?'

'For letting you down.'

'You didn't let me down, Az,' said his father with an exasperated laugh. 'How can I get that into your thick skull? I don't mind. Really I don't. It's enough for me that you're alive and well.'

'Well, I think I did. I mean, the wings would have worked. Almost certainly. Definitely. If I'd tried. I just didn't try. I didn't want to try.'

'Oh,' said his father. For his own pride's sake, it was what he had been hoping to hear. 'Well, anyway, you'll be pleased to learn that I've taken the damned things along to the scrapyard. Never again.'

'But you *are* going to carry on with your inventions.'

Az's father frowned. 'Perhaps. The fun's sort of gone out of it.'

'But what about making your million?'

'It's just a dream.'

'Dreams are important.'

'Az,' said his father, then paused. 'When your mother was pregnant with you, the doctors suggested she . . . she shouldn't have you. Health reasons. She wasn't so young any more. But she was prepared to take the risk. Quite determined, as a matter of fact. And because she was, I was, too. We both wanted you more than we'd ever wanted anything, no question about it. And when you came, we couldn't have been happier. We loved you the instant we set eyes on you. You were different, but that only made you special.' His father looked deep inside himself. 'Even so, it hasn't always been easy. You understand. For any of us. The looks we sometimes get, that mixture of compassion and disappointment, like we've somehow betrayed the whole race. Sometimes . . . Anyway, what I'm saying is, I was wrong to try and make you the same as everyone else. I'd convinced myself I was doing it for you, but of course I was just doing it for myself. And now I can't help thinking what would have happened if Michael hadn't been so quick off the mark, if he hadn't caught you when he did . . .'

40

'But he did, and I'm fine. It just wasn't meant to be, Dad. That's all there is to it.'

'Please believe me when I say that I had your best interests at heart. It simply never occurred to me . . . I just assumed that to fly must be your dream, your greatest, wildest dream.'

'Oh, it is, Dad, it is. I dream about having wings all the time. The thing is, I've got so used to the fact that it's never going to happen, it doesn't bother me so much any more. Sometimes it's better to have a dream and not have it fulfilled than make do with something that's like your dream but not quite as good.'

'Say I'm forgiven anyway.'

'You're forgiven anyway.'

'Thank you.' The old man thought about tousling his son's hair, but checked himself. That was something you did to little children. To boys. Instead, he patted Az's leg one more time, and left the room.

Az shut his book and turned over to look out of the window.

Cloudcap City, his home, lay suspended in the bright afternoon sunshine, shadowless and huge, its interstices busy with traffic, thriving with life. It pleased Az to think that, even if only for a handful of seconds, he had plunged through that city unaided, unsupported; that he had had a taste of flight, however brief and unwelcome. It filled him with a weird kind of serenity.

In this world he would always be a floorbound, wingless freak. There was no changing that. But in his dreams . . .

In his dreams, he would always be able to fly.

Satisfaction Guaranteed

When Nora stepped out into my headlights there was no way I could avoid her. The front bumper embraced her legs and she jackknifed over the bonnet, arms outstretched, face to the windscreen, staring at me through the glass, looking me straight in the eye.

She and I held each other's gaze for what felt like for ever, although it could only have been as long as it took for her to slither back down on to the road. My foot was squashing the brake pedal and my hands were squeezing the life out of the steering wheel; Nora was spreadeagled and already dead. Yet, in spite of this, in that protracted moment of eye contact sparks of recognition crackled between us, and I knew that our love was meant to be.

I was driving home from Janice's house, where I had been told that it was over between us, whatever we had was over, all over; where I had been called 'overbearing', 'too demanding' and 'an emotional cripple', for which I instantly forgave her because I was none of those things; where I had been accused of trying to run her life for her, and vilified simply because I liked to know where she was when I wasn't with her, as if that wasn't a perfect expression of my love for her.

I had left her in tears. *I* was in tears, that is, not Janice. *Her* eyes were as dry as bones, and as white and as hard. I drove away from her house along blurred, stinging streets where neon lights shone like starbursts and houses glowed like images in stained-glass windows; and then Nora stepped out into the glare of my headlights, and I didn't see her in time because I was blind with tears because Janice didn't love me any more. From which I can only conclude that fate intended that Nora come and throw her arms out to me over the bonnet, gazing at me in her death as though I was the only one who could ever make her happy again, before tumbling floppily out of sight. From the timing of it, the serendipity of it, I can only believe that Nora was *meant* to be mine.

I don't know how long I sat in the stalled car, hearing the engine tick as it cooled. I only know that when I opened the door and stepped out, I was as nervous as a virgin groom on his first night with his new bride.

I moved silently to where Nora's crumpled form lay flat on the tarmac. She was wearing a creamy-white suit, and her skirt had rucked up an inch or so above her knees. Her head was thrown back to expose the curve of her neck, and a small trickle of blood was leaking from one ear.

I stood over her for a long time in the empty street, waiting for her to stir, moan, breathe, flutter her eyelashes, twitch one manicured fingertip. When I was quite sure she was dead, I bent down, slid my arms under her, picked her up and carried her to the car.

She weighed next to nothing, and her lightness, along with the perfect scarlet O of her lips and the resilient rubbery stiffness of her limbs, made me think of an inflatable doll – the kind you get from those windowless shops in side streets, the kind that lie there without a life of their own until you inject your own animation into them.

No one saw me as I laid her across the back seat and drove her home with me. And no one saw me carry her, all dressed in white, across the threshold of my house. It was a private, special moment, marred only somewhat by the cracked-knuckles sound made by her head rolling around loosely on her shattered neck.

I took her upstairs and laid her out on the bed in the spare room. It was presumptuous of me to remove her clothes, but everyone hates to go to bed fully dressed, don't they? And I performed the deed as civilly as circumstances allowed, leaving her almost decent in her simple white cotton underwear. I arranged her body carefully, made her head comfortable on the pillow and wiped the blood from her hair with a damp cloth.

I skimmed through her belongings for a name but found only a credit card with a surname and two initials, the first of which was N. So I called her Nora, after my mother.

I switched out the lights and spent the night in the armchair by her bedside, keeping vigil over my Nora till dawn came. She slept soundlessly, peacefully. In the glow of daybreak, I saw what I thought was a smile spreading across her face, but it turned out to be just a wand of light that the sun had inserted through the gap in the curtains and was slowly running across her lips.

I went over and drew the curtains fully open, then spent a happy half-hour examining the new woman in my life by the light of the rising sun. Her lips and eye-sockets had turned purple and the contours of her bare stomach and thighs, which I remembered from the night before as being tightly muscled and sharply delineated, had blurred, losing definition as her flesh had thickened. Her left arm jutted at an ungainly angle over the side of the bed, and her knees and elbows were swollen with large blue-black bruises. It was then that I noticed a certain ripeness to the air in the room – but then what bedroom doesn't smell in the morning, of flatulence and the sleep-steam of bodies? None the less I opened the window a crack before heading downstairs to make my breakfast.

I thought about Nora all day at work. I signed documents and attended meetings and made telephone calls and dictated letters and thought about nothing but Nora. At lunchtime in the canteen Montgomery from Accounts asked me how Janice was, and I actually had to remind myself whom he was talking about. 'Janice,' I told him, with the look of a gladiator-in-love who has recovered from more wounds received in the arena than he can remember, 'is ancient history.' He wanted to know more, because my tone implied that I wasn't telling him everything, but I left him wriggling on the hook. It would have been premature of me to mention Nora when things weren't completely established between us, when a proper commitment had not yet been made. I'm superstitious about these things.

Back home, I bounded upstairs to see how she was getting on. During the day she had swollen up as though someone had inserted a bicycle pump into her mouth and inflated her. Her fingers, once slender, now resembled pork sausages. Her flesh strained around the waistband of her panties and the wiring of her bra and, though it pained me to do so, I felt obliged to remove these undergarments, cutting the elastic with a pair of blunt-nosed nail scissors. Naked on the counterpane, Nora was beautiful, Ophelian, delicately vulnerable. But she smelled worse than ever.

It was all right for a couple of days. I could bear the smell on account of her beauty and the fact that she made so few demands on me, and I would look in on her morning and evening without fail, but the duration of these visits shortened as the smell intensified. I bought a bottle of perfume from the chemist's, the brand Janice preferred, and sprinkled it all over Nora and all over the room, but its sickly-sweet scent only added to Nora's sweetly-sick stench to create a nauseating blend of man-made and nature-made.

We could not go on like this, and I told Nora so, and with masculine authority in my voice. The smell of her had pervaded the entire house. It was always there, always around me, in the atmosphere. Nowhere indoors could I get away from her. Even in the shower, lathering myself in shampoo- and magnolia-fragrance soap, I could smell her amid the clouds of steam, and was reminded of earthy mist over early-morning moors.

Janice noticed the smell when she dropped round, unannounced, to – in her words – 'see how you are'. She didn't mention the smell directly, but she kept casting her head to the side while she talked to me, raising her nose to the air like a cat.

I behaved impeccably in her presence. Nothing I said or did gave her any impression that I was upset at the way she had treated me or that I was worried she might discover I had found myself another girl so quickly. I didn't want to hurt her feelings and I didn't want her to think me shallow, so we sipped tea and talked sensibly, like two grown adults, and as she was leaving Janice said, 'I'm glad we can be sane and civilised about this, Gerald,' and I replied, 'Janice, I'm as sane and civilised as they come.'

And when she was gone, I went around the house spraying pine fragrance air-freshener into every corner of every room.

But the smell only grew stronger. It clung to me, to my skin, to my clothes. They began to notice it at work. Carver from the Legal Department asked me one day in the corridor if I'd trodden in something I shouldn't have trodden in, and old Horace who runs the stationery cupboard couldn't help wrinkling his nose when I went in for a ream of A4 and a ballpoint.

But what could I do? I wasn't prepared to ditch Nora. Our love was meant to be, and I would do anything to keep that love alive. (Isn't it funny how the bland clichés from popular songs suddenly burst out vibrant and true when you're in love, *really* in love?)

The smell permeated everything about me and everything I did, and no amount of soap or aftershave could shift it. My colleagues at work began shunning me in the canteen, and my secretary found every excuse to spend as little time as she could in my office, and I knew that the temps in the typing pool were whispering about me behind my back. The smell, in fact, was making me so unpopular that in the end I did the only thing I could: I handed in my notice. I quit. And when Mrs Haldane in Personnel asked me why I was quitting, I said it was because I wanted to spend more time with my loved one.

My loved one who was not so lovely any more, who was not at all the woman I had fallen in love with.

'Nora,' I told her, exactly a fortnight after we first met, 'I love you, I care for you, I want to be with you. But . . .' I drew a fresh breath through my handkerchief, lowered it and continued: 'There is something between us, something standing in our way, and I think it better that we clear the air now – spill our guts, so to speak – rather than bottle our feelings up, which only means that one or other of us will explode at a later date.'

I covered my mouth and nose quickly again, and raised the kitchen knife I had brought upstairs with me, tightening my rubber-gloved grip on the handle. I glanced at the copy of *Gray's Anatomy* which I had propped open on the pillow beside Nora's head and, using this as my guide, set about disembowelling her.

The illustrations in *Gray's*, with their fine lines and delicate cross-hatching, did nothing to prepare me for the clotted, reeking mess that was Nora's innards. Choking, I hacked and slashed and chopped with a singular lack of surgical precision, then plunged my hands in and sloshed fistful after fistful of intestine and inner organ into a bin-liner.

Finally, when Nora was empty and the bag was full, I carried the bundle of viscera downstairs and dumped it in the dustbin out in the back yard. Immediately three interested cats appeared and began sniffing around the base of the bin, but I shooed them away and, just to be on the safe side, secured the bin lid down with a length of washing line.

Then I returned to the spare room to inspect my handiwork. The sag of Nora's belly and the jagged slit running up her abdomen from mons veneris to solar plexus were – let's be frank here – unattractive. And as I looked more closely at her, I saw now that her whole skin was a chromatograph of spreading bruises, not the smooth expanse of milky white I remembered at all. And even though I knew that the worst of her was sitting outside in the dustbin waiting for Tuesday's collection, I realised that she wasn't the same any more and would never be the same again. She had changed. The one remaining constant in our relationship was the one thing about her that I couldn't stand: the smell.

I wondered what to do. How could I bring back the old Nora, the Nora who had only days ago thrown herself at me so openly, so blithely, so freely? How could I restore her to perfection?

I could not. But I could improvise.

I started by filling in the cavity in her belly with a tangled length of garden hose and giving her back her heart in the shape of my alarm clock, which I tucked inside her ribcage. It sat there snugly, ticking away the semi-seconds, beating perhaps a little too quickly for a healthy heart, but then that's love for you.

Once I'd done this, once I'd begun making improvements to Nora, it seemed unchivalrous to stop, so straight away I set to hollowing out her throat and inserting in it a portable transistor radio. If I wanted her to talk to me, all I had to do was flip a switch and she would give me Radio 4 (her conversation was wide-ranging and knowledgeable, but not notably feminine, except during *Woman's Hour*). If, on the other hand, I wanted her to sing, then she was only too happy to (and her repertoire was vast and the range of her voice was as broad as can be, from Classic FM to hardcore dance music). And if I grew tired of the sound of her, I always had the option of shutting her up at the touch of a button.

Her eyelids had peeled back to reveal milky-white orbs like ping-pong balls, so I substituted them with a pair of large paste diamonds. I would have given her the genuine article but, since I no longer had a job, money was tight. She didn't seem to mind. Paste diamonds are a girl's second-best friend.

Her left arm had to go. Stuck stiffly out over the edge of the bed, the hand would often butt against my crotch in an extremely crude and suggestive manner – perhaps this was deliberate on her part, I don't know. I replaced it with a broomstick, anyway, to the end of which I taped five table-knives for fingers. I was careful to position her new arm alongside her torso so that there would be no risk to my private parts. Soon after, I replaced her right arm with the hose and nozzle of a vacuum cleaner, for reasons of symmetry and aesthetics.

I bought a device from one of the aforementioned blank-fronted shops as a substitute for Nora's most intimate organ. I never did use it, although it was good to know that it was there; that I could make love with Nora any time I wanted to, if I wanted to.

Eventually her legs became so misshapen that it was a kindness when I replaced the left with a carpet sweeper and the right with a mop. I entertained fantasies of hoisting Nora upright and trundling her back and forth across the floor, her throat playing the theme tune from *The Archers* while she cleaned the carpet and the kitchen tiles. But I never dared. I never dared presume.

The drying rack from the sink drainer became her new ribcage. Unfortunately her breasts then sank in on themselves like badly set jellies. My solution to the problem was – if I say so myself – a stroke of genius. I wrung the gel from a freezer bag into a pair of pink polythene plastic sacks, topped each with the teat from a baby's dummy, and stuck these on top of the drying rack. Hey presto, a Hollywood starlet's dream come true: a bosom that would never sag.

But I think the pièce de résistance was Nora's brain. I scooped her cranial cavity clean, sawed off the top of her skull and fitted an electric blender there. With her hair glued around the blender's perspex cylinder, it seemed to me that I had come up with the perfect symbol for the mind of Woman: nimble, utilitarian, deceptively easy to use, lethally sharp if you aren't careful.

And all the offcuts and left-over fleshy pieces I dutifully bagged and binned for collection.

Come Tuesday morning, when I heard the dustbin lorry

rumble round, I felt profoundly sad to be losing so much of the old Nora, but drew comfort from the thought that the new Nora I had created would last for ever and would never need to be thrown away.

I heard the dustmen shouting agitatedly to one another. I didn't hear what they said. I was lying beside my Nora and had no thought but for my Nora – Nora whom I had restored to beauty, whom I had returned to her rightful place in my affections, as was meant to be.

I was still lying beside her when, half an hour later, there came a knocking at the front door and a loud officious voice asked me to open up. Even when the knocking turned to hammering, and then to splintering, I didn't so much as stir. There were footfalls on the stairs, but all I could think about was Nora and myself and our future together. I would want nothing from her and she would ask nothing from me (except, perhaps, a fresh bottle of perfume a week), and the longer we stayed together, the stronger our love would grow. We would stay together while our looks faded and our eyesight failed, and we would still be together long past the point when other couples lose interest in each other, when their love settles into complacency, when nothing the one does can satisfy the other. We would stay together until long past the expiration date of love's warranty.

Britworld™

Hi! Welcome to Britworld™. My name is Wanda May June and I will be your guide, hostess and compère for the duration of the tour. If you have any questions about anything you see here today, I will be more than happy to answer them.

Thank you for coming prepared with warm clothing. The temperature in Britworld™ is kept at a refreshing forty-five degrees Fahrenheit all year round. USACorp Entertainments have gone to great lengths to enhance the authenticity of your experience by reproducing the exact climate of the original. This also means a regulation four and a half hours of rain per day. If there is anyone here who suffers from respiratory ailments or is in any way inconvenienced by the Britworld™ environment, they should not hesitate to leave by one of the emergency exits, one of which you will see over there, marked 'EXIT'.

Now, has everyone got their umbrellas, or 'bumbershoots' as we call them in Britworld™?

Good. Then why don't you follow me to the first sector? Thank you!

Here we find ourselves in a typical urban situation. This is in fact London, which was the capital of Britworld™ and home to the famous Beatles.

The wind is a little gusty today. Look how it speeds the clouds along! There is a ninety-seven per cent chance of rain later.

A brief technical note. The sky you are now seeing is, of course, projected on to the underside of the geodesic dome. Now, whereas other theme parks use simple loop-sequences

57

of an hour or so in length, the clouds here are generated using the latest in Chaos Model programs. Thus no two are ever alike. Some are large, some are small. That one looks just like a duck, doesn't it? We at USACorp Entertainments are justly proud of innovations such as these which keep us one step ahead of the competition.

As you cross the street, mind your step on the piles of garbage – or 'rubbish' as it is known here.

Yes, it does smell kind of bad, doesn't it? But you must remember that in the real Britworld™ they had never heard of efficient disposal or recycling.

Whoops-a-daisy! Are we all right, ma'am? Good. I can see that you haven't sustained any serious injury, but I should take this opportunity to mention to you all that in the eventuality of an accident situation, USACorp Entertainments will accept zero liability. You all signed the waiver forms at the entrance.

Please try to keep up!

Let's wait here for a few minutes at this bus stop. If we are lucky, we may see a genuine double-decker bus. The word 'bus' is short for 'omnibus'. A double-decker bus is a bus with two decks. Hence the name. It is red and will have a number on the front, signifying its route, and a destination – perhaps the Houses of Parliament, where Guy Fawkes lived, or Hyde Park, named after the alter-ego of the famous scientist Dr Jekyll, or maybe the Globe Theater, which was built by Sir William Shakespeare.

Any minute now, there may be an omnibus. There may even be two. Or three!

Double-decker buses have a seating capacity of sixty-eight, forty-four on top, twenty-four below – not forgetting, of course, standing room for another twenty passengers.

Any . . . minute . . . now.

It doesn't look like one's coming. What a disappointment. Well, we can't hang around all day. Let's proceed along this road to the market.

Many historians consider the market to be an early precursor of our shopping mall. Notice how each stall sells a different product, what we now call franchising. Here is the fruit and vegetable stall, selling fruit and vegetables. It is tended by a cheerful man known as a greengrocer. The name is derived from the fact that a large proportion of his groceries are green in colour.

Listen.

'Apples and pears! Apples and pears! Getcha apples and pears!'

Isn't that clever? USACorp Entertainments have taken every effort to reduplicate the Britworld™ dialect, incomprehensible now to the great majority of the English-speaking world.

Little boy, the automata are *extremely* delicate. Please don't touch.

I would just like to show you this. A strawberry. Everybody! Look at this strawberry. This is the fruit from which we derive strawberry flavour.

Yes, sir, I suppose it does bear a slight resemblance to a wino's nose.

On the street corner we see the newsvendor, vending newspapers. Let's listen to his distinctive cry.

'Papcrrrr! Getcha paper heeeere!'

The cloth cap and raincoat he is wearing are the real thing, the genuine article, as is all the clothing you will see today, purchased at great cost by USACorp Entertainments from museums all over the world.

Beyond the newsvendor you may already have spotted the street musicians, or 'buskers', so called because they used to play on buses until the law banned them. The tune they are playing is a traditional folk ballad, 'Strawberry Fields Forever'. Remember that strawberry I showed you earlier on? Well, this song was written, so they say, about fields of strawberries stretching so far into the distance they seemed to go on for ever.

Don't the buskers sing well?

We are standing outside a pub, the Britworld™ equivalent of a bar. 'Pub' is short for public house, a house into which the public may enter whenever they wish. This one has a name. The King's Head. On the sign up there we see a picture of the head of the King. Notice his crown. Shall we go in?

Here we see the inhabitants of Britworld™ relaxing in the friendly, intimate atmosphere of the pub. At the bar we see the landlord and the landlady, so called because they rent out the house to the public.

This is Charly, a cheerful local. Cheerful locals in London were known as Cockneys because – so legend goes – they were born within the sound of the bells of Cockney Cathedral. Tell us, Charly, do you enjoy drinking here?

'Gor blimey, luvaduck, I should say. Crikey, strike me blind if I jolly bloomin' well don't! Lor lumme! Eh, guvnor?'

I think he does! And chim-chim-cheroo to you, too, Charly!

Now, follow me, everyone. Don't try that, sir. It's not safe to drink. It's a substitute for the popular pub drink, bitter ale, designed to maintain its colour and consistency and that distinctive frothy head for approximately eighteen years.

Let's hurry on to the next sector. But I must warn you, be prepared to be thrilled, chilled and spilled! Those with heart conditions or nervous complaints may wish to consider leaving by the nearest convenient emergency exit over there, marked 'EXIT'.

Where are we? Fog swirls along darkened streets and the gas lamps flicker, casting strange shadows on the sidewalk. Villains surely lurk in this fog-enshrouded place.

But look at that roadsign! 'Baker's Street'. How many of you know which well-known historical personality lived on Baker's Street?

No.

No.

No, not Chet Baker.

No.

No, it was Sherlock Holmes! And if we are lucky, we may just catch a glimpse . . .

Ah! There! The deerstalker, the cape, the pipe. It can only be . . . And yes, there is his friend and faithful companion, Dr Watson.

'The game's afoot.'

'Good heavens, Holmes! How on earth did you deduce that?'

'Elementary, my dear Watson. When you have eliminated the impossible, whatever remains, however improbable, must be the truth.'

And so the great detective sweeps past us on his way to solving another baffling, mystifying, perplexing mystery. So close, so realistic, you could reach out and touch him.

But who is that? A woman, wandering the night streets, vulnerable and alone. She must be careful. There's murder in the air.

Oh, look out! That man in the top hat and cloak! He has a knife! He is Jack the Ripper, that terrible fiend of the night and depraver of women. Who will save her? Who will save her?

Hooray! Here comes a friendly policeman, whose name is Bobby. He blows his whistle. That's seen that dreadful Ripper off! Look how Bobby is comforting that poor woman. How safe she must feel.

Well, I'm quite breathless with excitement. Everybody follow me to the next sector.

Oh dear. Bumbershoots up, everyone! As the saying in Britworld™ goes, 'It's raining buckets of cats.'

If you can't hear me over the rain, say so and I will speak up. OK?

Good.

This grand edifice is none other than the Buckingham Palace itself, the home of the King and Queen of Britworld™. USACorp Entertainments, sparing no expense, had the original building transported brick by brick and reconstructed here. See how the Union Jack, royal flag of

Britworld™, flutters proudly from the mast on the palace roof.

The palace has a small number of large rooms and a larger number of small rooms. All the interiors have been recreated down to the finest detail. However, as we're running a little behind, we'll have to skip that part of the tour.

If you *do* want a refund, ma'am, I'd advise you to take the matter up with USACorp's Central Office and not with me.

Trust me, they are *bee-yootiful* rooms.

Notice the Beefeaters standing guard at the palace gates with their fierce pikes and their mustaches. They get their name from their traditional beef-only diet. Yes, amazing as it may sound, they used to eat nothing but beef! Naturally, beefeaters had a disproportionately high rate of death from colonic cancer and Creutzfeld Jacob disease.

Twice a day the guards change their positions to avoid cramp. This is known as the Changing of the Guard.

Wait! Look! Up there! On the balcony! Why, the King and Queen have come out to wave at us! Wave back, everybody.

The King is wearing his crown. Remember the sign at the pub? The Queen, meanwhile, is wearing an elegant mid-length gown in taffeta, cut on the bias, with a lace hem and gold braid trim along the sleeves. To complete the ensemble, she wears a diamond tiara and earrings and matching accessories. Ladies, don't you wish you could dress as elegantly as that?

Oh, they're going in again. Goodbye, your majesties! Goodbye! Goodbye!

We are now entering the Shakespeare sector. You can put down your bumbershoots now, as the rain has been switched off. I know several of you have heard about the little difficulty we had in this sector some months back, but I am pleased to be able to tell you that the fire damage has been repaired and the tour can proceed as normal. However, please remember to observe the No Smoking rule at all times.

Sir William Shakespeare was known as the Bard of Avon, a

62

hereditary title handed down from one generation of bards to the next in the town of Avon, which was situated a few miles from London, capital city of Britworld™.

The Globe Theater was first constructed by USACorp Entertainments to the same specifications as the original, but since the fire a number of alterations have been made, for instance the use of steel and plastics in place of wood and plaster.

Let's go in.

Shhh. On the stage at this very moment a play is being performed. The play is *Macbeth*, about a barbarian king who goes on a rampage of slaughter and mayhem before being brought to justice by his best friend. You've all seen the old Schwarzenegger movie on cable.

'Tomorrow and tomorrow and tomorrow.'

We don't need to hear much more to get an idea of the genius of Sir William Shakespeare's dialogue.

And here, I'm sorry to say, the tour ends. Before we leave via the exit marked 'EXIT', may I say what a privilege and a pleasure it has been for me to share with you the sights, sounds and smells of Britworld™. As you will have seen, everything has been designed to the most rigorous of standards, including the automata, which incorporate a number of technological breakthroughs that allow for a wide range of facial expressions, body odours, minor blemishes and deformities, even perspiration!

On behalf of USACorp Entertainments, I would like to thank you for accompanying me on the experience that was . . . Britworld™.

The following souvenirs are available at the merchandise kiosks: reproduction bric-a-brac; a Cockney phrase book; Union Jack baseball caps; CD-ROM editions of the works of Sherlock Holmes and Sir William Shakespeare, abridged and modernised; *My Parents Went To Britworld™ And All I Got Was This Lousy T-Shirt* T-shirts; foam-rubber crowns for the kids; the fabulous *You Are Saucy Jack* computer game (all formats); and MiniDisc and CD recordings of favourite Britworld™ folk songs, including 'Strawberry Fields Forever', 'Jerusalem', 'God Save the King', and many many more. All major credit cards accepted.

And finally, may I remind you about our other Lost Worlds® experiences, all bookable. They include the Native American Experience™, Dreamtime: the Australian Aborigine Experience™ and Life Among the Bushmen of the Kalahari™.

USACorp Entertainment – where the science of tomorrow brings the past into the present.

Have a nice day.

© USACorp Entertainments
Britworld™ is a registered trademark of USACorp Entertainments

The House of Lazarus

Visitors were welcome at the House of Lazarus at all times of day and night, but it was cheaper to come at night, when off-peak rates applied. Then, too, the great cathedral-like building was less frequented, and it was possible to have a certain amount of privacy in the company of your dear departed.

Because it was dark out, the receptionist in the cool colonnaded atrium betrayed a flicker of amusement that Joey was wearing sunglasses. Then, recognising his face, she smiled at him like an old friend, although she didn't actually use his name until after he had asked to see his mother, Mrs Delgado, and she had called up the relevant file on her terminal.

'It's young Joseph, isn't it?' she said, squinting at the screen. She couldn't have been more than three years Joey's senior. The query was chased by another over-familiar smile. 'We haven't seen you for a couple of weeks, have we?'

'I've been busy,' Joey said. 'Busy' didn't even begin to describe his life, now that he had taken on a second job at a bar on Wiltshire Street, but he didn't think the receptionist wanted to hear about that, and, more to the point, he was too tired and irritable to want to enlighten her.

The receptionist folded her hands on the long slab of marble that formed her desktop. 'It's not my place to tell you what to do, Joseph,' she said, 'but you are Mrs Delgado's only living relative, and we do like our residents to get as much stimulation as possible. As you know, we wake them for an hour of news and information every morning and an hour of light music every evening, but it's not the same as actual verbal interaction. Think of it as mental exercise for minds that don't get out much. Conversation keeps them supple.'

'I come whenever I can.'

'Of course you do. Of course you do.' That smile again, that smile of old acquaintance, of intimacy that has passed way beyond the need for forgiveness. 'I'm not criticising. I'm merely suggesting.'

'Well, thank you for the suggestion,' he said, handing her his credit card. The receptionist went through the business of swiping it, then pressed a button on a panel set into the desktop. A man in a white orderly's uniform appeared.

'Arlene Delgado,' the receptionist told the orderly. 'Stack three thirty-nine, Drawer forty-one.'

'This way, sir.' The orderly ushered Joey through a pair of large doors on which were depicted, in brass bas-relief, a man and a woman, decorously naked, serenely asleep, with electrodes attached to their temples, chests and arms.

As they entered the next room, a vast windowless chamber, the ambient temperature dropped abruptly. Cold air fell over Joey's face like a veil freshly dipped in water, and his skin buzzed with gooseflesh. He craned his neck to look up.

No matter how many times he came here, the wall never ceased to amaze him. At least a hundred and fifty feet high and well over a mile long, it consisted of stacks of steel drawers, each about half as large again as an adult's coffin. Each stack began roughly six feet above the floor and rose all the way to the roof. The wall, comprising a thousand of these stacks all told, loomed like a sheer unscalable cliff, lit from above by arc-lights that shot beams of pure white brightness down its face. Sometimes it was hard to believe that each drawer contained a human being.

At the foot of the wall plush leather armchairs were arranged in rows, ten-deep, all facing the same way like pews in a church. About a quarter of them were occupied by people murmuring quietly, as if to themselves. Every so often someone would nod or gesticulate, and silent pauses were frequent. The human sibilance was echoed by the sound of machinery, thousands of cryogenic units all whirring and whispering at once, fans exhaling, unseen tubes pumping liquid nitrogen.

The orderly walked down the aisle between the chairs and the wall, with Joey in tow. Some acoustical trick carried the clack of Joey's boot heels up to the metal rafters but kept the squelch of the orderly's crêpe soles earthbound.

Arriving at Stack 339, the orderly gestured to Joey to take the nearest seat, then began tapping commands into a portable console the size of a large wallet. Without needing to be asked, Joey picked up the mic-and-earphones headset that was wired into a panel in the armrest of the chair and fitted the skeletal black device over his head. He took off his sunglasses and folded them into his breast pocket. The orderly glanced twice at the dark purple rings beneath Joey's eyes. Joey looked as if he had been punched, but the rings were just very heavy bags of exhaustion, packed with long days and late nights.

Realising he was staring, the orderly returned his gaze to his console. 'Right,' he said. 'I've given her a nudge. Can you hear anything?'

Joey shook his head.

'She may take a moment or two to wake up. Press the red button if you need me and push the blue switch to Disconnect when you're done. OK?'

Joey nodded.

'Pleasant chat,' said the orderly, and left, squelching along to a door set into the wall. The door was marked 'STRICTLY PRIVATE' and could only be opened by tapping a five-digit code number into the keypad set into its frame. It hissed slowly shut on a pneumatic spring.

Joey sat and waited, his gaze fixed somewhere near the top of the stack of drawers, where his mother lay.

The first sounds came as if from deep underwater, where

whales wail and the mouths of drowned sailors gape and close with the come and go of the currents. Up they surged in the earphones, these subaquatic groans, bubbling to the surface in waves. Indistinct syllables, tiny glottal clucks and stutters, the gummy munches of a waking infant, the wet weaning mewls of still-blind kittens – up they came from the darkness, taking form, taking strength, slowly evolving into things that resembled words, white-noise dream-thoughts being tuned down to a signal of speech, babel finding a single voice.

>wuhwhy the – dear? is that – huhhh – nuhnnnno, nothing, no, no, nothing – on the table, you'll find them on the – huhhhello? – she never said that to me – hello? is there someone – hrrrhhh – dear, I'm talking to you, now please – it's these shoes, you know – wuhwwwwell, if you want to buy it, buy it – someone at the door, would you – yes – hahhhhhello? is someone listening? I know someone's listening. Hello? Hello? What is that? Who's there, please?<

'Hi, Mum,' said Joey. 'It's me.'

>Joey! How nice of you to drop by. It's so good to hear your voice. Been a while, hasn't it?<

'Just three days, Mum.'

>Three days? It seems an awful lot longer than that. It's so easy to lose track of time, isn't it? Well, anyway . . . How have you been keeping?<

'I'm well. And you?'

>I must be all right, mustn't I? Nothing much changes in here, so I suppose I must be staying the same. Are you *quite* sure it's only been three days? I try and keep a count of the number of times they wake me. The news. And that dreadful music. Mantovani, Manilow . . .<

'OK, maybe not three. A few days.'

>You shouldn't feel you have to lie to me, Joey.<

'I've been meaning to get down more often, Mum, but what with one thing and another . . .'

>It's all right, Joey. I do understand. There are plenty of

things more important than your old mother. Plenty of things. How's work?<

'Oh, OK. Same as usual.'

>It's not a job for a bright boy like you, taking shopping orders. It's a waste of your talents.<

'It's all I could get, Mum. I'm lucky to have a job at all.'

>And have you found yourself a nice girl yet?<

'Not yet.'

>Don't make it sound like such a trial, Joey. I'm only asking. This isn't an interrogation. I only want to know if you're happy.<

'I'm happy, Mum.'

>Well, that's good, then. And the flat? Have you had the cockroach problem sorted out?<

'I rang the Council yesterday. They said they'd already sent a man round to deal with it, but he never turned up. I think he must have been mugged on the way. I read somewhere there's a thriving black market in bug-dust. You can sell it to rich kids as cocaine and poor kids as heroin.'

>Really, Joey, you ought to have moved out of the wharf district by now. Even with a job like yours, surely you can afford somewhere a bit nicer. There's lots of new property being built. I heard it on the news. Residential blocks are popping up all over the city like mushrooms. Why do you insist on staying where you are?<

'I like it there.'

>That's as maybe, but I don't like the idea of you being there.<

'I can't afford the down-payment on another place.'

>Oh, rot! There must be more than enough left over from the money your father left us.<

'Mum, it's not as straightforward as that.'

>Seems perfectly straightforward to me.<

'Well, it would, wouldn't it?' Joey was aware of raising his voice. In that great archetraved ocean of cryogenic susurration-and-sigh, it was the merest drop of noise, but to his mother, in the dark, cramped confines of her mind, it must have sounded like he was bellowing.

>And what's that remark supposed to mean?<

'Nothing, Mum,' Joey said softly. 'Nothing at all. I'm sorry.'

>What is it, Joey? What's wrong with you? We always start out chatting so nicely, and then I say *something*, I don't know what, but something, and all of a sudden you're shouting at me, and I don't know what it is I've done, I don't know what it is I say, but I wish you'd tell me, Joey, I wish you'd tell me what it is I do that makes you so angry.<

'It's nothing, Mum. Honest. Look, I've had a long day, that's all. I get a little snappish sometimes.' He decided not to tell her about the bar job. She would only worry that he was taking on too much, and if, with her acute sense of what was proper and what was not, she thought working for TeleStore Services was bad, what would she have to say about serving drinks in a glorified pick-up joint?

>Yes, well . . . < she said. >I'm sorry, too. But you must understand, it gets very lonely in here. Very, very lonely. It's just me in the dark, and you're my lifeline to the world, Joey. You're all that makes the solitude bearable. If it wasn't for your visits, I don't know what I'd do. Go mad, I expect. If I didn't know that you were coming, if I didn't know that you were going to visit me again soon . . . <

'I will, Mum. I promise. And I won't leave it so long next time.'

>That's the best I can hope for, I suppose. Off you go then, Joey. Thanks for dropping by. It was lovely talking. Come back when you can. Ha ha – I'm not going anywhere.<

'All right, Mum. Take care.'

>Bless you, Joey.<

'Goodnight, Mum. Sleep tight.'

He removed the headset, pushed the blue switch to Disconnect, and sat there for a while, listening to the hum of the electric tombs of fifty thousand slumbering men, women and children, his skin tingling with the icy chill that emanated from the wall of steel drawers, until the orderly arrived with his portable console to shut down Joey's mother's brain and send her back to sleep.

The receptionist presented Joey with a bill to sign.

'I took the liberty of adding the rent for this quarter. Seeing as it's due in a couple of days, I thought it wouldn't hurt.'

It did. Joey winced at the figure at the bottom of the slip of paper.

'I'm not sure my credit's up to this,' he said. 'I can afford the conversation OK. I just wasn't expecting the rest.'

The receptionist's smile of a lifetime's affinity lost perhaps a fortnight, but no more than that.

'That's fine,' she said. 'I just thought it would be easier this way. You do, of course, have a month to come up with the rent, although I should remind you that failure to settle the account by the end of that period could result in your contract being declared void and your mother being decommissioned.'

'I know,' Joey said, returning the bill to her.

'I just thought I should remind you,' the receptionist said, and tore up the bill and printed off a new one.

'How was she?' she enquired as Joey signed for the price of the conversation.

'Same,' he said. 'Same as she always was.'

It had been her last request.

I don't want to die.

Spoken in a small, frail, frightened voice by dry grey lips, while eyes too big for their sockets rolled, trying to find and focus on Joey's face.

Oh, Joey, I don't want to die.

On the bus bound for home, Joey pressed his face to the window and watched the city ease past. The black stone walls, the shopfronts behind their protective grilles, the blowsy smears of shop-sign neon reflected on the wet pavements, fast, gleaming cars and drab, slow-moving citizens – all sliding by with a steady, measured grace.

I don't want to die.

She had barely been able to talk. Each sentence had been an effort, gasped out between blocked-drain gurgles. Moving her head had been a Herculean labour, but she had done so, in order to fix those swollen, terrified eyes on her son – glassy marbles that were already losing their lustre, pale-blue pupils swimming in sepia-tinged whites.

Her arms, so thin. The veins, strings binding slender strips of flesh to bone. Brown parcel-paper skin.

The man next to Joey on the bus was watching a game-show on the screen set into the headrest of the seat in front. He chuckled and gave a little round of applause whenever a contestant answered a question correctly. He groaned if a contestant was eliminated. He groaned harder if he knew the answer to a question and a contestant did not. He was very drunk.

There are ways, Joey.

He remembered that her cheeks had been so sunken that she had appeared to have no teeth, no tongue, just a sucking vacuum where her buccal cavity used to be. Her skull had loomed beneath her face.

Outside, the city slicked by, silk-lined with artificial light.

In a hard hospital room, where there had been too much brightness, Joey had taken his mother's hand. It was the first time he had touched her in as long as he could recall. She had touched him often enough, held his arm, kissed his cheek – he had never been the one to reach out across the space between them and make contact.

She tried to squeeze his fingers. He felt the creak of her knuckles as they grated together.

We have money, she said. *Your father left us enough.*

A sales rep for the House of Lazarus had been around the hospital the previous week. He had left brochures and leaflets in every ward. There were leaflets by Joey's mother's bedside.

They had been well read. One of them contained an application form which she had half completed, filling in the blanks with scrawled handwriting like an EEG readout until the effort had become too great for her.

A girl sauntered down the gangway as the bus pulled into a stop. Earlier on she had given Joey a long, simmering look. Had he not been so dog-tired, he might have done something about that look. Might have taken her up on her silent offer.

'Next stop Eastport,' chimed a disembodied voice. 'Change at Eastport for the Satellite Islands and the Coastal Route.'

We have money. Were it properly invested . . .

It had all seemed so simple to her in the last dwindling days of her life, with her body failing organ by organ. It had all seemed so clear, during her moments of painful lucidity, at the ebbing of the tranquilliser tide. She didn't want to die, and here was her chance not to die.

I just need you to complete the form and give your consent.

What choice had he had?

It's what your father would have wanted, she had said.

She had been so sure.

There's plenty of money.

Had she known?

Isn't there?

Perhaps she *had* known. All along. Perhaps she had known, and had begged him to sign anyway, not caring what it might cost him.

I can't do it without your signature, Joey. They have to have the consent of a close relative.

And why hadn't he told her? Why had he kept his mouth shut? To spare her? Or to spare himself?

The game-show gave way to a commercial break, which included an advertisement for the House of Lazarus. Gordon Lazarus, sleek-haired proprietor, delivered his pitch from a well-appointed office. He sat, perched casually, yet in a bent-backed attitude of the utmost sympathy, on the edge of a walnut desk, with a marble bust of some patrician-looking Roman to his left and, to his right, a murky Augustan landscape in an ornate gilt frame. He gazed unwaveringly into the camera.

'There comes a time when each of us has to say goodbye to someone we love,' he intoned. 'For many, it is the most painful thing they will ever have to do.'

The camera glided slowly in.

'But what if you could be spared that pain? What if you were able to remain in touch with your loved ones even after they had been taken from you?'

A slow, snakelike smile. Cut to a moving craneshot of the wall of fifty thousand steel drawers.

Lazarus, in voice-over: 'Here at the House of Lazarus, years of research into cryogenic technology have borne fruit. The result? The actual moment of passing may now be delayed indefinitely.'

The camera continued its swoop, finding Gordon Lazarus at the foot of the wall, standing in front of a family who were clustered around a single headset in emulation of some long-forgotten pre-television tradition, taking it in turns to talk to grandfather or great aunt or poor little junior who was torn from this world far too soon. For bereaved people, the family looked remarkably happy.

'Until recently, communication with the departed was the province of mediums and clairvoyants,' said Lazarus. 'No more. Here at the House of Lazarus we can keep your loved ones permanently at the threshold of the hereafter. I won't blind you with science. Suffice it to say that by stimulating the neural impulses that remain in the cerebral cortex we can enable your loved ones to talk and interact with you long after the breath has left their bodies. Though departed, they won't be gone. Though lost, they will live on.' Another smile, this one ingratiating. 'To find out more, simply e-mail me, Gordon Lazarus, care of the House of Lazarus, or call the free-phone number below.'

A number appeared at the bottom of the screen in gilt-edged Gothic script.

With a spread of his arms, as if to say, *It's that simple*, Lazarus reached his conclusion: 'The House of Lazarus. Where nothing is inevitable.'

The image froze, and there was a brief burst of a jingle – a few bars of the chorus to 'Never Can Say Goodbye' – and then a caption appeared:

THE HOUSE OF LAZARUS
KEEPING THE MEMORIES ALIVE

'Poor bashtardsh,' muttered the drunk man next to Joey. 'Let 'em resht in peash, thash wha' I shay.'

It's for the best, his mother had said as he had signed the application form in the presence of the hospital-haunting sales rep. *You'll see.*

Through blurring tears Joey had appended his name to the form, which the rep had then taken and folded with a satisfied air, slipping his thumb and forefinger along the crease.

'We'll see to it that everything is in place,' the rep had said. 'For the final moment. It's essential that we are present for the final moment, in order to take possession of the body during the brief window of opportunity between physical shutdown and actual clinical brain-death. I'll make the arrangements with the hospital to alert one of our standby units when the time comes. Before that, we'll have to take tissue samples and carry out a few tests, including a full psychological profile. And then there's the question of payment . . .' He had raised his eyebrows meaningfully.

Joey's mother had strained and struggled to turn her eyes on her son again, to look at him, to beg.

Had she known? That there had been almost nothing left of the money his father had bequeathed to her? That after the government and the lawyers had taken their bites, there had been just a crust left over to pay for her treatment? That keeping her alive for six months had used up the very last of the capital?

Joey had to believe that she had not, that she had been too ill to make the calculations, that the sickness sucking on her like a spider had cocooned her from practical considerations. Otherwise . . . But the alternative was too awful to contemplate.

'Eastport,' chimed the bus's PA system.

No one except Joey disembarked.

He was almost too exhausted to undress. He barely made it down to his underpants before the weight of his tiredness dragged him down on to the bed. With the last ebb of his strength he switched off the bedside lamp, and then he was rushing down into a darkness like every curtain in the world closing at once.

And at some point during the night he dreamed that he was standing over his mother's grave. It was a traditional grave, dug in traditional ground, with a traditional headstone carved with the name ARLENE DELGADO. Beneath that were the dates that bookended her life, and then the inscription:

A GOOD MOTHER
LOVED BY HER SON

The earth that covered her had not yet been grassed over, and when Joey prodded the side of the shallow mound of soil with one toecap it gave softly and loosely, spilling in a tiny crumbling landslide around his boots. He reasoned – with the illogical certainty of dreams – that his mother could only have been buried within the past twenty-four hours. He even vaguely remembered a funeral service.

It was a large, tomb-crowded cemetery, stark in winter, lit by a bright, unclouded sun, and he was alone. In front of him, not two yards beneath his feet, the body of his mother lay. It was almost impossible to believe that she could be so close and yet seem so distant. (Perhaps this was an alert part of his consciousness gently reminding him that he was dreaming; that his mother really lay elsewhere, halfway across the city.) If not for the earth and the lid of the coffin, he could have reached down and actually touched her cold, placid face. The idea made him quite angry. What a ludicrous convention this was, to shove the dead under a few feet of soil. It was a kind of masochism, to allow your loved ones to be left so tantalisingly near. The dead ought to be thrown into bottomless pits, where they could disappear for ever and be forgotten. They shouldn't be put where anyone with two hands and sufficient determination could dig them up again . . .

As he was digging up his mother now.

He had no recollection of falling to his knees and starting to hand-shovel the earth away. The dream edited that bit out in a jump-cut. All he knew was that he had scooped aside a few handfuls of dirt and that he was already scraping the lid of his mother's coffin. Not even the full six feet down! What kind of cheapjack gravediggers did they employ at this cemetery?

The earth cleared easily from the lid, rattling down into the gaps between the sides of the coffin and the walls of the grave. Suddenly, with dream simplicity, the lid was free from dirt, shiny and clean. Its brass fixtures gleamed in the sun. Six butterfly nuts secured the lid. Feverishly Joey unscrewed them, tossing each over his shoulder as it spun free. As the final nut was removed the lid gave a little jump, as though eager to be opened.

Here, the dream allowed Joey to hesitate. Seconds away from seeing his mother's face again, it occurred to him that she might not be a pretty sight. Already, even after only a day, decay and worms might have begun their work. Did he really want to remember her rotten and halfeaten?

But no – he had to see. He had to see her for himself: lifeless, motionless, serenely and securely under death's spell.

He wedged his fingers under the lid and levered it up. It was surprisingly light, as though made of balsa wood rather than pine. It all but flew off, landing and bouncing on the graveside grass, finally settling upside down to lie rocking gently to and fro.

And now the unknown director of the dream decided to shoot everything in slow motion, and it took Joey what seemed like an eternity to transfer his gaze from the upturned lid to the opened coffin. He was anxious that he might wake up before he had a chance to look. So many of his dreams ended on precisely this sort of anticlimax. And having actually thought about waking up, he became more anxious still, because the thought usually preceded the reality. He forced his gaze towards the coffin, forced himself to stare in . . .

And even as he surfaced from sleep, to wake the customary three minutes before the alarm clock went off, he realised that he had known all along that the coffin would be empty. What else had he expected? His mother was lying in cold storage at the House of Lazarus. Of course she wasn't buried in any cemetery. Honestly, he did have the dumbest dreams sometimes.

But if only it had been that easy to dismiss the dream. All through the day, while he processed the orders that came through on the TeleStore computer and made sure that the correct packages were dispatched to the correct addresses, Joey couldn't shake from his head the dream's closing image: the gaping box, the lining of flesh-red quilted satin, the absence of any indication that his mother had lain there for even a second. Likewise at his evening job at the bar on Wiltshire Street, there was not a minute, not even during the headlong rush of happy hour, when he did not think of the coffin's mocking emptiness.

During a lull he mentioned the dream to Corinne, the bar manageress, who was into horoscopes and prediction and all that malarkey. She nodded authoritatively as he described the dream to her. 'It's a classic guilt/anxiety manifestation,' she explained. 'The empty coffin symbolises the loneliness you feel. The red lining symbolises your pain and grief, which are still unresolved. The fact that you dug her up means that you're trying to confront your dilemma, bringing your subconscious uncertainties to light.' Corinne smiled, glad to be of service. 'Does that help?'

'Yes,' he said. 'It does. Thanks.'

But it didn't help. Not one bit.

The trouble was, Joey could no longer remember his mother's face clearly. This had obsessed him all day, the obsession deepening as the day wore on and the work became more and yet more numbingly dull. In vain he racked his brain for an image of his mother that didn't involve her lying in a hospital bed with eyes full of fear and almost no flesh on her body. He tried to recall how she had looked when he was a child, and nothing came. He tried to think of a hairstyle, a shade of lipstick, a favourite item of clothing, anything that might jog his memory. No use. Any recollections he might have had of his mother before she fell ill had been supplanted by the image of the pitiful thing that had pleaded with him in the hospital, clutching a House of Lazarus leaflet in one skeletal hand. He could barely even remember what she had looked like *then*. His mother had become almost completely associated with an emotion, and that emotion was disgust, and the disgust smeared everything in dark, obscuring hues that hid facial features, expressions, gestures, kindness, love.

At midnight, when the bar closed, Joey mopped the floor, bagged the empties and left them out on the pavement for the recycling lorry, and then did not take the bus home. Instead, he took the bus across town to the House of Lazarus.

The receptionist was mildly surprised to see him, but no less displeased for that. This time she remembered his name straight away (it had, after all, been only a day since he had last visited). This made Joey feel uncomfortable. He preferred the formality of anonymity.

'Your mother will be delighted,' the receptionist said. She

obviously felt that, in successfully persuading Joey to come to the House of Lazarus more often, she had done her job well.

An orderly Joey didn't recognise took him through to the chamber. This man had either previously worked in a funeral parlour or else had decided that a sepulchral voice and a funereal pallor were appropriate to the job at hand. He talked with his lips alone. The rest of his face stayed immobile, like a wax death mask.

'Sir is familiar with the arrangements here?' he enquired as Joey sat himself down.

'Sir is,' Joey replied, fitting on the headset.

'Then,' said the orderly, tapping a last few instructions into his portable console, 'have a most enjoyable conversation.'

There were perhaps no more than three dozen living souls in the entire chamber (not counting the fifty thousand sealed in their sub-zero halfway houses), and while Joey waited for his mother's voice to manifest itself in the headphones, he looked around until he located the customer who was sitting closest to the door marked 'STRICTLY PRIVATE', through which the orderlies came and went as required. The customer was an old lady with whom bereavement clearly agreed. She was talking animatedly into the headset microphone, stopping only to listen briefly and laugh before continuing her side of the dialogue.

When he heard the first muffled murmurings of his mother's voice, he hit the Mute button on the chair's armrest, slid the volume control down to zero, and started to talk quietly.

'I know you can't hear me, Mum. If it's any consolation, I can't hear you either. I'm sorry about this. It must be very confusing for you. You're probably wondering what's gone wrong. You're probably complaining bitterly. I'm sorry. This is just something I have to do . . .'

All the while, as he apologised to thin air, his attention was focused on the old woman. He was waiting for her to finish her conversation and hit Disconnect with her gnarled old finger, which would automatically summon an orderly.

And at last, after about five minutes, the woman began gathering her belongings together, settling her handbag on her lap in readiness to leave. One final goodbye, and then her hand went to the armrest.

Joey snatched off his headset and got to his feet.

He hadn't had a plan when he had taken the bus here instead of going home. He had simply been obeying an instinct, an urge. And even now, when he was about to take action, he still didn't have a plan. He was extemporising, using situation and circumstance to get him where he wanted to be: on the other side of the wall. For, he believed, on the other side lay the means of reaching Drawer 41 in Stack 339, and not just reaching the drawer but opening the drawer and looking into the drawer.

It was the dream that had done it. The dream had in fact supplied the answer to its own question: the coffin had been empty because Joey could no longer remember how his mother had looked. Adrienne had been wrong. The coffin represented his memory. And so he had to see his mother's face again. It was no longer enough just to hear her voice, to talk to her and listen to the disembodied replies coming from an electric void. He had to fix her features once more in his mind. He had to see her once more in the flesh. This was something which a standard burial did not allow but which the House of Lazarus made possible (or so the dream had seemed to be telling him, if a little obliquely). All he had to do was get to the drawer, pull it open, take a good long look, and he was sure he would never forget her face again.

He was already moving towards the door when an orderly came out to shut down the old woman's relative. The orderly nodded politely to Joey as he passed, no doubt thinking Joey was merely making his way to the main exit. The door crept shut on a slow sigh of its pneumatic spring, and just as it was about to close Joey stepped nimbly into the gap, holding the door back long enough to insert himself through.

He found himself in a white corridor that reverberated with the throb of all the hardware overhead. About ten yards along, set into the left-hand wall, was a door which Joey presumed led to the place where the orderlies waited when they weren't attending to customers. Opposite it was another door, marked 'WC'. At the end of the corridor, about thirty yards away, was a lift.

Joey was almost certain that he had not been spotted sneaking in behind the orderly's back, but he couldn't afford to hang around, just in case he had not been as stealthy as he had thought. (Even now the orderly could be tapping in his door-code, alerted by some vigilant customer.) He set off along the corridor at a loping jog-trot, scarcely able to believe that he had had the audacity and the opportunity to get this far. He was on the other side of the wall. The lift would surely provide access to each and every drawer. He was going to see his mother again!

He smacked the button to summon the lift, and the heavy doors trundled open. He was just about to enter the lift when the lavatory door back down the corridor opened on a crescendo of flushing water. Joey froze, and then, realising that this was precisely what he shouldn't be doing, skipped smartly across the threshold of the lift. Turning to face the control panel, he caught sight of an orderly in the corridor. It was the same funereal fellow who had assisted him earlier. Blindly Joey hit the first button his fingers found. At the same instant the orderly turned and caught sight of him. A startled look discomposed the man's waxy features.

'Hey! What are you—?'

The lift doors closed, cutting off the rest of the question.

The lift ascended swiftly. Of the three floor levels listed on the control panel – Ground, Maintenance and Administration – Joey had, more by luck than judgement, pressed the button for the one he needed: Maintenance. When the lift hissed to a halt, the doors opened to reveal a gantry that travelled parallel with the wall, running some twenty feet above the ground floor. Like almost everything else Joey could see on this side of the wall, the gantry was painted white.

In front of Joey the drawers rose in their stacks, much as they did on the side he was already familiar with. The stacks stretched in both directions as far as the eye could see, and the mechanical hum was just as prevalent here. The major difference was that on this side the drawers were serviced by hydraulic cranes. In the distance two of them were moving with a slow and stately gracefulness up and down and along the stacks, each carrying a white-clad orderly in its cherry-picker. The cherry-pickers paused at each drawer to allow the orderlies to run diagnostic checks. Watching the two long mechanical arms rising and falling, Joey thought of a pair of long-necked dinosaurs engaged in some elegant, elaborate courting ritual.

Behind him the lift doors suddenly rolled shut and the lift began to descend. It required no great stretch of the imagination to deduce that the funereal orderly had raised the alarm. Joey realised he must move quickly now.

His gaze alighted on the nearest crane, which was parked a few yards along from where he was standing, its cherry-picker stationed adjacent to the gantry railing. A sign on the railing said:

STACKS 300–350

The next thing Joey knew, he was standing in the cherry-picker and examining its control panel. The On switch was easy to find, and once the small display lit up, operating the crane was simply a matter of following the onscreen prompts as they appeared. He tapped in the location of his mother's stack and drawer, then pressed Enter. The crane obediently began to move. First it extended forwards until Joey was within arm's reach of the wall. Then it began to glide horizontally past the drawers, heading for Stack 339. Joey noted that each drawer was fitted with an access panel and a rotating handle that was marked off by a hazard-striped circle. So much more convenient than digging through dirt, he thought. A twist and turn of the handle, and the drawer would slide smoothly open, and there she would be.

A shout from the gantry brought his head snapping round.

'You! What the hell do you think you're doing?' It was an orderly with an electronic clipboard. He was standing wide-legged on the gantry, with a look of outrage and incredulity on his face. 'You're not qualified to operate that!'

'I'm going to see my mother,' Joey replied straightfor-wardly.

Just then the lift arrived to disgorge another three orderlies, including the funereal one.

'There he is!' the funereal one shouted. His pale cheeks were flushed. Two pinks circles glowed unhealthily against his pure white complexion.

'Come back here at once,' said the orderly with the clipboard, striding along the gantry now, keeping pace with the progress of the cherry-picker.

'I pay to keep her here,' Joey said to him. 'I break my back to make enough fucking money to keep her here. So I'll fucking well see her if I fucking well want to.'

'But you don't understand,' said the orderly. 'The seal. If you break the cryogenic seal, the shock to her physiology could kill her.'

Joey shook his head calmly. 'I just want to take a look at her. It'll only be for a moment. She'll be fine.' He turned back to face the wall. The crane halted abruptly, and for a few heart-deadening, hope-dashing seconds Joey thought it had broken down – either that, or the orderlies had a means of overriding its controls. Then the cherry-picker began to move again, this time vertically. He had reached Stack 339 and was rising.

'Somebody go and fetch Mr Lazarus,' the clipboard orderly said, and there was the sound of running feet clanging on metal.

'Mr Delgado?' said the funereal orderly. He was pleading

now. 'Please come back down. I don't think you have any idea what you're doing.'

Ignoring him, Joey gazed upwards.

'I'm coming, Mum,' he said. 'I'm coming to see you.'

Gordon Lazarus was there when they finally managed to bring the crane back down from near the top of Stack 339. And it was Lazarus who first stepped into the cherry-picker, in which Joey was sitting hunched, his legs drawn up to his chest, his hands fisted beneath his chin, his gaze fixed somewhere on eternity.

'Joseph?'

Recognising the voice of the founder and proprietor of the House of Lazarus, Joey stirred.

'Come with me.'

Meekly Joey stood up and allowed himself to be taken by the hand and led back on to the gantry, through the crowd of a dozen or so orderlies that had gathered, into the lift and up to Administration. All the while Lazarus talked soothingly, encouragingly, reassuringly to him. In the commercial, Lazarus had come across as cold and vaguely insincere, but in the flesh he seemed genuinely caring. His dark suit stood out in sharp contrast to all the eye-watering whiteness. Joey found it strangely restful to look at that suit, when everything else was so painfully white.

Lazarus sat Joey down in his office – not the office shown on television. This was an altogether more functional place, rather like mission control for a space flight, fitted out with the very latest in communications technology. The chairs were comfortable but not extravagantly so. The desk was broad and spacious, but skeletally constructed from plastic and steel, not wood. There were no pictures on the walls and no windows.

Lazarus asked Joey if he would like a drink, and when Joey didn't reply, poured him one anyway. The chunky tumbler, quarter full of whisky, sat heavily in Joey's unfeeling fingers.

Lazarus poured himself a drink, too, and then sat on the edge of the desk and began talking. Explaining things. First he talked about faith. The transfiguring power of faith, the absolute necessity of faith when all else fails. Then he started talking about the unfeasibility of cryogenics, how it was impossible for complex organic systems to survive prolonged exposure to sub-zero conditions, and how for this reason cryogenics would always remain an unrealisable dream. Joey didn't quite understand what Lazarus was saying. Wasn't that the entire principle on which the House of Lazarus was based – keeping the dead alive on ice? So what was the deal here? Then Lazarus started using phrases such as 'connectionist networks' and 'subcognitive modules', 'rule-based symbol manipulation' and 'Gödel's theorems about enclosed formal systems'. None of these would have meant anything to Joey even if he had been thinking straight, but when Lazarus said the words 'artificial intelligence', Joey remembered what he had discovered in the drawer that was supposed to contain his mother's body, and things began to fall into place.

After he had talked some more, Lazarus fell silent, obviously expecting a reply. When none came, he spoke again: 'Well, Joseph. I've said all I've got to say. I've been as honest as I can. The question now is, what are *you* going to do?'

Joey made several hoarse false starts before finally finding his voice. 'I don't know.'

'Are you going to go to the police with this information? The media? I have to know, Joseph. It determines how I . . . deal with you.'

'She was just wires and chipboards and a hard drive and—'

'But she's *real*, isn't she, Joseph?' Lazarus said, with a glint in his eye. 'She's *real* to you. That's what counts.'

Joey couldn't deny the truth of that statement. 'What did you do with the body?' he asked.

'We gave her a proper send-off.'

Joey looked at Lazarus doubtfully.

'I swear,' said Lazarus. 'We employ a multi-denominational priest full-time at our private crematorium. I'm not a monster, Joseph. I have a healthy respect for the dead. After all, one day I'm going to join that club myself. But you still haven't answered my question.'

'I don't know what I'm going to do,' Joey said finally. 'I need some time to think.'

'I can't give you time, Joseph,' said Lazarus, glancing at his wristwatch as if considering whether it might not actually be conceivable for him to shave off a portion of the universe's relentless tick-tock and hand it to Joey. 'Time is the one thing I do not have. If you are prepared to be reasonable with me, however, I can make you an offer.'

'An offer?' said Joey.

'A very generous offer. As I said, I'm no monster.'

And Lazarus explained.

'Mr Delgado. How good to see you again.'

Joey was such a regular these days, perhaps the receptionist's smiling familiarity wasn't feigned after all. And now that he had privileged-customer status and was entitled to talk to his mother for however long he wanted, free, her smile seemed less patronising, more deferential.

'Go on through.'

Into the chamber of gleaming steel drawers. Into the mechanical exhalation of thousands of fans, chilling the skin, bringing a tincture of winter to the air – a marvellously bogus touch, the confirmation of a mass preconception, like a stage magician's top hat and wand.

Stack 339. Drawer 41.

'Mum?'

And telling her everything he had done that day, everything he was doing tomorrow.

'I'm thinking of moving. I've applied to the Council for a transfer. They say the chances are good.'

Building up a life for himself. For her.

'Still looking for a new job, but there's enough left from the money Dad left us to tide me over.'

Some of it false, but most of it real, and the real encroaching on the false day by day.

'I've found someone. You'd like her. I'll bring her along some time so you can meet her.'

Because all along, without his realising it, he had needed his mother just as much as he had believed she had needed him.

'I'm happy now, Mum.'

Because he hadn't wanted her to die any more than she herself had wanted to die.

'Honestly I am.'

And because sometimes an illusion is so enchanting, so alluring, so life-enhancing, it is infinitely preferable to the truth.

'And I'm glad that you are, too.'

Isn't that so?

'Very glad.'

Isn't it?

The Driftling

The morning after the storm, Jane/208 set off down the beach to see what the ocean had surrendered overnight. Flotsam was always more plentiful in the aftermath of a storm. It was as though the sea was trying to make up for having battered and buffeted the island all night long by offering up gifts, compensation for the dark, roaring hours of fear and sleeplessness.

The sky was ragged and torn, and an onshore wind gusted at Jane/208, forcing her to lean into it in order to keep her footing on the shingles, but the sun flared intermittently through gaps in the clouds, promising warmth to come. In its rays, the foam that flecked the wavetops was shot through with miniature rainbows.

Jane/208 passed clusters of seagulls squabbling over stranded fish and wave-crushed crabs. She was not looking for food. Others would be doing that, taking advantage of the harvest, scavenging above the tideline where the pickings were rich. Nor was she looking for fresh driftwood, though there was plenty of it about.

Sometimes, after storms, the ocean gave up something special; reached deep into its pockets and dug out something that been lying there for a long time, something precious and rare that only guilt and the desire to atone could have persuaded it to part with.

Jane/208 was searching for a gift for Jane/202. A piece of glass that had been smoothed and polished by the tide would, when hung on a braided length of sun-dried kelp, make a fine pendant. A mother-of-pearl shell could be transformed by a craftswoman into a comb to hold up Jane/202's beautiful hair. A shark's tooth would make for a brooch if Jane/208 took it to be scrimshawed; perhaps she could have her likeness engraved into it as a keepsake for her lover.

But what she was really hoping to come across was something made of metal. Gold, preferably, but since gold washed up once in a blue moon, she would happily settle for one of the duller, greyer varieties of metal. Any kind of metal, in fact, so long as it could be wrought into a ring.

Jane/208 had made up her mind to ask Jane/202 to be her sharer. They already lived together, had done so for seven bleedings, so it seemed the next logical step to solemnise their union with the ritual of exchanging gifts. And a ring, as Jane/208 saw it, was the ideal gift, representing as it did the beach that banded the island, the annular strip of shingle that shaped and limited the lives of the Parthenai.

Of course, it was by no means certain that Jane/202 would accept the ring and consent to become Jane/208's sharer. In fact, Jane/208 had a pretty good idea what Jane/202 would stay when she asked. *Why ruin what we have? We love each other, we're committed to each other . . . What difference will a couple of gifts and a ceremony make?*

No difference at all, and yet every difference in the world. Rituals and symbols meant a lot to Jane/208. Emotions, like the sea, were apt to change. A symbol gave permanence to a feeling. A ritual pegged a moment in memory, meaning it was less likely to be forgotten. Though Jane/208 was sure of her love for Jane/202, and almost as sure of Jane/202's love for her, still she wanted something tangible that would show Jane/202 how she felt and allow Jane/202 to demonstrate that she felt the same. That wasn't a lot to ask, was it?

As a matter of fact, knowing Jane/202, it probably was. But Jane/208 was none the less determined to go through with the ordeal of getting down on her knees before her and uttering the formal declaration of sharing – *You are my sister, my lover, my reflection, my matching half, the fullness of my moon* – even though there was a chance that Jane/202 would decline, even though it might conceivably mean the end of their relationship. Frightened though she was of rejection, Jane/208 was more frightened still of insecurity.

Soon the huddle of driftwood shelters was out of sight, and the beach stretched ahead of Jane/208 and the beach reached behind her, a curved, narrowing strip of grey in both directions, bounded by the sea on one side and on the other by a wall of black cliff spattered with streaks of bright white guano. What lay beyond the top of the cliff no one knew, since its sides were unclimbably smooth and sheer, but it was generally assumed that the island was a flat-topped plateau of granite encircled by beach. Only the seagulls had any idea if this assumption was true or not, and they weren't telling.

Jane/208's hardened feet scarcely felt the pebbles beneath them. Even the sharp edges of shells were unable to penetrate the thick calluses on her soles. She crunched along, scanning the ground in front of her, stopping every so often when a glint caught her eye. Though she had long ago learned to distinguish between the gleam of a fish's scales and any other shiny object, this morning she made a point of not passing anything by, just in case, just on the off-chance.

She had been foraging unsuccessfully for as long as it took the tide to go out two body-lengths when she spied the congregation of seagulls up ahead. Instead of the usual three or four, dozens of them had gathered in one spot, and they were strutting and squawking and feuding the way they usually did when there was good food to be had, but none of them was actually eating anything. Which meant that whatever it was that had drawn them was not dead.

Immediately Jane/208 thought, *Dolphin*. And with that thought came a twinge of annoyance. If it was a beached dolphin, she was obliged to go back to the village and report it, so that a team of volunteers could come with sledges and knives to slaughter the creature and flense it of its meat and hide. As the dolphin's finder, Jane/208 would have to be a part

95

of that team, and this meant that, basically, the rest of the day was no longer hers.

She toyed with the idea of ignoring the dolphin, strolling past as if it wasn't there, but her sense of duty was too strong, her loyalty to the tribe too deeply ingrained. Cursing her luck, she dragged her unwilling feet forwards to where the seagulls were flocking.

The birds saw her coming and grudgingly cleared a path for her. Those that didn't waddle out of the way quickly enough she motivated with a kick. They closed ranks behind her until she was standing at the centre of a ragged circle of white wings and grey-feathered backs and tossing yellow beaks and jet eyes.

It was not a dolphin.

It was a woman, lying face down on the shingles, the waves seething around her legs.

Not just a woman, either. At least, she was like no woman Jane/208 had laid eyes on before. The contours of her legs and back were wrong. Her buttocks were covered in matted hair; so were her shoulders. And there was something down there, down between her thighs. Some kind of growth or goitre, such as sometimes developed on the bodies of older Parthenai.

Jane/208 could hardly bring herself to touch this strange being, but she had to make sure she was alive.

The woman had been in the water for quite some while. Her skin was cold, white and wrinkled. But in the flesh beneath, there was warmth. In the big vein at her neck, a flutter.

'Bad luck, my friends,' Jane/208 told the seagulls, and bent to drag the woman up the beach where she would be beyond the reach of the sea when it came thundering back in.

The sun had broken up the clouds, reducing them to a few tattered wisps of white, when Jane/208 returned with Jane/197, Jane/211 and Jane/211's daughter, Jane/243. It was just past the peak of the day, and the black cliff gleamed so fiercely it was almost painful to look at.

Jane/197 had scoffed at Jane/208's excited claims about discovering a woman, saying that the sea only produced fish and *things*, not people. Never mind that Jane/208 insisted that she had actually touched the woman, had pulled her up the beach; Jane/197 considered Jane/208 a dreamy sort whose imagination too often got the better of her. Nonetheless, she had agreed to come because she thought that what Jane/208 had taken for a near-drowned woman was a seal or a manatee, and she fancied the idea of a new fur tunic or a new pair of boots. Hence she was equipped with two kinds of knife – one with a whelk-shell blade for paring, the other with a clam-shell blade for hacking, both fitted with bone handles – and Jane/211 and Jane/243 were pushing a sledge.

The seagulls were still there, more of them than before, but Jane/208 saw to her relief that they were keeping a respectful distance from the woman. The seagulls, in common with most creatures whose diet consisted mainly of carrion, were as cowardly as they were patient. They could wait for ever for a meal to die but none of them was bold enough to hasten the process along.

Their cries turned raucous and angry as the four Parthenai beat a path through them to the body.

'Jane/208,' said Jane/197 stiffly, 'please accept my humble apologies.' She stared down at the woman. 'Well, this is news. No boots or tunic for me today, but a driftling thing to show the rest of the tribe, that's for sure.'

Jane/243 knelt and ran a cautious hand over the woman's hairy shoulders. 'It's soft,' she said. 'Like fledgling down.'

'Will we be able to get her into the sledge?' Jane/211 wanted to know.

'I *did* suggest we built a stretcher,' said Jane/208, 'like we do when we have to take someone to Mother Cave who's too sick to walk.'

'Never mind that,' said Jane/197. 'We'll have to make do with what we've got. Each of you take a leg, Jane/208 and Jane/211. Jane/243 and I will both take an arm.'

They hoisted the driftling up and carried her to the sledge, resting her on its rim.

'Ready?' said Jane/197.

The other three nodded, and carefully they rolled the driftling over and lowered her backside first into the sledge, bending and angling her legs so that she would fit.

'Ugh!' exclaimed Jane/243, pointing at the knot of bulbous fleshy lumps that nestled at the driftling's crotch. 'Mother, what is *that*?'

Jane/211 prodded one of the lumps tentatively. 'Some kind of wart?' she hazarded.

'Tumours, by the looks of it,' said Jane/197. 'And one of them's split open.'

'That must hurt,' said Jane/211.

'What about this?' said Jane/208, indicating the driftling's face.

They all peered at the fuzz of hair that coated her cheeks and jaw.

'Some of the elders have that,' said Jane/211.

'But none as dark and bristly,' said Jane/208. 'And besides, it can only be about a hundred bleedings since she was a girl.'

'There's another of those lumps at the front of her throat,' said Jane/243.

'And see the shape of her breasts?' said Jane/211.

'Are they breasts at all?' Jane/197 wondered, eyeing the muscular, hirsute planes of the driftling's chest.

'She has teats,' Jane/208 remarked doubtfully.

'All very strange,' said Jane/197. 'Come on, let's get her back to the village and away from these damned birds. They're making such a racket I can't hear myself think.'

They took it in turns to push the sledge along the beach. The driftling was heavy and the sledge's runners ploughed deep into the shingles, making the going hard. They rested on several occasions and gnawed on strips of fish jerky for strength. A train of seagulls followed them all the way home, gliding in their wake like wind-blown thistledown.

It was decided that Jane/208, who had found the driftling, should have the responsibility of looking after her. Jane/202 was not best pleased at the idea of having to share their shelter, cramped as it already was, with a third party, but Jane/197, whom Jane/202 respected, convinced her that there was room, reminding her that duty to others came before anything else. Jane/208 rolled out the bed matting on the shingle floor and they placed the driftling gently there. The driftling had not stirred or uttered a sound since Jane/208 had discovered her. The sleep that held her was profound, death-like. But still a pulse beat in her neck, faintly, like a kelp flea hopping.

They wrapped her in a patchwork blanket, hiding her unnatural flat-chestedness, her angular, hairy body and that deformity between her legs. Then they went outside, sat in the shade of the shelter's awning and debated in low voices.

Jane/208 was all for someone going to Mother Cave and asking her advice. Jane/211 agreed, since it was well known that Mother Cave had all the answers.

'Maybe,' said a surly Jane/197, 'but it seems to me she's forgetting more and more of them every day.'

Three bleedings ago Jane/197's sharer, Jane/190, broke her ankle and was taken to Mother Cave to have the injury tended to and mended. She did not return, and when asked Mother Cave could not explain what had happened other than that she had made some sort of error. She did not apologise; she seemed confused but not at all perturbed. Jane/197, under-standably, had been deeply suspicious of Mother Cave ever since, and never missed an opportunity to cast doubt on her wisdom and infallibility.

'Perhaps Mother Cave isn't all she used to be,' said Jane/208, 'but she still has more knowledge about more things than the rest of us put together.'

'Who says?'

'Everyone, Jane/197.'

'Not me. Not a lot of the Parthenai I talk to.'

'Still,' said Jane/211, 'what harm can it do if one of us goes?'

'But which one?' said Jane/202, in a tone of voice that suggested she was hoping it wouldn't have to be her.

'You're so keen, Jane/208,' said Jane/197. 'You do it.'

Jane/208, realising that if she didn't go no one else would, begged Jane/202 to accompany her. Jane/202 was initially reluctant, saying she had far better things to do, but Jane/208 was persistent, and finally Jane/202 sighed and said all right, she would walk with her as far as the entrance to Mother Cave but no further.

Jane/211 wished them good luck, and together they set off up the beach.

Finding the driftling had driven from Jane/208's head all thoughts of gifts and asking Jane/202 to be her sharer, but now, in turn, her excitement and curiosity were ousted by trepidation. A visit to Mother Cave was always associated with pain and difficulty. The Parthenai went to Mother Cave for one of five reasons: to get advice, to conceive a child, to give birth to a child, to be cured of an ailment, and to die. All of these involved some degree or other of suffering.

Mother Cave stood at the top of the beach overlooking the village like a giant, empty eye-socket. The well-tended rockpool garden that surrounded the cavemouth could only be crossed by a series of stepping stones. The bed of the delta-shaped rockpool was purple with pulsing anemones, its waters speckled with silvery winks of sprats.

Mother Cave herself hollowed unfathomably far into the cliff. No tribeswoman had ever dared to investigate beyond the first two chambers, but it was generally believed that on the other side of the second chamber's door Mother Cave continued for ever, like the beach, like the sea, whose only limits were those that the eye imposed.

Pausing at the edge of the rockpool garden, Jane/208

begged a good-luck kiss off Jane/202, then turned and walked across the stepping stones.

The cavemouth, three times as tall as she was, yawned around her, and she felt very small and pitifully nervous as she ventured into the darkness within.

In still air, hush and shadow she paused to allow her eyes to grow accustomed to the gloom. Gradually the dim outlines of stalactites became clear, and she could detect the faint hum of Mother Cave dreaming. She moved slowly to the centre of the first chamber, her feet whispering on the smooth floor, and there, before a rusted, thronelike chair, she halted and inclined her head respectfully.

'Mother Cave?'

There was a groaning and a stirring from deep within Mother Cave's walls, and something sputtered and sparked, and a glass sphere half encrusted with smooth nodules of sedimentary deposit flickered and began to glow. One bright green eye snapped into life on the side of a large metal box, and the rusted chair shifted its arms and seat like a living thing, its joints whirring. In the next chamber along lights stuttered then shone, illuminating a steel table over which needles and scalpels were poised on armatures, all lustreless and corroded. Jane/208 averted her gaze from that room. You didn't have to know what went on in there (although she did) to tell that it had played host to more than its fair share of agony. Dark stains patterned the floor.

Name/number?

Mother Cave's voice reverberated achingly through Jane/208's skull.

'Jane/208, daughter of Jane/151, granddaughter of Jane/93,' she replied, speaking softly, because then Mother Cave would adjust her volume accordingly.

State your purpose, said Mother Cave, her boom subdued.

'We need advice on a certain matter, Mother Cave.'

Sit.

Nervously Jane/208 lowered herself into the chair. Its cold, damp surfaces chilled her skin, sending waves of gooseflesh undulating across her arms and legs. She braced herself.

The chair altered its dimensions to accommodate her tightly, then, with a squeal of servomotors, a helmet shaped like a jellyfish descended from between two stalactites and came to a halt a hand's breadth above the crown of her head. On pointed tips its tentacles danced over her face and scalp, searching, testing, and she winced in anticipation, clenching her teeth.

'Ah!'

She gasped as her skin was pierced in a dozen places at once. Pins of pain prickled around her eyebrows, ears, temples and at the top of her spinal column. She forced herself to keep calm. This was the worst of it. What came next was unpleasant but at least did not hurt.

She closed her eyes, and with a sudden whoosh she was wrenched out of herself, hurtling upwards into the soul-womb of Mother Cave, diving dizzyingly up through a darkness lit with mercurial flashes of white. A surge of sparkles, like stars being cast across the heavens, fading to black, and then she was floating suspended in a warm, dark place where there was no sense of up or down, no night or day, just an eternal, lulling, tidal rhythm, and when Mother Cave spoke again, her voice came from all around Jane/208 and inside her.

What would you ask of me?

Jane/208 made a conscious effort not to frame her thoughts in words and to think in images, but all the same she suspected that her body, wherever it was, was speaking aloud. She explained to Mother Cave about the driftling woman, going over the events of the day in detail – her actions, her feelings, even, regrettably, her reluctance to report what she had thought to be a beached dolphin – until she felt she had provided every scrap of relevant information, and then she let her mind go blank to indicate that she desired a reply.

Mother Cave was silent for an unusually long time.

Then she said: A threat is posed to the tribe. The system will not continue to function peacefully and harmoniously while this random element remains unchecked. However, further deliberation is called for before an appropriate course of action can be determined. Consult me again when this 'driftling' regains consciousness. Disengaging.

A vertiginous plummet, and Jane/208 was back in her body again, feeling sick and woozy. The helmet disconnected its tentacles, and she reached up and rubbed the tiny tingling swellings on her skin where they had been attached. Then she clambered shakily to her feet, hurried out of Mother Cave, darted across the rockpool garden and fell, trembling with relief, into Jane/202's arms.

'And?' said Jane/202. 'What are we to do? What has Mother Cave decreed?' She laid a gently sarcastic emphasis on the last word.

'What we would have done anyway,' Jane/208 replied. 'We look after the driftling. For now.'

For three days and three nights the driftling lay on the bed matting, breathing shallowly, scarcely moving. In all that time Jane/208 never left her side. Visitors came to the shelter and were allowed to peer in through the door flap, but most found their curiosity easily assuaged. Wrapped in a blanket, the driftling's most unusual features were hidden, leaving only her facial hair and the lump in the centre of her throat as visible evidence of her strangeness.

Her provenance was another question altogether, one that was frequently discussed by the Parthenai as they went about their daily business. Since she wasn't one of them, that meant she must come from another tribe, another island. The received wisdom was that there were no other islands out there, that the Parthenai occupied the last spit of land left high and dry by the ocean. So Mother Cave maintained, at any rate, but plainly she had been misguided. (Some of the tribeswomen, not least among them Jane/197, suggested that Mother Cave might even have been lying.) And if there was one other tribe out there, might there not be several more? And if so, what were they like? Were they friendly? Hostile? The implications were enormous, and the village buzzed with speculation.

But for Jane/208 this kind of talk was irrelevant. For her, everything was reduced to the simple issue of whether the driftling lived or died.

She tried feeding her bladderwrack broth, spooning it between her salt-cracked lips, but the driftling swallowed only a few drops and the rest spilled out of the sides of her mouth. She massaged her limbs regularly, trying to work some warmth into her cold, resilient flesh, and at night she snuggled up to her, hoping to impart some of her own body heat. In this practice she managed to persuade Jane/202 to join her, although Jane/202 said she felt awkward and stupid doing it.

In fact, Jane/202 was enjoying the attention that the driftling was bringing her. Around the evening fires, when the whole tribe gathered for a meal and songs and stories, Parthenai young and old would bombard her with queries about the stranger lying unconscious in her and Jane/208's shelter, and during the days she was constantly giving updates on the progress of the patient's recovery to anyone who enquired. That there was little change in the driftling's condition from day to day presented no problem. The nature of her freakish deformities alone was enough to provoke a lengthy discussion, and Jane/202's descriptions of her unusual hair and growths became ever more elaborate and exaggerated.

Jane/208 was pleased that, even if only in a roundabout way, she was the one who had brought Jane/202 this popularity, but at the same time she wished Jane/202 would stop treating the driftling as just some bizarre novelty. For all her physical peculiarities, for all that she had been disgorged by the ocean more drowned than alive, the driftling was still a human being. She might not be Parthenai, but she was still a sentient creature.

On the fourth day, the driftling awoke.

It was noon. The air was still and unforgivingly hot, and most of the tribe sat under awnings or floated in the sea to keep cool. Jane/208 sweltered quietly indoors, naked but for a sheen of sweat. At first she didn't believe that the figure on the bed matting was moving; she thought confinement and the heat had begun conspiring to play tricks on her mind. Then the driftling gave a low groan and coughed twice, dryly. Her eyelids flicked apart. Her irises were green like the phosphorescence that glimmers within breaking waves at night.

Jane/208 crawled to her side, knelt, and smiled down encouragingly. The driftling frowned back, puzzled. Blinking, she raised her head, looked at Jane/208's breasts, then slumped back on to the bed matting.

The first word she said, in a voice like coarse shale, Jane/208 did not recognise.

Barely a whisper.

'Christ.'

The driftling then tried to raise her head again, but her strength ebbed and she abandoned the attempt. She rolled her eyes around, struggling to focus on the shelter's driftwood walls and the carved bone ornaments and the brittle dried-seaweed sculptures with which they were decorated. It all seemed to be too much to take in, so the eyes returned their gaze to Jane/208, asking questions that the driftling's throat, possibly on account of that solid-looking lump, was unable to iterate.

'I'll fetch you something to drink,' Jane/208 said, but by the time she had returned from the barrels with a cup of sea-cooled rainwater, the driftling had lapsed back into unconsciousness.

When Jane/202 came in from bathing shortly afterwards, Jane/208 told her what had happened and asked her to keep watch over the driftling while she went and consulted Mother Cave again.

'Must I?'

'Unless *you* want to visit Mother Cave instead,' Jane/208 replied, a little more irritably than she might have liked.

'But why should I have to do anything for her at all?' Jane/202 whined. 'She's *your* responsibility.'

'Now there's a surprise. The way you've been going on about her these past couple of days, anyone would have thought she was *yours*.'

'We can't all be as dedicated as you are to helping others, Jane/208. Some of us have lives to be getting on with.'

'I've only been doing what Mother Cave told me to do.'

'Some of us think that too much store is put by what Mother Cave tells us to do. Some of us think we should make decisions for ourselves.'

'By "some of us" you mean Jane/197.'

'Among others,' said Jane/202. Jane/197's opinions were gaining currency among the Parthenai, not because they were right, necessarily, but because Jane/197 stated them with an irresistible authority and charisma.

'I'm not going to get into that now,' Jane/208 said. She was too tired to prolong the argument. 'I'm just asking for *one* small favour, Jane/202. Please?'

Reluctantly, sullenly, Jane/202 consented.

Yes?

In the chair, in Mother Cave's soul-womb, Jane/208 mentally replayed the driftling's awakening.

That is good. Still, there is insufficient data to formulate a plan of action. More time and information is needed. The driftling must be brought to me for examination and interrogation.

Jane/208 made it clear that she had done her best but the driftling was still too weak to communicate with Mother Cave.

Understood. For now, continue to look after her. In addition, do everything you can to ensure that she has as little contact as possible with the rest of the tribe.

Jane/208 wanted to know why, but Mother Cave could not be coaxed to elaborate.

If anyone asks why you are keeping the driftling from them, say it is because I told you to do so. That will be explanation enough.

Jane/208 hoped so, but in her heart of hearts she was none too sure.

The driftling was lying on her side with her eyes open when Jane/208 re-entered the shelter. Jane/202 was hunkered on the shingles in the opposite corner, staring at her. The driftling was staring back. Between them hung an atmosphere of bemused antagonism.

'She squeezed me,' Jane/202 said.

'What?'

'I had my back to her, I was kneeling, bending over, wringing out my hair, and suddenly I felt this hand on my buttock and she *squeezed* me.'

She sounded so mortally affronted, Jane/208 had to laugh.

'It's not funny.'

'No, of course not.'

'Real.'

Jane/208 looked over at the driftling. 'I'm sorry?'

Hard-scabbed lips struggled to shape words. 'Real. Had to see if she was. Real.'

'Oh yes,' said Jane/202, 'she talks, too. Though I can't say I much care for her voice.'

'Who are you?' Jane/208 asked the driftling. 'Do you have a name?'

The driftling weakly waved a hand: either she couldn't remember or it didn't matter.

Jane/208 would have pressed her further had Jane/202 not chosen that moment for a dramatic exit, getting up and flouncing out of the shelter, tossing the door flap aside.

'Wait!' Jane/208 followed her out, seized her by the arm and turned her around. 'Wait. Where are you going?'

107

'I don't know. All I know is, I'm not staying in there with *her* a moment longer. I'll find another shelter. Arrange for a new one to be built, if I have to. I don't like having to share our space with a *freak* who doesn't have any respect for another person's body.'

'Ssh, keep your voice down.'

'Freak! Freak! Freak! Freak! Freak!' Jane/202 leaned into the doorway. '*Freak!*'

'All right then, Jane/202, if that's how you're going to be,' said Jane/208 calmly. She knew she ought to be imploring her lover to stay. That was what Jane/202 wanted. A little bit of abasement and she would soften. But just then Jane/208 was too exhausted, too irritable and too proud to want to play such games, and besides, given Mother Cave's instruction that the driftling should be kept away from the rest of the Parthenai, Jane/202 leaving was probably a blessing in disguise. For Jane/202's own good, Jane/208 decided to let her go. It hurt, but then so did all sacrifices, and she prayed that, when the driftling was well enough to fend for herself, there would be a chance for her and Jane/202 to make amends, to reconcile, to start over.

'Tell everybody,' she simply said, 'that Mother Cave has advised that for the time being no one but me is to have any contact with the driftling.'

'Did she give a reason?' Jane/208's coolness had disappointed Jane/202.

'She didn't have to. She's Mother Cave.'

'Of course,' Jane/202 said with a contemptuous snort. 'She's Mother Cave.'

Jane/208 watched Jane/202 stride away, tossing her damp blonde hair and stamping great dents in the shingles. She felt her eyes prickle with tears and she sniffed them back hard, telling herself to be brave, to think of the tribe rather than herself. It wasn't much comfort, but it was the best she could manage under the circumstances. She turned and went back into the shelter.

'I'm sorry about that,' she said to the driftling. 'Now, are you hungry?'

Warily the driftling nodded.

'Well then, let's get you something to eat.'

Thanks to Jane/208's ministrations, the driftling's condition slowly improved. Her eyes gained a lustre, she was able to sit upright for longer and longer periods of time, and after much straining she succeeded in squeezing out a couple of small stools which Jane/208 disposed of beneath the pebbles as conscientiously as a mother would her infant's. When, however, the moon waxed full and the time for bleeding came around, she realised that the driftling still had some way to go before her recovery was complete because, while every tribeswoman of child-bearing age went around stanched for three days, the driftling did not leak so much as a drop. No doubt the tumours between her legs were interfering with her menstrual functions, just as the lump in her throat was interfering with her speech, but that only added weight to Jane/208's diagnosis: in someone who was not pregnant – and the driftling was clearly not – the absence of bleeding was a sure sign of ill-health.

They talked infrequently. Conversation was hard for the driftling. Not only did she find it an effort to speak, but every question Jane/208 asked her about her tribe and her island and her village caused her agonies of confusion. She didn't know her name. She could remember nothing of where she came from or how she came to be floating in the sea. All she could recall was a storm and being thrown into waves that tossed her about and tore the clothes from her back like a child tearing the wings off a fly.

Jane/208 knew about amnesia: Jane/186, daughter of Jane/134, had stumbled once and concussed herself on a rock, and for several days afterward had been unable to remember her own name/number or recognise the faces of any of her sisters, until, of course, Mother Cave had restored her to her senses.

Once Mother Cave got her metaphorical hands on the driftling, she, too, would recall everything.

Jane/208 was too tactful and embarrassed to ask the driftling about her deformities and facial hair. She reckoned that the driftling herself would talk about those when she was ready.

The driftling seemed perpetually fascinated by her surroundings, and Jane/208 often found her peering out through the gaps between the slats of the shelter's walls, watching the village and the Parthenai who wandered by. She asked to be allowed to go out and walk around, but Jane/208 explained that this was impossible. When asked why, Jane/208 replied that Mother Cave had said so. When asked who Mother Cave was, Jane/208 found herself unable offer an adequate answer.

'Mother Cave is our nurse, our goddess, our keeper,' she said, but that didn't even begin to describe Mother Cave's importance, her significance, her influence over the Parthenai. How could you encapsulate in mere words the place/person were life began and life was maintained and life ended?

Jane/208's devotion to caring for the driftling was absolute. She left the shelter only to fetch food or water, and if visitors came she turned them away at the door flap politely but firmly, using Mother Cave's name to lend the rejections authority. She could not realise that, at the nightly fire gatherings, Jane/197 was using her selfless dedication as an example of the absurd lengths to which the Parthenai went to indulge Mother Cave's whims.

'What do we have to fear from this stranger?' said Jane/197 to the assembled tribe one evening. 'Nothing! Yet Mother Cave would keep her from us until she has resolved what to do about her, as if we are children incapable of making decisions for ourselves. And she gets Jane/208 – poor, innocent, faithful Jane/208 – to do her dirty work for her. Are these the actions of an entity we should trust? Does this fill you with confidence that Mother Cave is the one to whom we should look for direction?'

There were murmurs to the effect that Mother Cave's will was not to be disputed, her motives were not to be questioned, and it was unwise to risk incurring her anger because, if she so wished, Mother Cave could refuse to heal the sick and get would-be mothers with child, and *then* what would become of the tribe?

Jane/197 answered them with a haughty laugh and a glittering eye. 'I'm not saying that we should do without her altogether, for Mother Cave fulfils many a useful purpose. I'm merely saying that rather than devote ourselves slavishly to her as we do, we should have faith in *ourselves* to act wisely and independently, without feeling we have to run and ask her opinion every time one of us stubs a toe or cracks a fingernail. Mother Cave is old and not always reliable. Something that Jane/190, if you'll recall, found out to her cost.'

'And who would take her place as arbiter and chief decision-maker?' someone grumbled. 'You?'

'I can think of worse candidates,' said Jane/197.

Restless in the shelter, Jane/208 and the driftling listened to the distant voices of the gathering, as they had on previous evenings.

'I would like to meet. These other women some. Time,' said the driftling.

'Until Mother Cave says you can, it is impossible.'

'I. Would like to meet. Mother Cave too.'

'That will surely happen.'

'What are. They talking about out there? It sounds. Like they're arguing.'

'They are, although I can't quite make out what they're saying.' Jane/208 thought, however, that she had a pretty good idea what the topic of discussion was. One voice was dominating: Jane/197's. 'They should start singing the songs and telling the stories soon, I hope. Would you like me to join in when they do, so that you can hear them?'

'That would be. Nice. Jane/208, you've. Been very kind. To me.'

'My duty.'

'I find myself. Thinking very fond. Thoughts about you.'

'Thank you.'

The debate eventually subsided, and the songs and stories began. Jane/208 recognised each by its tune or by the cadence of its opening lines, and she knew them all, word for word. 'The Tale of a Turtle', 'the Ballad of the Lost Albatross', 'Lila and the Little Whale', 'Why Seagulls All Look Alike', 'How the Walrus Won Her Whiskers' – she sang or spoke along to each, to the driftling's evident delight.

The climax was, as always, a retelling of the story of the creation of the Parthenai. Four generations ago, the First Jane came to the island, travelling alone across the swelling sea in an ark of iron, the rusting remnants of which could still be found among the Parthenai's shelters: here a strut used to prop up a doorway, there a scrap of tarpaulin offering a rainproof roof. With her she brought the raw materials required to build Mother Cave, and also the egg, extracted from her own body, that became Jane/2, whom she raised up wise and strong. Mother and daughter lived happily on the beach together, their every need tended to by Mother Cave, but as time went by the First Jane grew old and unwell, until soon she was sick beyond the power of Mother Cave to cure. When the day came that she was so ill she could barely breathe, she begged Jane/2 to help her walk up to Mother Cave, and there she bade her only daughter farewell, assuring her that Mother Cave would continue to look after her and any daughters she might have. And then the First Jane disappeared into the second chamber of Mother Cave, and was never seen again.

'We Parthenai are the descendants of Jane/2,' said Jane/208, intoning the words along with the other tribeswomen outside by the fires, 'and through her we are all joined to the First Jane.'

112

With that, the Parthenai fell silent, and Jane/208 with them, her throat dry and her tongue tired from so much talking.

'Thank you,' said the driftling.

'You're welcome,' said Jane/208, and lay down on the shingles, curled up and closed her eyes.

The gathering dispersed, and the Parthenai drifted back to their shelters, muttering amongst themselves. Jane/208 heard nothing: she was fast asleep.

So deeply asleep that when she felt a hand touch her between the legs, she assumed it was Jane/202's, forgetting that Jane/202 no longer lived in the shelter, and she let the hand caress her and murmured her lover's name sweetly. Somewhere between dreaming and waking she imagined she saw Jane/202 crouching over her, the glossy swoop of her blonde hair hanging around the curve of her neck and down over one breast, the other breast standing proud in all its firm, conical glory, and at this the rubbing at her crotch summoned a delicious, blooming warmth.

Jane/202 had come back. Her lover had come back.

The caressing stopped, and Jane/208 moaned softly in disappointment, and then she heard a grunt and a shifting of pebbles and smelled a strange, sharp scent she didn't recognise. Somewhere in the atavistic deeps of her mind the scent awoke an ancient anxiety. She stirred. She ordered her eyes to open, but her body was too enervated to obey her brain straight away.

Hands rolled her roughly onto her back. Something jabbed at the soft intimacy of her genitalia. Not a finger. Too blunt, too thick.

Now her eyes snapped open and she found herself staring up at the driftling.

The driftling, frowning in concentration, was crouched between Jane/208's legs and fumbling with the tumours, the uppermost of which, the split one, had become grotesquely distended while the lower pair, by contrast, had shrivelled tightly up, as though the other was sapping the lifestuff out of them.

And Jane/208 realised, with a shock of horrified disgust, that the driftling was trying to shove the raw-looking head of the split one *into her*.

It was a simple matter for Jane/208 to deliver a stunning blow to the side of the driftling's head. All the Parthenai, by virtue of their harsh lifestyle, were lithe, wiry and sinewy-strong. The driftling slumped to one side, groaning, and Jane/208 aimed a revolted punch at the three throbbing tumours.

The driftling shrieked horribly and clutched herself into a ball. A spurt of vomit coughed from her mouth.

Jane/208 did not need to raise the alarm. In heartbeats, a dozen of her sisters had appeared at the entrance to her shelter.

'What's going on?'

'What happened?'

'Who was that screaming?'

Jane/197 shouldered her way through the crowd, Jane/202 in her wake, and crawled in through the doorway. She took one look at the writhing driftling, and then at Jane/208 (flushed, furious, fearful), and nodded as if she had suspected all along that something like this might happen. As Jane/208 haltingly explained the nature of the driftling's assault on her, Jane/197's nods only deepened.

'Clearly those tumours are some kind of parasite,' Jane/197 said. 'They were forcing her to spread their infection to another host: you, Jane/208. That must be why she was thrown out from her own tribe and abandoned to the mercies of the sea. Well, *we* can cure her of what ails her.'

Jane/197 drew a knife from her belt and gestured to a couple of the tribeswomen outside to come in. They obeyed her unhesitatingly.

Jane/208, looking at the driftling, pitiful in her pain and helplessness, said, 'Shouldn't we at least wait until someone has talked to—'

'Don't say it, Jane/208,' Jane/197 snapped. 'Mention the words "Mother Cave" within earshot of me again, and so help mc I'll use this knife on *you*. Let's do something by ourselves for a change, eh?'

'Yes,' said Jane/202 viciously. 'Shut up about Mother Cave, Jane/208.'

Jane/208 flinched as if whipped.

Jane/197 told the other two Parthenai, Jane/201 and Jane/217, to take an arm each. They spread the driftling out flat on her back. Spittle and vomit were strung across her facial hair and her eyeballs twitched dementedly in their sockets. Gradually she became aware of what was happening around her, *to* her, but by the time she had fully recovered her wits from Jane/208's two savage blows, Jane/197 was straddling her thighs, Jane/202 was holding down her ankles, and Jane/201 and Jane/217 had her outstretched arms pinned securely beneath their knees.

In the streaks of moonshine that angled in through the chinks in the walls, the razor-sharp whelk-shell blade of Jane/197's knife glinted. Everyone – those inside, those standing outside the doorway looking in, Jane/208, Jane/202, the driftling – was briefly mesmerised by the play of silvery light over the blade's nacreous inner surface.

Then the driftling started to scream. Shudder and scream. Twist, squirm and *scream*.

'I don't think we should be doing this,' said Jane/208.

'Doing what?' said Jane/197. 'We're doing nothing more than your precious Mother Cave would do herself, were she capable of making up her mind. We're sending her a signal that we don't have to rely on her any more. A symbolic gesture, you might say. Besides, we won't be harming this poor, diseased creature. We'll be making her better.'

Jane/208's misgivings continued to grind away inside her belly, but she understood that there was no way she was going to be able to alter the course of events. She and all the Parthenai would simply have to live with the consequences of Jane/197's actions.

Jane/197 seized the bunch of bulbous tumours, now

restored to something like their original dimensions, and wrenched them away from the driftling's pelvis, stretching taut the skin that attached them.

The driftling let out a heart-rending howl and began to buck, her spine arching like a leaping dolphin's back, but the Parthenai were easily able to restrain her. Her eyes were swollen with terror and her face was scarlet and the veins in her temples pulsed fatly.

Jane/197 brought the edge of the blade to the base of the tumours.

'Keep a tight grip on her,' she told her accomplices, then added over her shoulder, 'Somebody go and fetch a brand from the fire so that we can cauterise the wound.'

The driftling's frantic gaze found Jane/208, and hoarsely she begged her to help, please help.

Jane/208 slowly shook her head, as powerless in her own way as the driftling.

Before Jane/197 made the first cut, she glanced at the lump in the driftling's throat, which was working convulsively.

'That will have to go next,' she said.

There followed two long, feverish days during which the driftling raged and writhed with the pain of her wounds, uttering tiny glottal clucks that were unborn screams. An infection set in beneath her bandages, and Jane/208 arranged for her to be taken to Mother Cave for healing.

If Mother Cave was angry that the Parthenai had taken matters into their own hands, she did not show it. She said nothing, and cured the driftling on the steel table with her corroded scalpels and needles.

Shocking as Jane/197's act was, Mother Cave's silence on the subject was even more alarming, and the tribe feared that they had mortally offended her. An atmosphere of dread enveloped the village, and grew so thick and oppressive, so full of averted gazes and nervous mutters, that finally Jane/208, out of frustration more than anything, went up to

Mother Cave, sat in the chair and asked her what she was thinking.

What has been done is for the best.

But, Jane/208 insisted, hadn't the Parthenai acted disrespectfully?

A spark of independence is not disrespect. Absolute independence of me is impossible. I am Mother Cave. I am your nurse, your goddess, your keeper. Without me there is no life. My daughters have defied me, but they will never be free of me. Our relationship has changed, that is all. The children want their mother to know that they have begun to outgrow her. It was inevitable.

So the driftling's arrival had been a bad omen?

All omens are open to interpretation, Jane/208, daughter of Jane/151, granddaughter of Jane/93. She was an omen of change perhaps. Perhaps not. It makes no difference. A change has occurred, and changes cannot be amended, they can only be endured. The driftling must take her place among the Parthenai. What happens to the tribe now is up to the tribe.

Not up to Mother Cave?

I have done as much as I can.

Jane/208 left Mother Cave far from reassured. It sounded as if, in her secret depths of thought, Mother Cave was sad and troubled. But the news Jane/208 conveyed to her sisters was good news. Mother Cave had forgiven them.

Despite her barbarous appearance and her muteness, the driftling was quickly accepted into the tribe and was assigned chores which she performed well but without a spark of enthusiasm. She was docile and inoffensive, to such a degree that Jane/197 suggested that Mother Cave had done more than heal the driftling's infected wounds and had, in fact, effected some permanent alteration to her brain. Whether this was the case or not, what was indisputably true was that the life seemed to have been drained out of her, and the trauma

117

caused by Jane/197's impromptu operation lingered for a long time in dark purple shadows beneath her eyes.

Around the evening fires the driftling would sit and listen to the stories but would not, because she could not, join in. A shelter was constructed for her with all the usual ceremony and celebration, decorations were donated, and she moved in and, as far as anyone could tell, seemed content. Pained and melancholic, but content.

Though she was not the youngest, they called her Jane/267, because they could think of no other name for her, and everyone did what they could to make her feel welcome, part of the tribe, not least Jane/208, who took Jane/267 with her whenever she went beachcombing. Jane/267 proved not to be the sharpest-eyed of scavengers, but she made for good company despite (or perhaps because of) her lack of conversation, and as the two of them roved together along the grey, island-girding strip of pebbles between the black cliff and the creamy waves, Jane/208 would sometimes catch Jane/267 gazing out to sea, her phosphorescent green eyes wistful, as though scanning the horizon for something she had lost.

Jane/208 shared that sense of loss, but for different reasons. Already there was talk, fomented by Jane/197, of building some kind of seagoing craft out of dismantled shelters, something like the First Jane's ark, and venturing out in it to discover other islands. Knowledge of how to put such a craft together existed in Mother Cave, and though she would be unwilling to impart it, she would do so if enough Parthenai demanded. Jane/208 herself had no urge to take part in the expedition, but many did, and whether they came home empty-handed or never returned, making the journey at all would destroy the beach-bound simplicity of the Parthenai's lives for ever.

Changes, Mother Cave had said, could not be amended; they could only be endured.

Was that true?

Only Jane/267, who could not speak, knew the answer to that question.

Dead Letters

Bert was a big man who looked like he could have been a rugby forward or a professional wrestler or a nightclub bouncer but was too gentle of nature to have been successful in any of those violent occupations. In fact, Bert worked for the Post Office. He possessed a slow, methodical brain, which made him ideal for sorting, and for thirty-seven years Bert did just that, sorted, until machines came along that read and classified and separated and distributed mail in a fraction of the time it took Bert – conscientious, reliable old Bert – to perform the same task.

When the machines came along, it seemed to Bert that that was that. He was near retirement, and the Post Office was taking on a lot of younger men and women now, people who actually understood how the sorting machines worked and could operate them. It was time for Bert to bow out nobly, the last of the old guard; take his pension and his fishing rod and move to a bungalow by the coast to watch telly and read novels and the newspapers.

His bosses had other plans for him. In the extending, expanding, full-speed-ahead-rocketing industry of mail delivery there was still a need for slow, methodical workers to do the jobs that required efficiency without urgency. Bert's bosses sent him a letter. They enjoyed sending letters. It made them feel that they were getting their hands dirty, actually touching the greasy cogs of the engine.

The letter, when it finally arrived, described Bert in glowing terms (he was 'a valuable, if not indispensable, asset') and

123

went on to enquire if he would be willing to accept a transfer to a different department where he would be 'in charge of and/or solely responsible for the distribution and/or disposal of undelivered and/or undeliverable correspondence'.

Bert's brain churned this one over for a while and came up with the translation: dead letter office.

Dead letter office? He'd rather retire!

But then he thought about friends who had retired. He thought of how they measured their hours with pint glasses and hip flasks; how they faded day by day; how boredom sucked the essence out of them, leaving them wrinkled husks of men. He thought about their rheumy, dreamy eyes that begged a question: *where did it all go?* Theirs was the shock and surprise of a punter who sees all the horses gallop past the finishing post and his isn't among them, hasn't even left the starting gate. *Eh? What happened?*

Bert thought about this the way he usually thought about things, long and hard, and gradually his mind changed, turning over like one of those snowstorm-globe novelties that tourists like to buy, slow-swirling confusion settling again to clarity. He composed a reply to his bosses and started at the dead letter office the following Monday.

The job banished him to the lower basement of the depot, where every morning he was greeted with canvas sacks full of undelivered correspondence. For the most part this consisted of circulars, shrinkwrapped catalogues and all the other junk mail that accumulated inside the front doors of abandoned shops and the homes of the recently deceased. Bert thought it was a shame, what with trees being whisked off the face of the planet at a rate of knots, that so much paper should be wasted selling products that people could go out and find for themselves if they really wanted them. Wearily he marked it all to be consigned to the incinerators.

Business letters he opened and read and gauged as to their importance. Usually these were junk mail thinly disguised, further pieces of sales pitch dressed up in formal brown envelopes with the name and address of the target customer framed in a little cellophane window. Bit of a nasty trick that, Bert thought.

Private correspondence, on the other hand, was sacred. It deserved respect for the effort that had been put into it, the care taken, the time spared. Bert regarded opening and reading private correspondence as very much a last resort, when every attempt to decipher the handwriting on the envelope or make sense of an insane address had failed. Even then, Bert looked only at the name and address of the sender (if there was one) at the top of the letter inside, then copied this on to the envelope, folded the letter back into the envelope and taped the flap shut. He would never have pried into another person's words. In fact, Bert wished he could write on every envelope, *I haven't read this – honest*. But who would believe that? Besides, it amounted to a confession that the temptation had been there.

The letters which he did read, and was delighted to read, and read because no one else would read them, were those addressed to *Santa Claus, The North Pole*. He loved the lists, painstakingly detailed in case Santa should go to the wrong shop or buy the wrong brand or type of toy. He chuckled over the requests for trips to the moon and wishes no parent could fulfil ('Please could you send my little brother to Timbuktu and make sure he never comes back?'). He smiled at the protestations of goodness that bordered on saintliness and the apologies for crimes committed during the past year, wishing that his greatest worry in life was that he had knocked over a vase and blamed it on the cat. He delighted in the spiky cacography, the way the lines of writing veered more and more from the horizontal the further down the page they went. Although December was Bert's busiest month, it was also his favourite. He took all the Santa Claus letters home with him and placed them in box-files. Each year he bought new box-files to fill.

Cynics might scoff, but Bert – the big, timid man, hidden

away from daylight in a chamber in a lower basement in a depot in a city – was perhaps the closest the world would come to a real Father Christmas.

Three years almost to the day that Bert was shunted off to the dead letter office, it arrived.

It was compact, lighter than an aerogramme wafer, with no stamp, and was addressed simply:

Dearest
There

That was all, two words on two lines. Bert tutted as he slid his finger under the flap. Honestly, there weren't half some odd sorts around.

The sender's name and address at the top of the page turned out to be even less illuminating than the recipient's. It said:

From Your Darling
Here

Bert scratched his head and was preparing to crumple the letter up when he found himself reading the first line. Well, it was only one line . . . But once his eye had begun to wander, he found he could not call it back.

My Dearest,
My heart grows sick while we are apart. It aches as it beats and with each shuddering throb seems ready to burst. When will you reply? When will this winter absence turn to spring? While you are there and I am here, snow surrounds me, the landscape is stripped of its beauty and I am cut off from everything that makes living bearable. A word from you, a single syllable, would be more welcome to me than the first bud on a branch, the first song of a returning bird, the first blade of grass. When will I see you again? When?

All my love,
Darling

Smiling, Bert read the letter again. Someone, he decided, had been buried too long in books of poetry. Perhaps a lovelorn student had hunted through pages of verse for these pearls of love-wisdom; perhaps an ageing spouse, hoping to rekindle love's first fading flame. Bert couldn't tell. The sentiments were immature, but their expression was adult. Or was it the other way round?

He held the letter up to the unshaded lightbulb that hung from the ceiling on a length of plaited flex. You know, he hadn't seen paper of this quality in . . . oh, ages. It captured the light. The light suffused it from corner to corner, from edge to edge, so that the lines of writing stood out like black bars against the sun. It fluttered dryly yet felt as smooth as cream, and it was thin – so thin it all but disappeared when turned sideways. The nib that wrote on this delicate stuff would have to be flawlessly smooth.

The letter should not have been sent. It was a mistake. Nothing this precious and delicate should have been surrendered up to the mangling jaws of the Post Office. Nor, by any rights, should it have survived intact the lugging and manhandling that every letter had to endure.

Bert took the frail miracle home with him, keeping it for the same reason he kept the letters to Santa, as a thing of simple faith that flew in the face of common sense.

About a month later, the second letter arrived. Again it was for 'Dearest, There' and again it was written on the same translucent paper. Bert opened the envelope with what he hoped was reverence tainted by forgivable eagerness.

My Dearest,
Time passes, and slowly your face decays in my memory. I can see its outline and know it to be handsome, and I remember the colour of your eyes and know them to sparkle, but I cannot mould the parts together to create a picture of you. I am left with a shape without form, an idea of beauty, and a hint of sadness.

Without you and without your words to inspire it, my memory is a clumsy, blunt instrument, and my heart the poor craftsman who blames the inefficiency of his tools when he ought to blame the failing of his art.

Send me words, send me art, send me love.

As I send you mine,
Your Darling

Several things about the letter puzzled Bert, most of all whether Darling was a man or a woman. The handwriting, normally a dead giveaway, was rounded italics, a product of learning rather than nature, and therefore not obviously belonging to one sex or the other. And the words 'handsome' and 'beauty' could be applied equally to a man as to a woman, so that didn't help – assuming in the first place that the letter was being sent by a member of one sex to a member of the opposite sex . . .

Bert showed this letter and its predecessor to his friend Harry (retired, widower, dismal) over a pint of bitter. Harry squinted at both letters for a while, slipping one behind the other, one behind the other again, while Bert searched his face for a glimmer of enlightenment. Eventually Harry set the letters down in the empty ashtray to keep them from getting soaked by the wet eclipses left behind by their pint glasses. Then he took a swig of bitter and said, 'Pretty.'

'Pretty?'

'The paper. Must've cost a bob or two.'

'But what about the words? What do you think? Do you think someone's playing a joke?'

'On you?'

'On me, on the Post Office, I don't know.'

'Don't make much sense as a joke, does it? Looks more like a headcase to me. I mean, the words are pretty, too, but a bit . . .' Harry tapped his temple. 'If you catch my drift.'

'They make sense to me,' said Bert. 'He, she, whoever it is, is in love. Really, truly in love.'

128

'My point exactly, Bert, my point exactly,' Harry said with a half grin, and waved his froth-streaked glass at Bert with significance.

Bert sighed. 'Same again?' he said, reaching into his pocket.

The letters from Darling started arriving regularly, once a month, usually towards the end of the second week, at the latest by the beginning of the third. They traced Darling's mounting desperation, the increasing urgency with which he or she longed for an answer from Dearest. Dearest's reticence was 'like the Arctic wind that cuts to the bone with innocent malice'. Dearest was 'the kindest and cruellest creature that ever lived'. Dearest was by turns 'beautiful' and 'beastly', 'exquisite' and 'evil', 'ravishing' and 'ruinous', 'tender' and 'tormenting', sometimes both in the space of a single sentence.

When Harry cast his expert eye over each new instalment, he would look sly, tap his temple as before, and say, 'Now, what did I tell you? Headcase. And getting nuttier by the month.'

And Bert would wonder (but never aloud) who was the biggest headcase here. Darling, for writing to an imaginary lover letters that would never reach anywhere? Harry, for dismissing love as a madness? Or himself, for being captivated, swept up, swallowed whole by the letters? Was there something wrong with him because he looked forward to Darling's next missive with the excitement of a schoolkid counting down the days until the end of term? No, he decided. Not when the letters made a dull job a little brighter, his confinement to the bowels of the depot that little bit more bearable.

Then one morning Bert received a letter from his bosses similar to the one which had informed him of his transfer to the dead letter office. This one informed him that his services would no longer be required as of next Friday. (The letter gave him the statutory month's notice, or at least it would have, had it arrived when it was supposed to.) The bosses added that they very much appreciated the decades of hard work and unstinting loyalty Bert had given to the Post Office, but owing to circumstances and/or situations beyond their control the dead letter office was to be closed down. He would receive his full pension, of course, and would he accept their deepest sympathy and/or sincerest hopes for the future?

Bert bent his head, gritted his teeth, and lodged a protest. What about the children's letters? What about the private correspondence? What about the arrows of love that never reached their intended targets? (He cribbed the metaphor from Darling's most recent outpouring.)

The smooth running of the mail delivery industry, replied his bosses, was their greatest concern, and they were gratified to see that it was his too. The sorting machines, they told him, could now be programmed to spot such mistakes and/or anomalies and direct them straight to the incinerators, thereby making immense savings all round in effort and/or time and/or care. They appreciated his drawing their attention to the problem and/or were moved by his display of company spirit right to the very end. Might they again offer their deepest sympathy and/or sincerest hopes?

Bert's final days at the dead letter office drifted by. The flow of letters began to dry up. The sorting machines were already hard at work tossing away the unwanted catalogues and the lists for Santa and the private correspondence without a second glance, with barely a blink of an electronic eye. It pained Bert to think that Darling's future letters would, once sealed, never be read; that the strange, delicate paper would be lumped in with the rest and burned to ashes. When it pained him too much to think about it, he went to the pub with Harry, drinking for the sake of drinking, even though drinking didn't do much except get him drunk.

Bert's last day arrived, and there was going to be a party that afternoon when the whole depot would turn out to present him with a gift they had all chipped in for. Then they would wheel in a cake that said, in letters of piped icing, 'To Bert, Best Wishes On Your Retirement'. And when everyone had eaten a slice they would stand in a circle, shuffling with embarrassment, and sing 'Auld Lang Syne'. The prospect filled Bert with dread. These rituals, these last rites that Bert had himself helped administer to the old men and the old women before him, feeling vaguely sorry for them as everyone was no doubt feeling vaguely sorry for him today – his really was the end, wasn't it? Now he had nothing to look forward to except beer and oblivion. He nearly called in sick, but decided that he had to attend. It would have been rude not to.

There was a letter waiting for him in the dead letter office. A small envelope. That extraordinary paper.

Bert snatched it from the table and attempted to drive his trembling finger under the flap. Then he felt a peculiar twinge at the back of his mind, as though his thoughts had snagged on a thorn. He looked around. Had a piece of furniture been moved or something? No. Then he looked down at the envelope in his hands. He turned it over.

The handwriting on the front was not Darling's. The letter was addressed:

Darling
There

Bert had to restrain himself from tearing the envelope apart. He fumbled out its contents and began to read, his eyes gaping wide to drain every last drop of prose from the page:

From your Dearest
Here

My Darling,
What can I say? I must reply. Your sweet words have moved me and my love cannot stay silent for ever.
I have abused you as no lover has abused a love before. I have ignored you when I should have cherished you. If my face has

131

grown faint in your memory, it is because the real me is wan with shame and pale with remorse. Would that I had vanished from your memory altogether, for I deserve to be forgotten, never forgiven!

But I beg you now, and will if necessary beg you to the day I die . . .

Forgive me, forgive me, forgive me.

All my love,
Your Dearest

A Taste of Heaven

Think'st thou that I that saw the face of God
And tasted the eternal joys of heaven,
Am not tormented with ten thousand hells
In being deprived of everlasting bliss?

— Mephistophilis
(Marlowe, *The Tragical History of Doctor Faustus*)

Harold hadn't been down to the homeless shelter for several weeks. I asked about him, asked anyone that I knew to be a friend of his if they'd seen him, and got only shaken heads and frowns in reply. 'Think he might've gone up north,' was one suggestion, but I knew Harold: with winter approaching, the last direction he would be heading in was northwards. London, for all its faults, at least had the advantage of being a few degrees warmer than Manchester or Newcastle, and once winter set in Harold stayed here usually until the first buds appeared on the trees. More to the point, he never left the city for long. A week or two, three at the most, and then, his wanderlust satisfied, his footsteps would turn towards the capital again, London a Saturn whose heavy gravitational pull he could not escape.

No, there was definitely something wrong, and once I had begun to fear the worst, every little symptom of poor health that Harold had exhibited the last time I'd seen him took on a new and sinister significance. That cough of his – it had been getting worse, hadn't it? Had been turning bronchial, definitely. And the sore on his forehead – just a lesion? Or a sarcoma? God, I'd lost count of the number of times I'd heard about one of the shelter regulars turning his or her toes up overnight, for no reason other than that the unending hardships of the vagrant lifestyle had finally taken their toll. Harold had been in no worse shape than most of them, but that didn't mean he couldn't still be lying undiscovered beneath a shambles of newsprint in an alley somewhere, clenched in a foetal knot of death.

I missed him, and though I didn't give up hope that he might still be alive, quietly, privately, I began to mourn him. Of all the strange and mad and sad and extraordinary human beings who passed through the doors of the homeless shelter, Harold was perhaps the most remarkable. In his time, before answering the call of the road, he had been a fireman, a trawlerman, a professor of linguistics at a minor provincial university, war correspondent for a French magazine, and campaign manager for a Colombian presidential candidate; he had worked as a missionary in Zaire and had also enjoyed a career as a petty criminal back here at home; he had fitted curtains, carpets and men's suits, had sold double glazing, life insurance and Jesus door-to-door, and had earned an Olympic bronze for pistol-shooting, a gold disc for a song he co-wrote that was made popular by Marty Wilde in the sixties, and the respect of a number of peers of the realm for his sound advice on the preservation of British wetlands (his suggestions led to a Bill being passed in Parliament). And these were just the achievements I knew about. Harold darkly hinted that there were more, and that he had done some things so shady, so hush-hush, that if he told me what they were he would have to kill me. He said that he had run errands for people so nebulously important and powerful that even politicians in the highest echelons of government didn't know they existed, and that his eyes had passed over official documents the contents of which were so alarming they would have turned my hair white. He said this in that calm, cultured voice of his that only served to reinforce the impression that he was truly

136

au fait with the secret workings of the world, the unseen cogs which turned the hands on the clockface of everything that ordinary people perceived.

He was, of course, lying his arse off. Everybody knew that. Even I, who was born with the word 'gullible' stamped across my forehead, had ceased to believe anything Harold told me after the first couple of fables I had fallen for. Harold lived to lie. It was his craft, his art, his true vocation. He did not do it idly or maliciously, to start gossip or spread a rumour or destroy a reputation. He lied the way you or I might collect records or read books. It was his recreation. It took him out of himself. It cleared his head of mind junk, spring-cleaned the attics of his brain. It was a diversion, an entertainment, a stage act. Harold didn't expect anyone to believe his stories, but he told them anyway, and out of politeness or admiration or a weird kind of gratitude no one turned round to him and said, 'Shut your mouth, Harold, I can't breathe for the stink of your bullshit.' Once you'd been seduced by a tale of his – and Harold was always careful to hook a new listener with one of his more plausible lines – you couldn't help but admire the eloquence and the unselfconscious audacity with which he wove his webs of untruth, and marvel at the lengths he would go to in order to keep you, and himself, amused. Nothing in Harold's imaginary world could be proved. Nothing, equally, could be disproved, so it was foolish to try to reason or argue with him. Any objection would only be met with a bigger lie, and if you persisted in protesting, claiming that what he was telling you contradicted another story he had told you earlier or else was blatantly impossible, his tales would just grow taller and taller and taller until he had built a wall of mendacity so high it could not be scaled, and you gave up, exhausted. Resistance was futile. It was easier simply to accept what Harold said at face value and, if you were in the mood, perhaps let drop a well-chosen question that would encourage him to yet more outrageous flights of fancy. And maybe, just maybe, if you got lucky, this lifelong liar might trip himself up and accidentally find himself telling the truth. You never know.

I've always thought that Harold would have made a fine novelist or playwright. He had the vocabulary for it, the skill with language. He spoke the way most people write, in well-formed, thought-through sentences, which made it all the more logical for me to suggest, as I did once, that he set the story of his life down on paper (by which I meant compose a work of fiction). Harold's reply was uncharacteristically straightforward and self-effacing: 'What would be the point, Mark? If I wrote it down, who would believe it?'

And now he was gone, or so it seemed. As the days shortened and the trees shed and the sky turned hazy like a cataracted eye, and still Harold did not show, the hope that I had been nurturing like the last ember in a grate gradually dwindled and cooled. Every evening, having left the office and arrived at the shelter in time to help with the dinner shift, I would walk slowly along the rows of tables, checking each bearded face I saw, smiling if its owner caught my eye and offered a greeting, but smiling without any joy or conviction. And then, as I doled out food to the shuffling, murmuring queue, each face would come under scrutiny again. Harold might, after all, have shaved his beard. He might have got rid of – far more likely lost – the battered, greasy Homburg that never left his head, even on hot days. He might even have had to part company with his army-surplus greatcoat. But however he looked I would have recognised him instantly, had he shambled up to me, plate outstretched, to receive his helping of mashed potato. You do not easily forget the face of a friend.

Finally I became so concerned that I called the police, though I knew they would tell me that there was about as much chance of tracking down a missing vagrant as there was of finding a lost sock at a launderette. Which they did, albeit somewhat more tactfully. I gave them a description of Harold and a list of his known haunts, and was assured that an eye would be kept out for him. This was the best I could hope for, but it didn't prevent me from feeling aggrieved and frustrated. Vivian, the shelter supervisor, sympathised but pointed out that someone like Harold, who had fallen through a hole in the net of society, would always be in danger of slipping out of sight altogether. 'These people have already, to a certain degree, disappeared,' she said, raising a wise eyebrow. 'There's little to stop them taking a last little hop, skip and jump to the left and vanishing completely.'

I didn't understand precisely what she meant, but I accepted the basic truth of the statement. In desperation, I pinned my home and office phone numbers to the shelter noticeboard, with a request to the other volunteers to get in touch with me, no matter what time of day or night, should Harold show up. And winter deepened, and a rare December snow came down in thick flurries and left London with an ankle-deep coating of sooty slush, and Christmas came and went, and a New Year crawled over the horizon filled with the promise of much the same as last year, and January turned bitter, and the last spark of hope that Harold might still be alive winked out, and I learned to live with the fact that I would never see him again.

Then one morning, around about four o'clock, the phone rang, and the voice of one of the damned croaked my name.

The tiny portion of my brain that never goes to sleep knew who it was straight away, but the bit that thinks it does the thinking needed longer to place the identity of the caller, so, playing for time, I muttered something about the ungodliness of the hour and told whoever it was that he had better have a bloody good reason for waking me up. There was a long silence at the other end of the line, but even though I thought the connection had been cut, something prevented me from putting down the receiver. Then the voice spoke again. It sounded as though each word was being forged only with great effort and pain.

'I saw your note on the board. I must speak with you.'

My conscious brain finally engaged gear with my subconscious. 'Harold? Jesus, is that you, Harold?'

'It is.'

'Well, I mean . . . What's happened? Where have you been? Are you all right? No, OK, listen, you're at the shelter, right? I'll be straight over. Man, I really thought I was never going to hear from you again. Wow. OK, Harold, stay put. I'll be right there.'

'Listen,' Harold said and, from the effort of concentrating so much energy into the command, left himself speechless again. There was breathing – sore, laboured breathing – and then the pips went. I shouted at Harold to give me the number of the payphone so that I could call him back, but he managed to insert a coin in time.

'This is how it is, Mark,' he said. 'I'm not at the shelter now. I've been there and I got your number there, but I didn't stay long – I didn't want anyone seeing me. I'm coming round to call on you at your place. I need the address.'

'OK.' I gave it to him and said I'd have a hot cup of tea waiting for him when he arrived.

Either he didn't hear or he didn't care. 'I'll be about an hour,' he said, and hung up.

After a shower and a shave, I sat down in front of the television. A Bollywood movie was showing. The hour passed slowly, with me drifting again and again towards the threshold of sleep and just managing to snap myself awake each time, with the result that my impressions of the film were a bewildering, fragmented chaos of blue gods, portly heroes in polyester shirts and women dancing sinuously. At last the doorbell rang. I switched off the television, lit the gas beneath the kettle, and buzzed Harold up, leaving the flat door ajar. The concrete staircase that served all the flats in the building was uncarpeted and Harold's slow shuffling footfalls echoed all the way up. When he reached the landing outside my door he hesitated, pondering, breathing hard, and then, with a feeble knock, he entered.

Nothing could have prepared me for the profound change that had come over him. It wasn't just that he had lost weight, more weight than a man in his circumstances can afford to lose. Nor was it the unkempt stragggliness of his hair and beard, which he was normally at pains to keep brushed and trimmed and tidy. It wasn't that his once-pristine greatcoat was mud-stained and had a number of torn seams, or that frostbite had left three of his fingertips black, shrivelled and hard. It wasn't even the way he walked, stooped over where once he had carried himself with dignified erectness, bent as though bearing an invisible boulder on his back. It was his eyes that shocked me the most. While the rest of him had been somehow *lessened*, his eyes were larger and wider than I remembered them, and stared, crazy-veined, with a despairing emptiness from oyster-grey sockets. They looked without seeing, and when they finally found me standing by the stove in the small kitchen area of the living room, it took them a while to focus on me and make sense of me.

Forcing on a smile, I pretended that there was nothing different about him. 'Hey, man, how're you doing? It's good to see you. I'm glad you're alive.'

His reply was dragged up from a moss-encrusted well of misery: '*I'm* not.'

Without saying another word he plodded over to the living room window and, with some effort, drew back the curtains. The street was misty, the milky air tinged orange by the streetlights, the houses opposite blank-windowed and cold-shouldering. It was the dead hour of the night, when the pavements belong to cats and foxes, when no cars disturb the stillness and you can almost hear the burn of the neon bulbs in their casings. Harold gazed out for a long time. It was almost as if he couldn't bear, or didn't dare, to take his eyes off the city for a second. The kettle burped steam and I made us tea, and it was only when I nudged Harold on the shoulder with a full mug that he turned away from the window and, with a nod of thanks, accepted the mug, made his way over to the armchair and settled down. I took to the sofa, and in the eerie small-hours quiet we sat without talking and sipped without tasting. The pain that had been clearly audible in Harold's last remark kept me from asking him anything. Though I burned to know what had happened to him, and though I was deeply concerned about the state of both his physical and his mental health, I realised I would have to wait for him to speak; the only way he was going to give up any information was by volunteering it. And while I hated myself for even giving them head room, the words 'cancer' and 'AIDS' did flit across my mind. What else but a terminal illness could so ravage a man, suck so much of the juice out of him, make a husk of him in such a short space of time?

'You want to know where I've been, don't you?' Harold said at last, haltingly, like a man treading barefoot over sharp stones. 'Gone all this time – must be dead, right? Sometimes, you know, I think I am dead. I *feel* dead, that's for sure. If this isn't how it feels to be dead, I don't know what does.'

'I was worried. We all were, all of us at the shelter. You'd never been away for so long before.'

Harold didn't seem to care that someone cared. 'I'm going to tell you something now, Mark, and you'd better listen, because I'm never going to tell another living soul. I'm not even sure I should be telling you.'

'If this is a matter of national security,' I joked, 'perhaps I shouldn't be—'

'This is real.' From beneath the brim of his Homburg Harold fixed me with his eyes. Briefly they gained a lustre, though it was not the pleasant twinkling light that accompanied his forays into falsehood; this was a mean light, bitter in its brightness, harsh and hard. 'This is something that actually happened to me, and I'm telling you because I have to tell someone. Because I'll go mad if I don't. I regret, for your sake, that it has to be you, but of all the people I know you're the one I trust most to remember and believe. Everyone else will think I'm making it up. Everyone else will think this is just another of Harold's stories.'

It was the first time I'd heard him even come close to admitting that the tales he told about himself, the tales he maintained in the face of all opposition were true, were lies. While it didn't amount to an outright confession, it was near enough to one to make me sit up and pay attention, which was perhaps what Harold had intended.

'You know me, Mark,' he continued. 'I've been wandering London for a fair old number of years now. I think I know this city pretty well. As well as a husband knows the body of his wife, you might say. There's not a street I haven't been down, not a square inch of pavement in the Greater London area that hasn't seen the soles of my feet. I've worn parts of this city away with walking. It's worn parts of me away in return. I really thought there was nothing new in it, nothing that could surprise me. It turns out I was mistaken.

'It happened last October. Nice, wasn't it, October? Mild, mellow, calm. Trees putting on their autumn firework display. Lovely weather to be out in, all the more lovely because you know it's not going to last. Well, I'd strayed into the suburbs, south of the river. Down Balham way. There's a couple of churches round there that open their crypts at night to let us sleep in them. One of them has a health-care place attached to it, you can get seen by a doctor almost straight away, and I'd had a cough that had been bothering me for weeks, you probably remember. The doctor said it was nothing serious and gave me some antibiotics for it, and I left the health-care place feeling pretty good about myself, the way you do when you're ill and you've just been to see the doctor and he's given you something that you *know* is going to make you well again. I'd got a meal inside me, too, from one of those charity vans that do the rounds. Soup and sandwiches: God's way of saying, "Cheer up, old fellow, things aren't so bad." And I'd picked up a pair of trainers from a skip – these trainers I've got on here – and they happened to fit me just right. Air-cushioned soles, nearly new. That put a spring in my step, all right. So I had just about every creature comfort you could think of, nothing whatsoever to complain about. I wonder if that had something . . . ? No, never mind. I'll just tell you the story straight. It hurts too much to think too hard about it.

'London lives. You know that, don't you? Perhaps you don't. It's true of every big city, of course, but it's something you're only aware of if you know that city well, and the way to get to know a city well is not to travel across it by bus or tube, not to drive around it in a car, but to walk through it. That's when you're moving at its own pace, do you see? Contrary to popular opinion, there's nothing fast about cities. The people who live in them may rush around all the time, but cities themselves grow and change so slowly, it's hard to see it happening. It's like mould forming, like a rising-damp stain spreading across a patch of wallpaper. A building goes up, a building comes down, and most of the time we're whizzing by too quickly to notice. Haven't you ever found yourself strolling down a street you know well, only to be caught up short because a house you didn't even realise was being demolished has gone? Whish! Like a conjuror has magicked it away. And I'm sure there have been times when you've stumbled across a brand-new block of flats or a brand-new shopping centre and, when you stop to think about it for a moment, you realise you've been passing that site every day and not once did you spot even one piece of scaffolding. Shops are changing hands all the time, aren't they? Façades get repainted. Sooty brickwork gets sandblasted clean. And all this goes on around you, and yet only occasionally – usually when you're out on foot – does it ever strike you that the city is constantly renewing and reshaping itself, that it's not just a great mass of brick and stone that sits there mouldering and decaying, that the place you live in is something that breathes, pulses, has a heartbeat, may even have some dim kind of sentience.'

Here Harold paused, giving me an opportunity to take in

what he had been saying so far and prepare myself for what was coming, which, judging by the ironic purse of his lips, was going to be harder still to swallow. I don't think he appreciated how immune I had become to his fictions and fabrications. Neither his savagely altered appearance nor his insistence that this story, of all his stories, was true gave me any reason to suspect that I wasn't just being spun another yarn. I'd decided to hear him out because I thought it would be good for him to get whatever was plaguing him off his chest and because I hoped that this unburdening would be a stepping stone to getting at the real problem, the real reason why he looked and spoke like a soul in torment. I'd also decided that when he was done I would bundle him into a taxi and get him to a hospital. Even if his spirit was beyond repair, his body could be mended.

Harold drew a deep breath and sent it hissing out through his nostrils. 'I was coming up through Streatham when it happened. At first I didn't know what was going on. I felt it all around me, like something vast and unseen turning over in its sleep, but I'd no idea what it was. The sky rumbled like a jet was passing overhead, though one wasn't, and the air turned a different colour, darkening several shades. The street I was walking down was busy, full of mid-morning shoppers and pedestrians, and for a few seconds, while this "shift" was taking place, while the city twitched and stirred and scratched its nose, everyone paused and looked up and around and at each other like there was something they were supposed to be communicating, some thought, some vital piece of information they were supposed to be sharing. And then the rumble faded and the light brightened again and, the moment now past, everyone dropped their heads again and carried on with their lives. A few children, for no apparent reason, started crying. A dog that was barking fell silent. That was it. Nothing else was different. Yet I knew – *knew* – that things had changed. Ever so slightly, but perceptibly. And I started walking again, warily now, glancing around me in every direction, hoping to find what was new about the city, what London had done to itself.

'It didn't take long. I hadn't gone more than half a mile when I came across a street I didn't recognise. I said I knew London as well as a husband knows his wife, didn't I?'

' "Knows the body of his wife," were your precise words.'

'Right. Well, imagine you discovered a mole – no, a tattoo, an old faded tattoo on your wife's right buttock that wasn't there before, couldn't have been there or else you'd have noticed.'

My bachelor status made it difficult to empathise with the metaphor, but dutifully I made the imaginative leap. 'OK.'

'Same thing,' said Harold. 'What I found was a street that I would be willing to swear on the Bible, the Talmud *and* the Koran hadn't existed before that odd moment, that "shift", occurred. Leading off a road I'd been down dozens of times before: a new, perfectly ordinary-looking, perhaps somewhat seedy little street. One that appeared to have been there for ages, for as long as all the other streets around it, at least a century, perhaps longer, but a new street all the same.

'Well, what would *you* have done? You'd have investigated, wouldn't you? And that's what I did. I wasn't scared. I was curious, and part of that curiosity was fear, but not enough of it to make me turn and walk away, as I should have done. Things would have been so much better if I'd simply turned and walked away. But then we don't do that when we're confronted with a mystery, do we? And it was also a challenge. A stretch of road I'd never been down before, a virgin piece of the city just begging for me to trample all over it – how could I resist? Me, who's known London so intimately for so long? How could I not walk down those fresh pavements and make my knowledge complete?

'The most peculiar thing about that street was it felt and smelled and sounded just like any other street. Radios were playing, and there were cars parked along the kerbs and net curtains in the windows of the houses, and people had done different things to their houses, whitewashed them, pebble-dashed them, had paved over their front gardens, made little glades out of their front gardens, or not bothered at all with their front gardens and let the weeds grow up and the low front walls crumble and sag. Lives had been lived there on that street. Children had been born, old people had died. Dogs had filled the gutters with their droppings. The street had a history – and yet less than quarter of an hour ago it hadn't existed.

'And that wasn't all. At the end I came to a pair of huge wrought-iron gates, topped with spikes, wide open. And beyond them was the park.

'I couldn't tell how large the park was when I first stepped through the gates. It was as big as I could see, it stretched in every direction to the horizon, but there were trees and low hills that made it hard to make out exactly how far it extended. It was larger than Hyde Park, that's for sure. Larger, maybe, than Richmond Park. But I wasn't wondering about that at the time. Certainly that was at the back of my mind, but what I was really thinking about was how this place couldn't possibly fit into the map of London I have etched in my head. There wasn't room for it in the network of densely packed suburban streets in that area. For that park to exist, thousands of houses would have to have been shunted aside, acres of built-up land would have to have been levelled and planted. It was a municipal impossibility. But there it was. I was standing within its perimeter, my feet resting on a solid asphalt path, and I was inhaling the damp sweet autumn aroma of its trees and grass, and I was staring at flower beds and small swelling hills and neatly clipped bushes and hedge rows, and I wasn't dreaming and I wasn't hallucinating – I hadn't had a drop of alcohol all week. It was all perfectly real, perfectly there. I couldn't have created a whole park out of nothing. No one's imagination is that good.

'I must have stood there like a zombie for the best part of

twenty minutes. People were strolling past me, giving me curious looks – questioning, not wary. A jogger almost ran into me, checking his watch. He apologised and carried on panting along the path. A dog veered away from its owner to sniff at my shoes, tail wagging, and then got dragged back by a tug on the lead, and its owner, a pretty young girl, gave me a brilliant smile and said sorry. She wasn't scared or suspicious of me. She simply smiled and said sorry, and I said there was no reason to apologise, and she smiled again and carried on her way. Some pigeons strutted over to me and pecked expectantly at the ground around my feet. And then the sun came out.

'It had been overcast all morning, not cold, just grey, but the clouds had been threatening to part for an hour or so, and now at last they did, and the sunlight came down like a blessing and suddenly everything was aglow. The trees were no longer weighed down with yellow leaves, they were dripping with great gleaming flakes of gold. The breeze had been nagging and chilly and a little unpleasant, and now, suddenly, it was warm and wild and playful. It was amazing, the way the clouds rolled away across the sky and left everything below bright and sparkling. Like a TV advert for floor polish, you know what I'm talking about? One wipe of your mop and your linoleum is gleaming. Only on a giant scale. I didn't take my hat off, of course.'

'Of course.' Harold never removed his Homburg outdoors, and seldom indoors. He had worn it ever since the day he had been struck by lightning in the Sudan (yeah, right). He believed the hat protected him from being hit again, and so far no one could deny that as a talisman it had been an unqualified success.

'That was what finally got my feet moving,' he continued, 'that sweep of sunshine. It was an invitation. "Come on," it said, "come and explore." So I did. Any sane man would have done the same.'

Harold took a swig of lukewarm tea and set the mug down

on the coffee table. For the first time since arriving at my flat he smiled. It was a wan smile, a tenth-generation photocopy of the real thing.

'What can I say about that park? It seemed to have been designed with one thing in mind, and that was to please the human eye. The shapes of the flower beds, the shrubs and the roses that were still blooming even in October, the patterns made by the hedgerows, everything just so. Where you expected to see a tree, there was a tree. Where you expected a pathway to turn or fork or intersect with another, so it did. The lawns were immaculate, clipped to an inch, rolled, and springy underfoot, the perfect resilience, and where a path cut through there was a clean division, a ridge of sheared-off earth the colour and texture of chocolate cake. And whichever way you looked there was always something to catch your eye: a little Roman garden, a yew maze, a cupola perched on a low hill, a small windowless Georgian house at the end of an avenue of cypresses that was there not to be lived in but because it looked right, a wooden bandstand straight out of an American town square circa 1958, painted blue and cream . . . Did I mention a maze?'

'You did.'

'I stood for a while at the entrance and watched people go in and out, hearing exasperated cries and peals of laughter coming from inside. No one got lost for long. Everyone who went in emerged after about ten minutes, grinning and satisfied, saying that the maze was just the right difficulty, puzzling but not perplexing. I didn't try it myself. There was too much else to see.

'There was a boating pond where a dozen amateur admirals – young and old, from eight to eighty, the boys as serious as grown men, the grown men as blithe as boys – were sending their precious craft on perilous voyages across an Atlantic twenty yards wide. Destroyers and ducks were engaged on manoeuvres side by side. Hopes were pinned on the whims of the wind to bring sailing yachts safely back to shore. A lone submarine glided underwater, popping up every so often and surprising everyone.

'And there was a playground, a playground like you only ever dreamed about when you were a child. There were swings, there were roundabouts, there were slides and see-saws, and best of all there was a climbing frame as big as a house, a sprawling fantasy of ladders and portholes and turrets and fireman's poles, its various sections joined together by wooden suspension bridges hanging from knotted ropes. To the children clambering all over it, it was Sherwood Forest, the *Marie-Celeste*, the Alamo and the Death Star all rolled into one, and they were having so much fun I had to fight the urge to join them. And do you know what? In any other park in the country, if I'd stood for as long as I did watching those children, at least one of the adults present would have come up and asked me to leave, if not threatened to call the police. But in that park the mothers and fathers and nannies and au pairs just smiled up at me from the benches that surrounded the playground, understanding that I was simply sharing their delight at seeing children at play.

'Not far away there was an ice cream van. I didn't have much change on me, and it wasn't what you might call a blistering hot day, but right then I could think of nothing nicer, nothing that would cap my mood better, than a vanilla cone with a Flake in it. I joined the queue, and, can you believe it, they were giving the stuff away. A promotional offer, the man in the van called it. A new brand, apparently. I don't think I need to tell you how much sweeter that ice cream tasted for being free.

'I took my cone to a bench on a rise just above the playground and gazed out across the park, licking slowly, savouring, nibbling the Flake to make it last. I looked for houses, but there were none. Their rooftops were hidden by trees. I couldn't even see a tower block. There was just park whichever way you looked. Park to the north, park to the south, park in every direction. There were bright green tennis courts, and men and women in clean white sports clothes running backwards and forwards, and the yellow balls arcing over the nets. There were three teenage boys tossing a Frisbee to each other, and with them a red setter that rushed to and fro and every so often leapt up and snatched the Frisbee from the air in its teeth and wouldn't give it back without a long, grinning tug-of-war. There were young couples wandering hand in hand, pausing now and then for a lingering kiss. There were other young couples lolling on blankets on the grass, legs entwined. There was even an elderly couple behaving like a young couple – walking a little more slowly, to be sure, but taking more time over their kisses, too.

'Who were these people? Were they Londoners who, like me, had strayed into the park by accident? Or did they belong there? That might have explained their universal cheerfulness – the fact that they were the park's people, embodying the delight of every spring, summer or autumn day anyone had ever spent in a city park. The ones I'd exchanged words with – the jogger, the dog owner, people in the queue for ice creams – had all been kind and gracious and generous with their time. They didn't shy away from me like most people do, worried that I'm going to ask them for money and that they won't know how to respond. These well-dressed, smiling human beings had without exception treated me as an equal. Much like you do, my friend. You don't know what that means to a gentleman in my position.

'And at no point during that long, happy, sunlit afternoon did I ask myself if this was possible, if a place like this could really exist. Exactly the question you're asking now, Mark, with your eyes. What you must realise is that I wanted it so badly to *be* possible that I wasn't going to let a little thing like common sense get in the way. So a vast park had appeared where a park could not possibly be – so what? Sitting there with the sun on my face, a free ice cream in my belly and a view of dozens of happy people in front of me, why would I want to disturb the illusion with questions?

151

'I stayed there all afternoon, heavy with contentment, the kind of contentment I haven't felt since I was a very small child. A peace that, to coin a phrase, passed all understanding. A sense that the world and I had come to terms with each other, shaken hands and declared a truce. And the sun rolled down and shadows fell, and gradually people began to gather up their belongings and move off. One by one the tennis courts emptied of clean, white-clothed players. The young couples suddenly found a purpose after a day's dawdling and hurried off to the pictures or a pub or a bedroom somewhere. Supremacy over the boating pond was given back to the ducks. The ice cream van whirred away along the pathways, headlights on against the clustering dusk, tinkling a mournful tune. The climbing frame was abandoned. Beside it the swings swayed vacantly to and fro. And finally, when there was no one else in sight and I felt like the only person left alive in the entire world, I hauled myself to my feet, stretched the cricks out of my spine, and set off down the hill in the direction of the gates. Everything was hushed, that twilight a sacred hour. The only sound I could hear was my own reluctant, dragging footsteps. Had it been summer I might have thought about spending the night there, perhaps on the very bench on which I'd been sitting all day, but what with my cough and the dreadful dampness of autumn nights, I thought it would be best if I found somewhere indoors, one of those church crypts perhaps. And I could always come back to the park tomorrow, couldn't I? I could keep coming back as often as I wanted.

'There seemed to be only one way in or out of the park, and that was the way I'd come in, through those gates. And now, as darkness was beginning to fall, one of the gates was shut and there was someone standing by the other. A plain-faced man in uniform. A park-keeper. He had on a cap and a courteous smile.

' "Last one out, eh, sir?" he said to me. Someone in uniform calling *me* sir!

' "Am I?" I replied, glancing around. I really thought there would be others like me, stragglers unwilling to leave. No one. "I'm sorry. I was enjoying myself so much, I entirely lost track of the time."

'And the park-keeper said, "That's all right, sir. We deserve a little enjoyment in our lives, don't we? One day of happiness to make up for all the other miserable ones."

'I told him he couldn't be righter, thanked him for the use of his park and said I'd be coming back soon. It was too wonderful a place not to revisit. And he just smiled again – a little sadly, I realise now – and ushered me through the gate and closed it behind me with a heavy, ringing clang and wished me good night and strode away. I was halfway down the street when I realised I had forgotten to ask him the name of the park, but by then it was too late. I looked back, and he was nowhere to be seen.

'I slept well that night. The crypt was warm – once a hundred or so bodies had heated it up – and a mattress makes all the difference, doesn't it? A mattress and the memory of a day so strange and delightful you can hardly believe it happened.

'And then, near dawn, I woke to the sound of the "shift" taking place again. A great groaning, far off, like the bellow of a dinosaur in pain. A grating noise like a huge stone being rolled across a cavern entrance. And up and down the length of the crypt sleeping people stirred and moaned and rolled over, as though sharing a bad dream. I lay there for a moment frozen in horror, then leapt out of bed and threw on my hat and coat – of course I'd kept my new shoes on in bed; even amongst beggars there's precious little honour – and I sprinted out of there filled with a panic I couldn't explain, a sense of foreboding, of abrupt and irredeemable loss. I dashed through the dawn streets like a madman, driven by fear and the need to know, and finally I reached the street from which the other street, the street that had come from nowhere, led off. Gasping for breath, I staggered down it to where the junction with the other street had been. But I knew, even before I got there, that . . .'

I completed the sentence he couldn't finish himself: 'That it was gone.'

'As though it had never been there,' he sighed. 'The street was gone, the houses were gone, the iron gates were gone, the park was gone. What had been unearthed by that first shift of the city had been buried again, packed neatly away back where it came from, like a toy no longer wanted.'

He paused there, as if unable to contemplate the magnitude of his loss.

'I don't understand the hows or the whys of it,' he said eventually. 'Perhaps the street and the park belong to a London we don't normally see, a secret London that exists alongside the city we know, a second London, a ghostly twin that's made up of all our hopes and dreams and longings of what this city should be like, and sometimes the two, for some reason, overlap and you can move from one to the other. I don't know. Or perhaps everyone, once in their lives, is allowed a glimpse of how things *should* be. Perhaps that's what the park-keeper was telling me when he said that everybody deserved a day of happiness to make up for all the miserable ones. Perhaps he meant we should never forget that true contentment is possible and, whatever our circumstances, we should keep striving to achieve it. I don't know.

'All I know is this. I've been searching for that park ever since. For four months I've been roaming London in a state of shock. I've hardly slept, I've hardly eaten, I've hardly communicated with anyone – I've talked more this past half-hour than I have in the entire past four months. I've just walked and walked and walked, gradually coming to look like a cartoon parody of a tramp, and hoping constantly, with the desperation of a fool, that somehow I'll find a way back to the park, or another park like it, another pocket of perfection in an otherwise ruined world.

'At times I think I've been close. Once or twice I've heard a distant rumbling, but so far away, too far away to be sure that it wasn't just a bus revving in the next street or a tube train thundering below my feet. Once or twice I've detected a change in the quality of the light, but how can I know for certain it wasn't just a cloud passing in front of the sun or my eyes playing tricks on me? I can't. I can't be sure of anything except that the park was real, that the peace I felt there was real, and that I will never stop looking until I find both that park and that peace again.

'What do you call it, Mark, when you get a taste of heaven and realise that nothing will ever be that sweet again?'

'Growing up? Growing old?' I hazarded.

Harold lowered his gaze to look at his cracked, frostbitten hands. 'I call it Hell,' he said, simply.

There wasn't much else to be said. The alarm clock trilled in the bedroom, slowly winding down to silence. Outside the street had become marginally brighter, and every so often a car swished past. Lights were on in some of the windows opposite. London and its inhabitants were gearing themselves up for another day.

'Harold,' I offered tentatively, 'how about I take you to a doctor? Get you looked at?'

'What's the point?' he said, after a moment of actually looking like he was considering it.

'The point is, frankly, you're in awful shape, and in my opinion if you're not careful and you carry on the way you have been, you're going to do yourself irreparable harm.'

'And in *my* opinion I think I should be going now.' So saying, Harold rose stiffly to his feet.

'Harold,' I said, 'you're crazy.'

'Mark, I wish I were,' he replied, and turned to go.

I didn't stop him. I know I should have, but really, what could I have done? Manhandled him down the stairs and wrestled him into a taxi? Knocked him unconscious with a candlestick and called for an ambulance? I had no right to force Harold to do anything he didn't want to do. Or so I justified it to myself then, and have been justifying it ever since. The fact is, I watched Harold shuffle out of the flat and listened to him make his way painfully down the stairs and didn't lift a finger to prevent him because right at that moment I hated him. I hated him for having sat there in my armchair and manufactured a story of utter preposterousness – possibly the most ludicrous and pointless story he had ever told, not to mention the hardest to disprove – rather than simply owned up to the truth. What the truth was I had no idea (I fear he actually *had* contracted a terminal illness), but whatever the real reason for Harold's physical and spiritual deterioration, I hated him for not having the courage to share it with me. Until then his stories had been a source of amusement and wry pleasure, but that morning I saw Harold clearly for the first time, saw him for the pathetic, deluded, degraded man he was, a man so vain and yet so devoid of self-esteem that he felt he had to lie to make himself interesting.

And I'll tell you this, too. I have never seen Harold since that morning, which is getting on for half a year ago now. Neither has anyone else, and it seems to all intents and purposes that he has vanished off the face of the earth. And while an ungenerous part of me thinks good riddance, another kinder part hopes that wherever Harold is, he has found his park again.

In the meantime, whenever I'm walking around London, I find myself half listening out for what Harold called a 'shift', a faint, far-off rumble that will mean that the city has in some way reconfigured itself to show another facet briefly to the world, revealing the truth behind the façade – or the façade behind the truth (Harold would have known the difference). And for all my cynicism, for all my scepticism, I find myself hoping that, in this one instance, Harold was on the level.

Well, you never know.

Nana

Nana was nobody's mother and a mother to everyone on our street.

Asking Nana her age was like asking why the sky was blue or the grass green. She would reply, 'I'm *my* age,' and that was the best answer anyone could hope for.

I have always thought of Nana in terms of her wrinkles – contour lines on a map of a well-known, much-loved treasure island.

Nana had been a young woman when Queen Victoria died, and she was all of Edwardian England bound up in a bundle of bones, skin and woollen clothing.

Nana was like mountains: ancient, craggy, awe-inspiring and always there.

If you stayed awake, gummy-eyed, till midnight and dared to peek out of your bedroom window, you might well see Nana pacing slowly along the pavement, inspecting beneath cars and hedges, a brown paper bag in her hand. Nana cared for everyone in our street, even the stray cats. She would lay out fish heads and chicken legs for them and then walk away. A cat would sniff the food. Nana would look round. The cat would vanish beneath the hedge or car where it had been hiding. Nana would resume walking. The cat would ease its body out again. Nana would look round. The cat would vanish. Nana would carry on. The cat would appear again, snatch the titbit, wolf it down in three gulps, then vanish again. Nana would smile to herself.

I used to imagine she bore an iron weight on her shoulders –

a hundred pounds or more, invisible – that bent her neck horizontal so that cats, children and the ground were all she could see. Not forgetting, of course, Hamish, her little Scottie who fancied himself a Great Dane.

That was Nana, and to be honest I did not expect her to be alive when I returned to the street. Nor, from my frequent and enthusiastic descriptions of the woman who had looked after me on countless afternoons between the ages of three and six, did Jill, who pointed out that while women as a rule live longer than men – and a very sensible rule it was, too – there were few people living, of either sex, who could remember the nineteenth century as anything more than stories handed down to them by long-dead grandparents.

Trust Jill to get in that crack about men.

'You don't know Nana,' I said, locking the car door.

'Maybe,' was all she said.

It was teatime, and the street was empty except for parked cars. It was a broad street in an area of the suburbs which, if not exactly well-to-do, had a nodding acquaintance with respectability. Each boxy house sat in its own half-acre of garden, with a garage to the side and its front door protected by an arching porch. The road itself was made up of huge sections of concrete joined with strips of tar.

'Changed much?' Jill asked, adding, 'Dumb question, I suppose.'

'A question is only as dumb as she who asks it,' I said, going round the front of our car and extending an arm across her back to rest my hand in the curve between rib and hip.

'Answer me,' she threatened.

'Yes, it's basically the same. The houses are the same bricks and mortar, though the paint's new on most of them, but all the elms have gone. This used to be a tree-lined avenue, you know. I guess Dutch Elm Disease must have got them and no one thought to replace them with anything else. Oddly enough, it seems much narrower now without them.'

She gave me that funny-quizzical, crinkled-nose look, the

one I had fallen for a year and a half ago, the look that said, *You're a fool but then so am I, and if we both insist on being fools then let's at least be fools together.*

'Thanks for coming with me,' I said. 'It's as if there's something I've got to lay to rest before I can move on to the next stage.'

'I understand.' She pecked me on the cheek.

'I couldn't do it on my own. I wouldn't have the courage.'

'I know. You're a complete wimp.'

I dug my fingers into her side and she folded over, giggling and trying to poke me in the balls, but once I had started tickling her she was hopelessly in my power and, my physical superiority having been established, all that was left to her was verbal violence. Between laughing gasps she said, 'If you don't . . . bloody stop . . . you'll be spending the next month . . . sleeping on the bloody . . . sofa!'

I stopped. That kind of blackmail you do not mess about with.

She made one last attempt to jab her fingers into my crotch, and I stepped smartly back and banged my calf on the car's bumper.

'Bugger!'

'Serves you right.'

We found the old family homestead. Number Eleven. Whoever was living there now had reglazed the downstairs windows with mottled glass and covered the walls with stone cladding. A cartwheel leaned against the door and – another rustic touch – the porch was adorned with a pair of carriage lanterns.

'Another victory for your mother's appalling bad taste,' Jill said.

'Screw you, sweetie. Nothing to do with her.'

'You surprise me.'

'You know, I bet my initials are still chalked on the inside of the fireplace.'

'They'll have bricked it up, stuck in a coal-effect gas fire and surrounded it in fake marble.'

'Maybe, but my initials are still there, even if nobody can see them. Anyway, we're not interested in that house.'

'Oh, we aren't, are we?'

'No.'

'Where did she live?'

'Number Thirty-six.'

We looked both ways, and nothing was coming, and we crossed the street.

I had turned thirty-six last February. When I last saw Nana, just before my father's work took the family away from this street and this city, I had been six. Thirty-six being the square of six, I decided to share this numerical coincidence with Jill. 'Funny how it all adds up, isn't it?'

She was unimpressed. I don't think the Apocalypse will impress Jill. As Hell spews forth its demons and the Four Horsemen gallop across the land and the armies of Good and Evil battle it out on the plain of Megiddo beneath a purple thunderous sky, Jill will shrug, yawn and say she's seen better.

Thirty-six had further magical properties for the amateur numerologist like me. Divisible by three and four (both lucky), and by twelve (three times four, ultra-lucky), with its two digits totalling nine (the trinity of trinities), it was, in fact, the number of numbers.

And it was the number of Nana's house.

And as we neared Number Thirty-six, I myself square-rooted. I became six again, and the hedges sprouted and grew tall until their tops were unseen plateaux, and suddenly the gate to Number Eighteen once more caged a gigantic barking Alsatian, and outside the door to Number Twenty-two I knew there was a red scooter flipped over on to its side, propped at an angle by ram's-horn handlebars.

Some of these houses were safe ground, the homes of

162

friends. There was Jimmy's house, and there Annette's, and there the twins', Jeremy and William, or Ger and Bil as we used to know them. But one was enemy territory, home to the street bully Fergus, bastard son of Torquemada and Lucrezia Borgia, nephew of Genghis Khan and favourite godson of Attila the Hun. At the thought of Fergus my ears started to sting from his pinches and my shins to ache from his kicks, and though I was thirty-six and a little over six feet tall, I still tiptoed past the gate to his house, Number Twenty-eight . . .

Just in case.

Jill sensed the change that had come over me, the boy still quivering in tumultuous fear of Fergus and his pinches and his jeers and his bruisings, and she hugged me more tightly.

Number Thirty-six

'Here we are.'

Jill said it, peering at the rusty numerals on the gatepost. She said it because I was saying nothing. Anything I said would have emerged as the reedy treble of a six-year-old. I knew for a fact that I was six years old now because here was Nana's house as if the intervening three decades since I had last been here had never happened, as if time was an irrelevancy and growing old just a figure of speech. The grass might have been a little shaggier than I remembered and the fence that ran alongside the stone path to the front door might have developed something of a sag in the middle, but in every other respect Nana's house was exactly as I had last seen it. The brick-lined arch over the doorway was just as weather-beaten and the paintwork was that same unmistakable rust-red, the colour of cough drops, and yellowed lace curtains frilled the windows.

Eventually I did speak. 'My God.' My own voice, thank Christ. Cigarette-tuned, whisky-pitched.

'Where are you going, Martin?'
'Nowhere, Nana.'

'*Then you won't mind coming straight back here and sitting down while I tell you about Springheel Jack.*'

'*You've told me about Springheel Jack a million billion times.*'

' *"Springheel Jack was a murderer of fallen women . . ."* '

' *" . . . who terrorised the fog-bound streets of Old London." I know I've heard it all before. What's a fallen woman, Nana?*'

'*Keep still and listen to the rest of the story.*'

'*When are Mummy and Daddy coming back?*'

'*Later.*'

'*Not soon?*'

'*Later. But later can wait until it's good and ready. For now, you are to listen to me. "Springheel Jack . . ."*'

'Where are you going, Mart?'

'To ring the doorbell. What else?'

'You don't seriously think . . . You can't just . . . Oh, for heaven's sake.' Jill rolled her eyes and chased after me up the path. 'If you're so set on making a complete prat of yourself, I suppose I can always pretend I'm your care-in-the-community social worker.'

I travelled the length of the path in a few short strides, where once it had taken a mean fourteen (avoiding the cracks, naturally). And I reached down, not up, to press the doorbell.

A chime tolled deep within the house. I honestly expected Hamish to come yap-snarl-yapping up to the door and push his wet black nose through the flap of the letter-box, which was at shoe height. I had to remind myself that dogs do not live that long. Nor do humans, not even the female of the species.

'And what, pray, do you intend to say when a complete stranger opens the door?' Jill whispered.

'That we're Jehovah's Witnesses.'

But no stranger opened the door.

Nana did.

She blinked in the sunshine, shielded her eyes, said, 'Who is it?' and then said, 'Oh, it's you. I remember you. Martin. Martin from Number Eleven.' She lowered her hand to reveal her face in all its wrinkled splendour: the lines that shaped the dormant volcanoes of her eyes and the bottomless crevice of her mouth. Here, and here, and here, was treasure.

In an ecstasy of remembrance I gasped, 'Nana, you haven't changed a bit.'

It was no lie: she had not. I'm prepared to swear an oath on it. She was still wearing the same old housecoat with its floral pattern of indeterminate era, gaudy and sun-faded, and she was still labouring under the same invisible weight that had raised the vertebrae in her neck to form a reptilian ridge that creaked audibly as she looked inquisitively up at my face.

'You have.' She flashed yellow denture. This was her smile. 'I preferred you when you were smaller. At least I could see you properly then.'

'Nana, this is my wife Jill. Jill, Nana.'

Jill's hello was guarded but polite.

Nana turned to me. 'You always come with your wives and husbands,' she said darkly.

'Who do?'

'You children. Suddenly, when you get married, you remember me.' Her expression shifted, brightening abruptly like a hillside no longer shadowed by cloud. 'But where are my manners? Come in, come in. Enter freely and of your own will.'

I followed Nana's stiffly swaying form into the hallway, but Jill hung back, not sure whether she belonged here. I beckoned to her, and she came.

'A vampire, Martin, cannot enter a house unless he has been invited by a member of the household. This is useful to remember should the vampires come knocking at your door, demanding entry so they can SUCK YOUR BLOOD!'

165

'Ssh, Nana, you're being scary.'

'Vampires ARE scary, Martin. They're not to be taken lightly. They come into your life and won't leave you alone until you're drained and wasted, a pale shell of yourself. Not that a chubby fellow like you need worry too much about that. But never, ever let one into your house.'

'How will I recognise a vampire when I see one?'

'By its pale face and pale skin, its blood-red eyes and blood-red lips, its night-black hair and night-black cloak. But you don't need to see these things to know if somebody is a vampire. You sense it. Every hair on your body stands on end. Hamish here met a vampire once, and he howled and his coat went stiffer than a wire brush, didn't it, boy? Yes, it did, it diiiid . . .'

'Tea, of course,' said Nana. 'Tea for three. And cakes. I have some cakes in the kitchen.'

Nana shuffled out of the front room leaving Jill and myself sitting on the sofa in doubt-filled silence. The sun shining through the shroud of lace curtain tinted the air sepia. The old clock in its case of walnut had stopped at five to ten. (Its steady, reverberant tick used to sneak whole hours past me without my noticing.) The furniture and bric-a-brac were too old to have gone out of fashion. Antique porcelain dogs danced with china ballerinas, as they had danced when I was six, across clean varnished surfaces, leaving no footprints. I tried to see the room through Jill's eyes, which had never beheld all this before and so found nothing special about it, nothing that triggered off a dozen memories brighter and more explosive than fireworks. For her, that tray had never framed a jigsaw in the making. For her, that table had never been the scene of countless games of gin rummy that continued until I finally won a hand. For her, that carpet, those dusty Turkish swirls, had never been a battlefield for battalions of plastic soldiers.

'Are you uncomfortable?' she whispered.

'Why, are you? Is there a spring sticking into your bum or something?'

'No, you clot. Uncomfortable about being here.'

'No,' I lied. 'Are you?'

'Yes.'

I only touched her. A kiss would have been too furtive, too adult. 'I wonder how many visitors she's had in the past thirty years.'

Jill shook her head.

Nana returned with a teapot and a plate laden with jam tarts and coconut macaroons and French fancies and bakewell slices, each fresh and separate, clean from the wrappers. I offered to fetch anything else that needed fetching from the kitchen.

'No, Martin, I'll get the cups myself. I *can* still walk.'

Her tone agitated me. 'I thought I might help, that's all.'

'I don't need help.'

'Crikey, she's pushed the boat out, hasn't she?' Jill said when Nana had left the room again. 'Can she afford this?'

'Maybe I should offer her some money.'

'Do. She'd hate that.'

'Martin, you're good at drawing. Draw me a homunculus.'

'What's a halum—a halumculus, Nana?'

'Homunculus, Martin. A little man, an evil little man.'

'What crayon should I use?'

'Grammar, Martin. WHICH crayon. Use the red. Monsters are always red.'

'Mummy says I shouldn't do everything you tell me. She says it's bad for me. She says you fill my head with funny ideas.'

'She should say it to my face. Who's been around longer, do you suppose, Martin? Your mother or me?'

'You, of course.'

'Then I know better than her. I know what's good for you. Draw me a homunculus.'

167

'How big is it exactly?'

'It should be a little bit larger than a child. It should bend and stoop and walk with a limp. Its eyes should not look in the same direction as each other.'

'Crossed?'

'No, the other way.'

'I suppose I should ask what you're doing now.' Nana could have sounded more enthusiastic.

'I'm a cartoonist.'

'And what do you cartoon?'

Grammar, Nana, I thought to myself, although I remembered someone saying once that the noun didn't exist that couldn't be verbed. I said, 'Comic books. Horror stories, mostly. I have a knack for drawing horror stories.'

Nana's wrinkles made more wrinkles. New valleys and hills appeared on the island of her face, as though the island was in fact a vast sea monster on whose back a shipload of unwary travellers had staked their claim. Now the creature was awakening. Make for the boats! The ground is alive!

'I think it was because of what you encouraged me to draw,' I said.

'Nice to know my advice lives on after me. Though it's hardly art, is it?'

'It's a living.'

'Cake, dear?' Nana extended the plate to Jill, who refused. Nana tutted. 'Girls these days worry too much about their weight. Take plenty of exercise and you can eat as much as you like, that's what I say.'

'I do take exercise.' Politeness buried the sneer deep down in Jill's words where it could be detected but was too deep to be remarked upon.

'I'll certainly have one,' I said. I chose a strawberry tart – a single fruit perched on a iceberg of cream that bulged as I bit into it and foamed over my chin. The sharpness of the jam pricked nostalgia out of its hidey-hole. Melancholy beast that it was, the Eeyore of emotions, it prompted me to say, 'Where do you find these, Nana? I didn't think they made them any more, not this way, not this good.'

'The bakery's still going. Any reason it should have closed?' There – the flash of dentures that indicated that Nana had said something she was pleased about. 'Do you remember our trips to the bakery, Martin? You used to look forward to them all week.'

'I did?'

Nana tilted her head back and regarded me with minute satisfaction. 'I'm glad you said that, Martin, because I never took you or anyone to the bakery, I always went on my own. You'd be surprised how many of you say you did go. Say that and plenty of other things. I can twist you around and about and upside down until I have you remembering things that couldn't possibly have happened to you. I can invent whole new childhoods for you, if I want.'

'You won't do that with me. I can remember it all. How you used to feed us and the cats and break up fights and tell us stories and everything.'

Jill had begun to fidget. I had told her this morning that she need not come, but she had insisted, and when Jill put her foot down she put it down so hard it went through the floorboards. So in a sense she deserved to be bored, but the fact that she was showing it irritated me.

'Are you successful?' Nana asked.

I said that if she meant in terms of income, just barely, but in terms of artistic satisfaction I was exactly where I wanted to be, although I was forever searching for new and better techniques, greater skill, dexterity, refinement.

We fell into silence, an awkward lock in which no key seemed to fit.

Then, slowly, ponderously, the old clock gave a tick – a single, solitary tick, loud as a gunshot, and the minute hand clicked on to four to ten.

'It works!' I yelped.

'It does,' Nana replied evenly.

Jill looked as if she had been stabbed in the leg with a needle. 'That gave me a fright. I thought I was going to have a heart attack.'

'A young, slim, well-exercised person like you?' said Nana.

By her eyes I could tell that Jill was contemplating murder. Why *had* I brought her along? No, more accurately: why had I allowed her to convince me to let her tag along? Come to think of it, why was I here at all? Was I really so insecure, in myself and about the future, that I needed some reassurance from yesterday before launching myself into tomorrow?

Nana, as ever, knew what I was thinking. 'Why have you come, Martin? Be honest.'

'I came to see you.'

'I said be honest. You didn't believe that I'd still be alive, surely.'

I wasn't prepared to answer that.

Jill was. 'No.'

'But here I am.'

'And you haven't changed a bit,' I said. It was trite, but it was all part of an effort to patch up the damaged atmosphere in the room.

'That's what you all say. You've all been back. You're the last of your lot, Martin. Jeremy, William, Jimmy, Annie, even Fergus, and the others, they've all been back to gloat over old Nana's grave and found old Nana isn't quite as dead and gone as they expected.' Her eyes glimmered in the sepia light that was growing dimmer as the sun sank over the rooftops on the shadowy side of the street. 'You thought I'd disappear when you grew up and left. You thought I'd stop living because supplying you with cakes and games and stories was the only thing that kept me alive, the only thing I considered worth carrying on for. You and all the others. But you forgot something.'

'Hormone replacement therapy?' Jill was never one to resist a barbed comment if she felt the recipient was deserving.

Nana glared at her. For a second her eyes swelled in their leathery pouches.

'You,' Nana said to me exclusively, 'forgot that children are immortal.'

'They grow up, they die like everyone else,' I pointed out.

'A child does, yes, of course, but *children* do not. For every one that leaves, a new arrival steps in to fill its shoes. Did I ever tell you about the Hydra, Martin?'

'Yes, Nana, dozens of times.'

'How if you cut off one head two more appeared in its place?'

'Yes, Nana. I understand.'

'And do you remember telling me that you believed that, if you shut your eyes, no one else could see you?'

'Yes,' I said, vaguely embarrassed. It had seemed a reasonable enough assumption at the time.

'You still believe it. You still believe that the world grinds to a halt whenever you leave a room and people cease to exist whenever you drift out of their lives.'

As a matter of fact, whenever I leave a room I believe that people are sniggering about me. *There goes the arrested developer who draws comics for a living!* But I didn't say anything.

'But I'm still here, Martin,' said Nana. 'So I ask again: why have you come?'

I had no answer to that.

Someone rapped at the front door. In the seconds that followed I heard – probably from a neighbouring garden, although I could have sworn it came from just outside the room, in the hallway – the skitter-scratch of claws and the yapping of a little dog pretending that it was a big dog. Jill heard it, too. She cocked her head. Nana gazed wisely at both of us. The yapping died away. Nana set down her cup.

'You'd better leave now. I have visitors.'

We rose to our feet, sending chalk-scented curls of dust

boiling through the air. Nana peered upwards, the effort stretching and straining the tendons in her neck.

'It was good to see you, Nana,' I said.

'Was it? Then I'm glad. For your sake. And I'm glad to have met your wife. It's nice to know how my old children are getting on with their new lives.'

The door was rapped again.

On an impulse I asked, 'Could I take a cake, please? One for the road. They're so good.'

'You always used to, Martin. You always loved to munch on a cake on the way back to your house, didn't you? Yes. Which would you prefer?'

'Strawberry tart, definitely. Please.'

'You used to put them in your pocket to take them home, didn't you? And your mother always complained about the mess.'

'Some things never change,' Jill muttered. 'You're still a pig.'

'We'd better wrap it,' Nana said. 'I have some greaseproof paper. Give.'

I took a tart from the plate and handed it to her. She disappeared and returned a minute later with a parcel of paper containing the tart. Shiny stains were already forming on the paper, and the colour of strawberry glimmered through.

At the front door Nana welcomed in a girl and a boy aged around six or seven, twins with carroty hair and a smattering of freckles. They regarded Jill and me with curiosity and suspicion.

'Gemma, Dean, you go into the front room and get out a jigsaw. These grown-ups are just leaving. And help yourself to cakes. I've put them out ready for you.'

'OK,' chorused Gemma and Dean as one, and they ran down the hallway and into the front room.

'Their mother died recently,' Nana explained, 'and their father doesn't get home till six, so I look after them between school and then.'

'Goodbye, Nana,' I said.

'Yes, lovely meeting you,' Jill said.

'At least we've said a proper goodbye,' said Nana, brushing my cheek with a monkey-paw hand.

As she closed the door on us, her head lowered to its usual position. Tendons slackened, wrinkles relaxed. Her eyes were no doubt relieved to return to the ground.

'Here I am,' I heard her say, her voice diminishing as she turned.

The street had grown life while we had been indoors. A petrol-driven lawnmower was droning, pulling along a man in vest and braces. Kids were holding skateboard races, though they spent more time falling off their boards than actually racing. A radio sang to the sunset. Somewhere a pigeon fluted and purred.

Jill and I walked solemnly back to the car. I laid the tart on the back seat.

As we were strapping ourselves in, she broke the silence.

'Can you look me straight in the eye and say, sincerely, that you feel better for that?'

'No, I don't. But I do feel less guilty.'

'Did you used to feel guilty?'

'About deserting her? I guess so.'

'I bet she'd have liked that.'

'Don't be so hard on her.'

'Like she wasn't hard on you!'

'That's how she is. That was always her way. She was always a bit stern, a bit fierce, even when she was being kind. *Especially* when she was being kind.'

Although the argument was far from won, Jill called a truce by saying, 'Well, you ought to know.'

I started the car and pulled out, careful to avoid the children hurtling along the rippled concrete.

About a hundred yards down the street I had to stop.

'Damn her.'

'What is it, Mart?' Jill asked.

'Will you drive?'

'Of course. What is it? What's wrong?'

I turned to her. Tears were brimming in my eyes, ready to spill. Tears of anger mixed with sorrow.

'I've just realised,' I told her. 'What Nana said about taking cakes home in my pocket. I never did. It never happened. Never. Never!'

The Gift

They never knocked, just came right in. Didn't kick down the door, nothing so thuggish as that. A universal key unit could pop the lock in an instant, and so save them from a suit for unlawful damage.

They could turn up at any time of night or day, but they preferred to come at night, when there was more chance of finding you in. Either way, it was best to be prepared. Aaron had taken to wearing pyjamas even when the darkness sweltered and he had to sleep with the air conditioning full on. There was nothing more humiliating than to wake up with a flashlight blazing in your face and half a dozen men and women in cream-coloured suits staring down at your vulnerably naked body, then to fumble your way into a pair of undershorts and a T-shirt while the same men and women in cream-coloured suits looked on, like bored scientists observing yet another run-through of a tried-and-tested experiment. It wasn't so much that they didn't know the meaning of modesty, it was the fact that they didn't care. So the pyjamas stayed on, even if Aaron felt he was in danger of sweating to death inside them.

Like so many people in his line of work, Aaron had developed something of an instinct about the raids. In the same way that you often wake up a few seconds before your alarm clock goes off, so Aaron would usually snap out of sleep just before the door lock went. Perhaps he was responding to some subliminal cue – a stifled breath, a stealthy footfall – which his ears picked up while the rest of his body slumbered.

Perhaps he just knew a raid was coming the way wild animals sense an impending thunderstorm.

Tonight, though, his instinct failed him. It wasn't until an FPP officer was shaking him by the shoulder and aiming half a hundred watts of candlepower at his eyelids that he emerged from the Land of Nod, pawing at the air, curled and mewling like a ragged kitten.

More than the grabbing hands and the rough voices, Aaron was acutely conscious of the clamminess of his pyjama jacket as he awoke, and also of the need to urinate, a need that was going to become an urge very soon. It was this, more than anything, that concerned him as he rolled upright, swung his legs over the side of the bed, sat up, rested his elbows on his knees and his forehead in his hands, groaned, ground the heels of his palms in his eye-sockets, and finally looked up, squinting grittily into the miniature sun of the flashlight. His need to pee was a weakness, and he didn't want to show weakness, any weakness.

'Aaron Novak?'

'What do you think?'

'Aaron Novak of Apartment a hundred and seventeen B, Seaview Tower?'

Aaron shuttled his fingers through his hair. 'Do you see the sea out of that window?'

'Answer the question.'

'Yeah. Yeah, that's me.'

'Stand up, please.'

'I was just pointing out the fact that whoever thought to call this building Seaview Tower either had a lousy sense of humour or X-ray vision,' said Aaron, getting to his feet.

'Please keep your comments to yourself, Mr Novak.'

'Sure. Just trying to break the ice, you know?'

The bedroom light came on. There were only four FPP officers tonight. Each was wearing the de rigeur cream-coloured two-piece and the brass badge with TRUST written on it in letters and manufolded hands. In deference to the weather, one had undone his shirt collar button beneath the knot of his tie. As ever, it was the Englishman, Captain Silas Gregory, leading the raid.

'Mr Novak,' Gregory said, with a formal nod.

'Captain,' Aaron replied, with a respect that wasn't entirely feigned.

'You know the drill.' Gregory held out a hardcopy warrant. 'Read this and sign.'

Aaron waved a hand. 'Just get on with the search. I know what it says.'

'You must sign it,' said Gregory, thrusting the warrant under Aaron's nose. 'It absolves us of any responsibility for breakage or loss incurred during the execution of our duty. Without your signature we leave ourselves open to a lawsuit.'

'And if I refuse to sign?' As if he wasn't going to.

'Signatures can be coerced.'

'Yeah,' said Aaron, 'painfully. And then, of course, I'll have signed a document that says that I can't have any comeback for something already done to me.'

'Procedure must be observed,' said Gregory. A dry smile bristled below his moustache, revealing a glimpse of typically bad British dentistry. 'Please, Mr Novak.' He held out the warrant again. 'For your own good?'

Aaron took the document and also the pen Gregory offered him, and signed.

'You won't find anything,' he said, returning pen and warrant.

'That remains to be seen.' Gregory produced an FPP-issue organiser from his jacket pocket, keyed up a digital facsimile of Aaron's signature and compared it with the one on the warrant. 'Close enough,' he said. He turned to his three subordinates. 'Off you go.'

The FPP officers set about the task of ransacking the apartment with an enthusiasm that neither professional competence nor job-familiarity nor their habitual impassivity could entirely disguise. They opened, they overturned, they scattered, they emptied, they peered behind, they looked under, they crawled over, they fingered, they flicked through, they unfolded, they shook out, they prised apart, they undid, they unscrewed, they held up to the light, they squinted at, they scanned, and all the time they grinned, to each other, to themselves, gleefully.

Meanwhile Captain Gregory stood by the uncurtained bedroom window with his hands clasped lightly together behind his back, gazing out through the huge sheet of glass at the night-time city. The lit windows of the buildings opposite shimmered in the billows of Floridan heat rising from the broiling street. Rooftop parties thumped away around sapphire swimming pools. A huge pleasure dirigible glided across the sky; festooned with fairy-lights, it resembled some giant floating chandelier. A dozen microlight aircraft buzzed in its wake, riding the bumpy currents of its slipstream like scavenger fish following a shark. From beside the bed Aaron watched the captain watching the city, and observed a humble silence while the pressure in his bladder slowly mounted in an exquisite crescendo.

'You're wrong, you know,' said Gregory, without looking round.

'About what?'

'Whoever named this building didn't have a lousy sense of humour, or X-ray vision, for that matter. Whoever called this building Seaview Tower understood that the difference between having a view of the sea and not having a view of the sea but living close to it is so small as to be insignificant.'

'Meaning?'

'Simple psychology. You know in which direction the sea lies, don't you, Mr Novak, and sometimes, when the wind blows right, you can hear the engines of motor launches and jet-skis, am I right? And it can't be denied that the air in this area is just that much clearer, that much fresher, for the sea's proximity. And so, even though you can't see the sea, even though it lies two or three buildings away, you are still constantly aware of it. The view is in your mind's eye, and the building's name reaffirms and refreshes that image.'

'Yeah, well, if only that made a difference to the rent.'

The remark won a smirk from Gregory. 'What I'm getting at,' he said, 'is that something as simple as a name can have a powerful effect on the human psyche. If well-chosen, it can stick like a grain of sand in the mind, and around it can form a pearl of unconscious thought, a gorgeous, self-created mental mirage. Music can do that, too. Good music has the power to seed pearls of the imagination, wouldn't you agree?'

Aaron was about to answer when something shattered in the living room.

'Sorry!' one of the officers called out, with very little apology in his tone of voice. The other two officers, in different rooms, snickered.

Aaron winced. It could have been one of his Foreign statuettes, but he suspected, hoped, prayed it was only the sheet of glass that topped the coffee table. There had been no hum beforehand, had there? And the FPP, for all their thoroughness, were notoriously careful about handling Foreign artefacts.

'I am sorry,' said Gregory sincerely.

'Fuck that,' said Aaron.

Gregory turned his ocean-blue eyes on Aaron, not in anger but in curiosity. Where had this spark of resentment come from? Of all the Sirens he regularly raided, Aaron Novak was among the most passive, the most subdued. Some harangued the FPP from the moment they arrived to the moment they left. Others sat sullenly in a corner talking to their lawyers on the phone, or followed the officers around with a palmcorder scrupulously taping everything they did. Aaron simply accepted the intrusions and the officers' behaviour. Almost as if he expected to be caught with contraband and was resigned to the fact. Either that, or he thought that to act submissively was a good way of avoiding suspicion.

'Why do you do it?' Gregory asked. 'Sing for Foreigners?'

The enquiry was casual, as if Gregory was merely making conversation.

Aaron shrugged. The pressure in his groin was making him irritable, but he regretted having snapped at Gregory just now and wanted to regain the captain's favour, so with an extra effort of will he kept his voice calm and level and friendly as he said: 'Because I can. Because I'm good at it. Because it makes me a lot of money.'

'There are many other more respectable trades a young man could turn his hand to.'

'I don't think singing's unrespectable. It's no less respectable than being a hotel owner and charging the golden giants a fortune for Foreign-scale rooms. Everyone in Bridgeville, whether they realise it or not, is making money off the Foreigners. Cabbies, street vendors, tour guides, garbage collectors, even . . .'

Gregory raised his eyebrows. 'You were going to say?'

'Nothing.'

'You were going to say, "Even FPP officers." '

Aaron shuffled embarrassedly. 'Yeah,' he murmured. 'Even FPP officers.'

' "Everybody else is doing it so why can't you?" That's what you think, yes?'

'Yes.' Defiantly. Aaron had nothing to be ashamed of.

Captain Silas Gregory of the Foreign Policy Police, Bridgeville division, parted his hands, turned around, rested his backside against the windowsill and folded his arms across his chest – all with the deliberate slowness of a schoolteacher who has just stumbled across some hitherto undiscovered vein of ignorance in his class.

'I won't deny that Bridgeville has a lot to be thankful to the golden giants for,' he said. 'Nor will I deny that almost every one of this town's citizens, in one way or another, benefits from their generosity. There are, however, different levels of complicity. My role as an officer for the FPP, for instance, is to ensure that Foreigners are not conned, victimised, intimidated or mistreated in any way during their visits. That, I would have said, was a respectable and, more to the point, a respect*ful* way of profiting from the Foreign input into the Bridgeville economy. Not only that but it serves a useful function as well. Whereas singing, it seems to me, preys on the Foreigners' most basic instincts.'

'They enjoy it.'

'Of course they do. And how handsomely they reward Sirens like you, the men and women whose voices bring them such pleasure. Look at all this, Mr Novak.' Gregory gestured around the bedroom, at its walnut fixtures, at the plush divan, at the mood-attuned wall fabric which was currently attempting to soothe Aaron's emotional and physical discomfort with a deep midnight blue. 'How many twenty-four-year-olds live in this kind of splendour?'

'Twenty-five,' Aaron said.

'I'm sorry?'

'I turned twenty-five last week.'

'Congratulations. Your first quarter-century. I myself am approaching the end of my second.'

'You look good on it.'

'Thank you.' Gregory seemed genuinely flattered. He spread out his arms. 'And that's my point. Here I am, nearly twice your age, and I've not earned in my whole lifetime nearly a tenth as much as you have in yours.'

'That must make you very unhappy.'

'No.' Gregory frowned, as though giving the facetious comment serious thought. 'No, I don't resent you at all, Mr Novak, if that's what you're implying. I'm envious of your talent, perhaps, but I think that even if I was equipped with a magnificent singing voice, I wouldn't squander it on Foreign music.'

'Have you ever heard me sing?'

Gregory shook his head.

'Then how do you know my voice is magnificent?'

'Isn't it?' said Gregory simply.

Aaron laughed, even though the action elicited a twinge of pain from his bulging bladder. 'Fair enough. And what would you sing, Captain Gregory, if you could sing as magnificently as you say I do?'

'Songs with words, for one thing. Words and tunes. Songs that have something to say, that mean something. Operatic arias. Beatles numbers. Old show tunes. Standards. Not this meandering, monotonous muck the Foreigners like. Songs that stir emotions in the heart.' He slapped his chest. 'The human heart.'

'Well, I guess that's the difference between you and me,' said Aaron. 'You want to stir emotions, I want to earn a living.'

'Yes,' sighed Gregory. 'I suppose that is the difference.'

The urge to urinate had now become an imperative. Fearing that the only alternative was wetting himself, Aaron asked the captain's permission to answer the call of nature. It was granted with a nod, and Aaron skipped to the bathroom, where one of the officers had just finished tossing the contents of the basin cabinet on to the floor and was now attempting to slash open the shower curtain with a razor blade.

'How on earth would I be able to hide anything inside that?' Aaron asked him.

The officer shrugged and started cutting along the seam of the curtain's lower hem.

Doing his best to ignore the man's presence, Aaron flipped up the lavatory seat and relieved himself.

When he returned to the bedroom, he found Captain Gregory overseeing the two other officers as they dismantled the bed. While one methodically palpated the pillows, his colleague was on his hands and knees busily unscrewing the bolts that secured the headboard to the base. The walls, mistaking all this activity as the prelude to vigorous sexual congress, had gone peach-pink.

Gregory asked Aaron if he knew what they were looking for.

'I do now,' said Aaron. 'A vocal enhancer.'

'Quite right.' Gregory narrowed his eyes. 'Was that, I wonder, just a lucky guess?'

'What else could fit into the hem of a shower curtain?'

'Ah yes, well deduced. Yesterday we arrested a greyware pirate who confessed to selling at least three dozen enhancers within the past month. He gave no names, just physical descriptions. One of those descriptions matched yours.'

'And what if I said I don't use one because I don't need one?'

'Coming from a young man of such self-assurance, I'd have said that was highly likely. However, these days, with so many Sirens competing for the Foreigners' attention, each of you needs every advantage he or she can get. Even you, Mr Novak, might be tempted to use a vocal enhancer if you thought it would give you an edge over the competition. And since my job is to see to it that all Foreigners are treated fairly and equally . . .' The sentence languished into a take-it-or-leave-it shrug.

'Or see to it that no one person is allowed to earn more money from the Foreigners than anyone else,' Aaron added.

'The FPP Council,' said Gregory, 'welcomes Foreign tourism in every resort-city and wants the golden giants to feel free to do as they please. They are our guests. But it also wants them to know that while they're on Earth they'll be safe from exploitation. That's why there are regulations – regulations it is my duty to enforce – against cabbies taking Foreign fares on unnecessarily circuitous routes, against tour guides showing Foreigners around anything other than the officially designated sites, and against Sirens using any means other than their God-given talents to charm the golden giants.'

'I never once met a Foreigner who complained because my voice was better than someone else's.'

'That's not the point,' said Gregory, stepping smartly sideways to avoid the mattress that one of the officers was heaving off the base of the divan. 'The point is that we mustn't give them cause to take offence. If one of them feels he's been defrauded, for whatever reason, and however mild the alleged deceit, it could have a disastrous effect. We know so little about this race, they're such a mystery to us, even after forty years, and yet we owe them so much. And it doesn't take much to scare them off, as we know from what happened at Koh Farang and New Venice. It's such a precarious situation. What if something drives them off from the entire planet, as it did from those cities? What if they abandon us altogether? *Then* where will we be?'

Aaron pretended that the thought had never once crossed his mind or caused him to lose sleep.

'So you see, Mr Novak, I'm not picking on you. I'm not picking on anybody. I'm just trying to keep everybody happy, humans and Foreigners alike.'

'There's nothing here, sir,' said the FPP officer kneeling by the bed. He straightened up with a grunt and smoothed the wrinkles out of his suit jacket. 'Either he's got a very clever hiding place, or he's as honest as the day is long.'

Aaron struggled to keep the gloat of vindication out of his face.

'Very well then, Mr Novak,' said Gregory. 'I'm sorry to have troubled you. Again. This will be the fourth time this year, won't it?'

'And it's only July,' said Aaron.

Following the four FPP officers into the living room, he glanced back over his shoulder at his wrecked bed. With the mattress half on, the pillows strewn, the sheets awry and the headboard detached, it looked like a discarded sandwich. He couldn't face having to rebuild it right now; he would sleep on the sofa for the rest of the night.

The living room looked as if it had suffered an earthquake. Pictures hung askew, pot plants had been tipped over, artfully arranged piles of unread vintage books had been spilled, and a vase of dried flowers had been emptied out on to the lid of the Steinway baby grand on which Aaron accompanied himself when he rehearsed. He saw, to his relief, that it *had* been the sheet of glass on the coffee table, after all, and not one of the statuettes that had been shattered. A snowdrift of fragments lay on the floor beneath the table's hollow frame, roughly enclosed by its legs. The glass could be replaced. The statuettes had a value uniquely their own.

'I love those things,' said Gregory. He had followed the direction of Aaron's gaze. 'May I? I'll be extremely careful.'

Warily Aaron gave his consent, and while the three officers looked on, neither impatiently nor with much interest, Gregory approached the statuettes, which were arrayed at assorted levels on the sideboard and on the shelves behind.

They ranged in size from handspan miniatures to three-foot-tall figurines as thick in diameter as a grown man's calf, and all were carved from the same opaque yellow quartz. The sculpting was rough, unfinished, primitive in its lack of finesse, yet at the same time artful and evocative. The statuettes represented Foreigners. As slender and elegant as African tribesmen, they stood in various ritual poses with their hands and their long, expressive fingers held at waist level to form manufolds, the elementary human/Foreign creole, a vocabulary of ninety-six words that every three-year-old child knew: TRANQUILLITY, GRATITUDE, APPROVAL, SALUTATION, RESPECT, and all the other examples of convoluted digit origami that could nowadays be found adorning everything from soft-drink cans to television station idents.

Gregory positioned himself in front of a medium-sized statuette and with an almost reverential care raised a finger to stroke its chest. Immediately a note filled the room – E flat below middle C. Pure and clear, the note rose in volume the more insistently Gregory stroked the statuette, and as he brought other fingers into play, so high and low harmonics appeared, like the blur around a vibrating violin string. You could almost imagine that the statuette had come to life and that the humming note was issuing from the oval double-bow of the lips on its upturned face, and that the more pleasure

187

Gregory's masturbatory caresses brought it, the harder it sang.

Gregory's expression was that of a child when shown the simplest of conjuring tricks, one part bewilderment to three parts wonder, and had Aaron been in a less distracted frame of mind he would have envied the FPP captain his easy delight. Gregory, in his capacity as UN-sponsored killjoy, only ever met Foreigners under trying and exacting circumstances, answering their complaints and arbitrating over disputes between them and humans. Foreigners were seldom happy to see him, and even when he helped them they were not effusive in their thanks. Where Aaron won the golden giants' approval and their gifts with his singing, Gregory earned little in return for his efforts except perhaps a manufolded GRATITUDE. No Foreigner would ever present Gregory with a statuette, or any other gift, in grateful recognition of his services.

Finally Gregory took his hand from the statuette, and the note ended.

'You could play a whole symphony on a collection like this,' he mused, eyeing the many different sizes of the statuettes. 'How do they do it, I wonder? How do they make crystal sing like that? Will we ever know? Will we ever make musical instruments half as cunning and as graceful as these?'

'I wish we could,' Aaron retorted. 'Then they wouldn't cost so damn much to insure.'

'Well, anyway.' Gregory turned away from the statuettes quickly, as though their hold over him could only be broken by force. 'We've two more appointments to keep tonight. My apologies for disturbing you, Mr Novak. Stay honest, and we'll stay out of your way.'

Aaron nearly pointed out that honesty was never any guarantee of freedom from FPP interference, not these days. But he thought better of it, and instead said, 'Captain Gregory?'

'Yes?'

'Would you like to take one of the statuettes home with

you? I could pick you out one. As a gift. That one, perhaps.'
He indicated a handspan-high example that could pipe out a
piccolo F.

Gregory blinked, glanced at his subordinates (whose faces
said, *What do we care?*), looked down at his toecaps, back to
his subordinates (they still didn't care), and finally said to
Aaron: 'No. No, thank you, Mr Novak. I don't think that
would be a good idea. Much as I would like . . .' He blinked
again. 'Much as I admire your collection, it would be
inappropriate for me to accept anything from you that might
be construed at a later date as a bribe. But a very generous
offer nonetheless. A very generous offer.'

After that, Gregory could not meet Aaron's gaze again, and
as the FPP captain hustled his three subordinates out of the
apartment, Aaron allowed himself a small and not altogether
agreeable chuckle. Conventional wisdom among Sirens was
that you didn't mess with the FPP because, if they felt like it,
they could bring a whole load of unnecessary shit down on
your head, but in the course of this encounter Aaron had
proved to himself that a man like Gregory was neither to be
feared nor despised. A man like Gregory, who lived a life
circumscribed by rules, regulations and subservience to
others, was only to be pitied.

That was the last time Gregory came to Aaron's apartment
before the Foreigners stopped visiting Earth.

The years after the Foreigners' disappearance were hard on
everyone. While it was generally held that no human was to
blame, suspicious glares were easy to come by and even easier
to cast. A friend, a relative, a neighbour, even a stranger in the
street might be the guilty one, the one who had scared the
Foreigners away, the one who had abused their sweetly naïve
generosity, the one whose carelessness had caused the golden
giants to bolt like a herd of skittish deer, the one who had
mortally offended one and therefore all of them.

Like all the other resort-cities, Bridgeville fell prey to rage and despair. Fights and brawls became commonplace. Random, motiveless murders abounded. The fears and frustrations of a populace, a large proportion of whom had relied solely on the Foreigners as a source of income and now found themselves without money or employment, fermented, seethed and ultimately boiled over.

As a direct result of the riots that left the FPP HQ at Gaijin Hello Friendly Island a burned-out husk, the Foreign Policy Police was disbanded and its component parts reconstituted to form the Resort-City Protection Department, an even more autocratic body whose powers were as wide-ranging as they were loosely defined. Out went the cream-coloured suits and the home searches and the forceful coercion. In came leather and street patrols and batons.

They were years of terror and fire and fury. But beneath the tumult, behind the wide, angry eyes, there lay a deeper, stranger sadness – a sadness that was shared throughout the world. It was as though humankind had been handed a very wonderful gift and then, for no clear reason, had had it snatched away again.

The Foreigners had gone. Without explanation, without excuse, without warning: gone.

Bridgeville itself came to embody this sense of loss. Its gleaming plazas and promenades grew tarnished and litter-strewn, and its many tourist attractions were allowed to fall into disrepair and decay. Alligators were a not uncommon sight, prowling the streets with plodding reptilian certainty. Fewer and fewer cabbies plied their trade, and the dirigibles that rumbled overhead carried not tourists now but refugees heading north to the cooler climates that had been less favoured by the Foreigners and so not as reliant on them to generate wealth.

As for Aaron, he weathered the lean times as well as anybody. Forced to give up his apartment in Seaview Tower, he moved from one rented accommodation to the next, each less salubrious than the previous. Gradually he shed his worldly goods along the way, selling valuables and objets d'art to black-marketeers for a fraction of their worth. First to go was the Steinway. The statuettes were last on the list; he was obliged to part with all but a handful of them. Eventually he found himself, like so many of his fellow Sirens, reduced to surviving on handouts and seeking menial labour wherever he could find it.

The golden years were definitely over.

It was after taking up residence in the Basin, which had always been one of the shabbiest quarters of Bridgeville, an area characterised by the quantity of waste – household and human – that littered its streets and floated in its canals, that Aaron first started hearing rumours of an English ex-FPP officer who had relocated there, too, and who was the object of universal scorn and spite: a moustachioed sad-sack of a man, with sparkling, startling ocean-blue eyes, who went from house to house offering his services as janitor in return for a meal and perhaps a small consideration of money if the home-owner felt that he had performed his duties well. The irony that a one-time ransacker of houses was now scraping a living through the restoration of domestic order and cleanliness was not lost on Aaron, and for this reason he initially dismissed the rumours as a vengeful urban morality tale.

At this point he was renting a one-room cold-water walk-up above a fishmonger's and working in one of the Basin's seedier drinking dens, earning meagre tips by singing old standards to bleary-eyed barflies who liked to slur gratingly along to the choruses, dogging the pure cadences of Aaron's voice with their hoarse, tuneless, nostalgia-choked drones. He thought he was handling the reduction in his circumstances reasonably well, but then as far as he was concerned his apparent submissiveness had always hidden a core of resilience. What others might see as compliance he saw as adaptability. And he felt that it was thanks to this quality that he had so successfully put the past behind him, abandoning it piece by piece with every possession he had parted with, all those belongings he had so unsentimentally sold. Once he had been wealthy, praised and prized. Now he led barside singalongs in a down-and-out dive in one of a depressed resort-city's most depressed corners, and while this life wasn't exactly everything he could have wanted, he had just about stopped comparing it with his old life. He had just about forgotten his old life.

But when he heard locals again and again talk about someone whose description matched that of Captain Silas Gregory in every detail, Aaron felt compelled to seek the old fellow out. For one thing, he was curious to know why Gregory had resigned. For another, he wanted to know why Gregory was making no secret of his earlier FPP affiliation. Few people had pleasant memories of that self-important bureaucracy, fewer still had anything but criticism of the army of leather-garbed, baton-wielding bullyboys that the FPP had become. In Gregory's shoes, Aaron would have done almost anything to distance himself from such past and present associations: emigration, reconstructive surgery, suicide, anything. But he had another reason for finding Gregory, too.

Finally, after days of following false leads and winding up in dead ends (one peripatetic janitor wasn't easy to locate in a city filled with a million such dispossessed wanderers), Aaron found himself one sullenly hot afternoon standing at the foot of a tall, fire-scuffed dosshouse that teetered at the edge of what had once been a pleasant green lagoon. Now half-choked with the rubble of a demolished concert venue and a repository for excrement and shopping trolleys, the lagoon made a well-appointed lido for rats.

The dosshouse didn't have a caretaker as such, but a man watching television in the main hallway, sitting on a plastic chair and shelling and eating peanuts from a supermarket carrier-bag, had heard of a resident by the name of Gregory and suggested Aaron try the ninth floor.

There was no elevator.

On the ninth floor, a profusely perspiring Aaron was told to try the eighth, but the eighth was a women's floor so he proceeded down to the seventh, and there was fortunate enough to encounter an emaciated octogenarian who was out in the corridor towelling himself down after a shower. The octogenarian knew a Silas Gregory, sure. Energetically rubbing the towel around his scrawny genitalia with one hand, he pointed down the corridor with the other.

'Room seven zero three,' he croaked, adding, 'You're in luck. He's in,' and also adding, 'But he never receives visitors.'

There was an electronically controlled lock on the door to 703, but Aaron could tell at a glance that it hadn't worked in ages. The glass that covered its infra-red eye was cloudy like a cataract. The door looked flimsy, and he was tempted to try and kick it down, just so that Gregory would know what it was like to have your home invaded, but in the end he merely knocked.

There was no reply, but the stifled silence from within told Aaron all he needed to know.

'Mr Gregory? Silas Gregory? My name is Novak. Aaron Novak. Perhaps you remember me?'

Aaron thought he detected a shuffling footfall.

'You ought to remember me,' he said. 'You tried to bust me often enough.'

The voice that emerged from behind the door was frail and tremulous, hardly recognisable as the same brisk voice that used to answer Aaron's irony-laden remarks with such blithe equanimity. 'I know who you are,' it said. 'Why are you here? Have you come to get even? You wouldn't be the first, you know. Not by a long shot. Seems like I gave half of Bridgeville a reason to hold a grudge against me.'

'I'm not here for anything like that. I just want to talk.'

'Why should I believe you?'

'No reason. Except that had I really wanted to do you harm, I'd have broken in and done so by now.'

'Yes,' said Gregory. 'Yes, you have a point. You were never that sort of a person, Mr Novak, were you? In fact, as I recall, you were usually quite agreeable. All right. Yes. I'll let you in.'

Bolts were withdrawn manually, and the door shuddered inwards, Gregory dragging it hard against a moraine of damp-warped linoleum.

Aaron had expected the former captain to have been reduced physically by his social abasement, but in fact in appearance Gregory was little changed. A little whiter of hair, certainly, but the moustache and the ocean-blue gaze were as proud and firm as Aaron remembered them. It was the first time Aaron had ever seen him without his cream-coloured suit on (it was hung neatly on a hanger on one wall) but even without it, in only a vest and slacks, Gregory had just as much presence. The room itself was small, shoddily furnished, its safety-glass window-panes murky and cracked, and the walls and ceiling painted a shade of brown that was clearly designed to foster suicidal depression, but for all this the place was free of dust and tidy. A ceiling fan rotated with a sluggishness that belied the strenuous whine of its motor. If there was anything apart from the room and his voice to show that Gregory had suffered in the intervening years or that the reduction in his status had left a lasting mark on him, it was the scar that ran from one armpit over his clavicle to the centre of his ribcage, curving around on itself at the tip. The skin around it was puckered and at its fattest the scar was at least half an inch wide. It must have been a deep wound, and it must have hurt and it must have bled.

Once Aaron spotted the scar, he couldn't help but stare at it.

'Ah yes,' said Gregory, rebolting the door and nodding as he moved back into the room. 'You've noticed.' He pulled out a chair for Aaron to sit on. 'I'm not surprised. It's very noticeable. An ex-cabbie gave it to me with a pocket knife. I suppose it served me right for citing him for overcharging.' He uttered a short bark of a laugh. 'I resigned the day after I was discharged from hospital. Used it as an excuse, really. It meant I lost my pension privileges and so on, but that didn't matter to me. I resigned because I didn't like what was happening. I didn't like the plans the FPP Council had for the FPP.'

He lowered himself on to the narrow iron-framed bed that occupied a good third of the available floor-space. Its stretched springs bellied beneath his backside.

'The attack taught me a valuable lesson, besides,' he went on. 'It taught me that there's no point trying to escape the past. Better to acknowledge it. Better to embrace it.'

'Why?' Aaron asked. 'Why cling on to the past if it only gets you into trouble?'

Gregory appeared to ignore the question. 'I'd offer you some kind of refreshment,' he said, 'but as you can see, I lack the facilities.' He gestured at the wooden table to Aaron's left, on which there was a kettle and a half-finished packet of cookies. The plug socket that could have powered the kettle had been wrenched out of the wall to leave a rough hole in the plaster inside which Aaron glimpsed rustling activity and the dim glint of light reflecting off dun-coloured carapaces. Seeing this, he decided he wouldn't accept a cookie if Gregory offered.

'But in answer to your question,' Gregory said, 'sometimes it's not possible. After all, *you* don't seem to have let go of your past either, have you? Not entirely. You're here, are you not?'

'What's done is done. What either of us did while the Foreigners were here no longer matters. Agreed?'

Gregory understood the implication. 'Very well. I can accept that for the purposes of this meeting there are to be no recriminations. Embrace the past but don't disturb the past, eh?'

'Sort of.'

'That still doesn't completely explain why you tracked me down to this place. Unless it's to crow.'

Aaron reached into his pocket, took something out and placed it on the table. The object hummed softly from the moment he took hold of it to the moment he let go of it.

195

'Recognise this?' he said.

Delight spread across Gregory's features. He reached towards the table, then drew his hand back. A frown clouded his face, not entirely extinguishing the delight. 'I'm sorry,' he said. 'It's just that it's been so long since I've seen one of those, I didn't even think to ask your permission.'

The statuette was about eight inches tall. Its hands were interlocked in an inverted steeple, thumbs outward, palms arched, little fingers interlocked. The symbol for TRANQUILLITY.

'Ah, but they're beautiful things,' Gregory sighed. 'Even just to look at.'

'You don't want to hear it sing?'

'Well, I do, and I don't, and I don't more than I do. I'm scared it'll . . .' He shrugged.

'I tried to give you this once,' said Aaron.

'This statuette?'

'This very one. You refused.'

'Yes, I did. Yes, I did.'

'You wanted it, but you said it wouldn't be appropriate.'

'It wouldn't have been. Very improper. More than my job was worth.'

'I have to say I felt bad about making the offer myself, afterwards.'

'Well, who would want to give away such a thing? Even you, who had so many of them.'

'This one in particular,' said Aaron, and he seized the statuette and turned it upside down. Its note, suddenly kick-started into life, wailed up an octave as it was inverted, and then broke off when its head was pointing directly downwards.

'You shouldn't treat it like that,' said Gregory.

Saying nothing, Aaron inserted his thumbnail into a notch in the underside of the corrugated base and after several attempts managed to lever open a panel the size of a postage stamp. The panel was so skilfully wrought that, when shut, it fitted undetectably into place.

Poking an index finger into the aperture thus exposed, Aaron drew out a coil of slender, rubber-insulated wire which was attached to a wafer of chip which in turn was connected to a microphone no larger than a match-head.

Gregory's ocean-blue eyes, which had grown wide at the sight of the hatch, grew wider still at the sight of a vocal enhancer.

'Oh, my,' he said. 'And you even offered it to me. How brazen of you.'

'I was pretty sure you'd never accept it,' Aaron replied. 'I was testing myself rather than you, seeing if I could pull it off, if I had the nerve to look you in the eye and tell you exactly where what you were looking for was hidden. I'd only just bought the enhancer, you see. That last time you raided me was the first time I actually had anything unlawful in my possession.'

'Well.' Gregory's mouth soured into a pout. 'I hope you're pleased with yourself. You pulled the wool over my eyes, that's for sure.' He delivered a slow, sarcastic handclap. 'Well done. Bravo.'

'No, I didn't come here to show you how clever I am. I came here, if anything, to . . . I don't know, to confess, I suppose.'

Gregory's eyebrows went up a notch.

'I never used it, you see,' Aaron said, toying with the wire that was the enhancer's sending antenna. 'I bought it on an impulse, because so many of my friends who were Sirens were saying how great it made their voices sound, how it could drive Foreigners crazy with pleasure. I paid some greyware pirate way too much for it, and I still don't know if it works.'

'Didn't you even once wind it around inside your collar and try it out?'

'Not once.'

'Why?'

'Because I thought I was a good enough Siren without one? Because I thought it would be cheating? Because I was scared of being shopped to the FPP by a rival? I don't know. A little bit of everything, I guess. Too much pride, not enough nerve.'

'And if I had accepted the statuette?'

'I'd have let you take it. It would have freed me from the moral dilemma. You'd never have found the panel, so you'd never have found the enhancer.'

'And then the Foreigners solved your problem for you by dropping Earth from their travel brochures,' said Gregory wryly.

'Exactly. I suppose you have a theory as to why they stopped coming.'

'I don't, as a matter of fact. They first chose us on a whim, so maybe they changed their minds on a whim, too. Maybe another planet became popular, another dimension. Maybe we'll never know. Maybe it was enough that they rescued us from the mess we'd got ourselves into, and now we either learn the lessons they taught us or else we go under again for the final time. Sometimes I wonder if they weren't actually some sort of divine visitation.'

Aaron had heard this sort of *Revelation*-myth talk before. He didn't think it a very helpful way of dealing with the Foreigners' departure. Leaving the vocal enhancer on the table, he closed the panel and set the statuette the right way up. Immediately its note sang out around his fist, the vibrations tickling his fingers.

'Would you like it now?' he asked Gregory.

'Are you sure?'

'It's one of the last few I have left, but I'm busy severing my ties, one by one. Casting myself adrift. I'm thinking of moving to somewhere a bit cooler. Canada, possibly. I've just enough left from my savings to cover the journey, and there I can reinvent myself. There I won't be an ex-Siren. I won't be an ex-anything.'

'I'm told there are plenty of jobs going up north. I'd move there myself, if I could afford it.'

'Sell the statuette and you could.' Aaron rose to go. He held out a hand. 'Thank you for your time, Mr Gregory. And no hard feelings?'

Gregory took his eyes off the statuette. He shook Aaron's hand. 'None at all,' he said.

Aaron had pulled back the last bolt and was preparing himself for a battle with the recalcitrant door when Gregory said, 'Mr Novak? I know this is going to sound terribly presumptuous, seeing as you've given me the statuette and everything, but I was wondering if you could do me another favour.'

'I can try.'

'It's more of a request, really.' Gregory blinked back his nervousness. 'I know I don't have a right to ask this, but would you sing for me? Just one song. Just so that I can hear you for myself, see if you're as good as I suspect you are. I wouldn't ask this normally, but' – the ocean-blue eyes were shimmering behind a film of tears – 'it's been a while since I've actually thought about the way things used to be with anything like pleasure.'

'I thought you said you'd embraced the past.'

'Embraced it like a drowning man embraces a lifebelt. Please. It would mean a lot to me.'

Aaron couldn't see the harm. 'OK, what do you want? I've perfected a nice line in rousing, sentimental show tunes recently.'

'No, not that. Not a song. Sing to me the way you used to sing to Foreigners.'

'Well, I'm a little rusty, but . . .' He gave a Las Vegas grin. 'I'll give it a go.'

Aaron took a few deep breaths to flex his diaphragm, then drew the high F out of the statuette with a fingertip. Taking this as his keynote, he began to improvise a series of arpeggios in his sweetest alto, his voice going over the runs like a child making its way carefully over stepping stones. Then he settled into a soft trill that spoke of ancient cathedrals and guttering ranks of devotional candles and a nightingale swooping through the hollows of a vaulted ceiling, something solitary in an emptiness, something sacred yet mundane. From this he developed a theme of glissandos that flowed in silky ripples of increasing depth and frequency – a vocal feat that had quickened many a Foreigner to a swaying, shuddering climax. Now he pictured in his mind's eye a field of corn and imagined his voice a breeze brushing across the golden swathe, gusting out in several directions at once to expose the undersides of the stalks in glossy swirls and curlicues. He sang inarticulate word-forms that sounded sometimes human and sometimes Foreign but never quite one or the other. Easily (though he hadn't sung like this for three years) he found himself slipping into that calm, hollowed-out state of mind where he was no longer the originator of his song but its vehicle, to be driven wherever the whim of the music took him. Time collapsed and elapsed, as images of seas and seasons and valleys and ancient green forests crowded through his brain and took flight on wings of vocal-cord-construed breath, emerging from the very heart of him, transmuted from thought to sound by an alchemical process he himself did not quite understand.

One by one these mental impressions flowed out of him and into Gregory, who saw them as if by telepathy, as if he were a television set and Aaron's voice the signal. A cloud of flamingos taking flight from salty marshes. A queen bee humming at the heart of a contented hive. A necklace of lights tracing the line of a coastal road through the thickening dusk. A sun-drenched park playing host to a summerful of children. Messages zinging through the wires of a nineteenth-century prairie telegraph. Two lovers moving against one another in the heavy lumbering flush of post-coition. Deep underground the bones of long-dead animals being cooled by a subterranean spring. A foundry from a bygone age gouting cinder-flecked smoke into the industrial night. A pack of wolves trotting down from the tree line to investigate the embers of a camp fire. In the tiniest fluctuations of his vibrato, with each variation and modulation he introduced into his voice, Aaron

200

drove these mental pictures like spikes of mercury into Gregory's mind. It was a song and yet not a song. It followed none of the conventions of musical composition. It was unearthly and rich and strange, and when it was over Aaron felt drained and satisfied. He had been worried that disuse would have dulled his talent, but it gleamed as brightly as ever. He was pleased.

Gregory was sitting gripping the edge of the bed, the tears spilling freely down his cheeks, his body motionless.

'I never thought . . .' he breathed. 'I never knew . . .'

All of a sudden the room was cramped and stiflingly muggy, and outside, in the streets of Bridgeville, men and women of a world that had once thought itself damned, then thought itself saved, and now wasn't sure what it was, men and women who had enjoyed times of plenty and doubted they would ever see them again, went about their business with a secret ache in their hearts which was dulled by the din of day but which throbbed into life at night.

They came at night, usually, the fears. Kicked down the doors of the soul and rushed in to find what guilt had hidden there.

Usually at night.

The Unmentionable

What follows is the transcript of a text I discovered recently while rummaging around in my attic. It is there that I keep, among other things, my great-grandfather's personal effects which, since his death some seven decades ago, have been passed from one branch of my family to another like a baton in a relay race, rarely staying in one place for any length of time owing to the quantity of the items involved and their inconvenient size. Finding myself in dire financial straits, I had been hoping to unearth something of value, but unfortunately my great-grandfather was an inveterate hoarder of junk, knick-knacks, gewgaws, trinkets, baubles and other ephemera, and the two dozen well-travelled trunks which had just over a month ago become my property contained little of any worth. Or so I thought.

The discovery took the form of a notebook, weathered, worn and torn. Inside I found several pages of text written in pencil, many of the sentences faded almost beyond deciphering. To judge by the handwriting the work was completed in some haste, and although no name is appended to the manuscript, given its age and the curious circumstances surrounding my great-grandfather's brief tenancy of Peculiar Manor (the house that provides the location for the events the text relates), it would be safe to assume that authorship lies with none other than him. I print the contents below in their entirety, with a few judicious editings which will, I trust, diminish neither the integrity of the work nor my great-grandfather's reputation.

A word about the man himself. M.H. Livegrave was that rarity, an impecunious lawyer. This is not to say that he was not successful in his chosen profession – a donkey in a wig and gown would be able to make a decent living by the Law – but almost every penny he earned went to fuel his passion for junk, which he accumulated with a mania. His particular enthusiasm was for sailors' scrimshaws of dubious authenticity. Indeed, many of these items which are now in my possession bear a manufacturer's stamp on the base, but my great-grandfather seems to have convinced himself that they were individually whittled by salt-caked sea-dogs and as a result paid well over the odds for them. He was also an amateur physician, and it was he who first championed the use of electricity as a stimulus for the flagging sexual appetites of the over-sixties, a treatment met with howls of derision by his contemporaries in the medical community but now, I believe, practised widely.

For such a man any marriage was surely doomed to failure, and under the circumstances it seems remarkable that his lasted long enough for him to sire two sons before his wife – apparently a woman of saint-like demeanour, no doubt driven to despair by my great-grandfather's bouts of eccentric behaviour and his accumulation of junk – finally expelled him and his belongings from the house. He travelled to North America, and after many Wanderjahren *in that great continent settled down in Boston where, finding himself unable to practise his profession, he obtained gainful employment in a bakery.*

I realise that in submitting this piece for publication I am laying myself open to accusations of profiteering. Nothing could be further from my intentions. I believe this to be a document of considerable historical significance, detailing an extraordinary episode in the life of an extraordinary man. It is true that I have approached a number of museums with a view to their purchasing the original manuscript – so far, it must be said, without much success – but I am of the firm opinion that

any monies which do accrue from its sale or publication are
simply a vindication of my faith in its importance.

However, before you commence reading, I must leave you
with a stern warning.

What follows is not for the faint of heart.

Ah God, can I bring myself to relate the events of these past few weeks? Yet I must, I must, for I shall surely go mad if I do not! E'en now I can hear the sinister tick of the deathwatch beetle in the walls of this very room, counting down the seconds that remain to me. Ah, how I wish I had never clapped eyes on that thrice-cursed book the *Encyclopaedia Culinaria*, that dread tome which, if my intuition is correct, was first set down over two thousand years ago by some mad heretic monk who wrote his foul enchantments on parchment made of human skin, using his own blood for ink. What have I unleashed upon the world? The very thought of it freezes the blood in my veins to ice-water.

But I must be calm. I must set down the events in order, as they occurred, so that I might make sense of my madness and leave a warning to others not to follow my example and seek that which they should not seek.

I came to Peculiar Manor in the county of Fetlock, Mass., in March of this year, 18—. I was still in something of a state of shock following the news that a relative I had barely heard of – Cyrus Livegrave, my third cousin once removed, a lifelong Classical scholar and the undisputed expert on the work of the critically overlooked Ancient Greek poet Uttatos – had died and that, as his only remaining descendant, Peculiar Manor was to be passed on to me. It was with a nervous but anticipatorily fluttering heart that I leaned out of the window of the carriage as it rattled through the Manor's imposing wrought-iron gates, framed by the louring branches of dark cedars, and caught my first glimpse of my new home. How my heart sank to behold that crumbling edifice, a pitiful mass of brick and creeping vine that loomed on the brow of a steep hill overlooking the town of Surgeon Mills. If I had known then what terrors awaited me within those four walls, my soul would have been plunged yet further into gloom.

The carriage drew up outside the Manor but the driver, for some inexplicable reason, declined to unload my cases, let alone hold the door open for me, so that I was obliged to perform both functions for myself. The fellow seemed wary, of what I knew not. Indeed, he had evinced nothing but mounting apprehension the entire journey, ever since our departure from Boston which, I may say, was somewhat hastier than I would have wished, but he had happened to be passing and I was fortunate to find a carriage at all in the district in which my straitened circumstances obliged me to live. Now he sat huddled in his seat with his cape wrapped tight about him and, when I came to render payment, was most unwilling to accept the money. I pressed it upon him until, at last, and with the utmost reluctance, he relented. I then asked him what affrighted him so.

''Tis not my vehicle, sir. I've stolen it,' replied he, and whipped the horses.

But even as the carriage clattered down the drive I was convinced that this was a mere ruse. His terror was not that of a man who fears the unmasking of a felony. Might it not be the Manor itself that was the source of his fright?

If, as I stood there in the driveway surrounded by the two dozen crates, trunks and packing cases that contained my belongings, I had had an inkling of the horrors that lay in store for me in the coming weeks, I might have pursued that carriage shrieking for help. However, with night fast closing in, I had no choice but to climb the Manor steps and ring the doorbell, whose sonorous echoes reverberated deep within the bowels of the building. A full quarter of an hour elapsed before the housekeeper arrived to open the door, during which time the sun's flaring orb fell below the western horizon and the shades of night engulfed the sky, but my dampened spirits dried and my heart lifted when I beheld the genial face of the woman who was to become my friend, confidante and companion over the coming weeks: the redoubtable Mrs Slugworthy. This lady was the possessor of a single eye, the other, as I learned, having been lost in a disagreement with a neighbour over the position of a garden fence. Hair-crowned warts proliferated on her face and vast forearms, but she had a welcoming smile and nearly all of her teeth.

'Master Mortimer Hereward Livegrave!' exclaimed this virtuous woman. 'Welcome, new owner of Peculiar Manor!' She took me in her arms and smothered me in her voluminous bosom. 'My, but you are a fine-looking gentleman.'

'And you,' I replied graciously, 'have marvellous ears.'

Mrs Slugworthy wasted no time in hauling my things indoors. I shall never forget my first sight of that great hallway with its sweeping staircase. Above all I recall the portrait of my distant relative that stared down at me forbiddingly from above the fireplace. Cousin Cyrus's expression seemed to be warning me about something, I could not conceive what. I could only stare back numbly, as though mesmerised.

'Come, Master Mortimer,' said Mrs Slugworthy, clapping a hand on my shoulder and breaking my reverie, 'let me feed you and get you warm. You must be tired after your long and wearying journey.'

I replied that I was, indeed, somewhat fatigued and hungry, having eaten nothing since lunchtime four hours ago, when I enjoyed a side of beef with a generous side portion of potatoes, several buttered bread rolls and a jar of ale at a roadside tavern at which I had insisted the driver stop en route. Mrs Slugworthy guided me to the kitchen, sat me down before a log fire and produced some comestibles – a leg of ham that was apparently the last thing my distant relative ate and a glass of wine from the very bottle he had been drinking before he died. While consuming this repast, my appetite not in the slightest diminished by the greenish hue of certain portions of the ham, I enquired of Mrs Slugworthy her recollection of my predecessor's last hours.

'Ah, that was some weeks back, Master Mortimer, but I do recall finding him at his desk in his study that fateful morning, sprawled over a book with this awful look on his face, a look of . . .'

'Of what?' I urged her, eager in my impatience.

'Terrible agony,' she whispered, and the hair stiffened at the nape of my neck. 'But then,' she added, 'he had always suffered from problems of a digestive nature. I fear that is what eventually killed him.' She sighed and tousled my hair. 'He was never the trencherman that you are, though in other respects you are as like as two peas in a pod. In fact, now that I inspect you more closely, Master Mortimer, I see that you are the spitting image of Master Cyrus, though you do not smell quite as bad.'

It had not escaped my notice that the late Cyrus and I shared many physiognomic characteristics, and my assumption was that the familial distance between us must surely have been less great than I had hitherto been led to believe. But I leave such conjecture to genealogists. My concern is myself.

I thanked Mrs Slugworthy for the compliment and, in an offhand manner, asked which book it was he had been reading that had brought on his demise. At this, her face was transformed into a mask of the purest anguish.

'Oh, Master Mortimer, don't ever ask such a thing! That book is not for the likes of you, oh no, nor any mortal man who values his soul. Whatever you do, do not ask me to show you that book. That book, which you must never demand to see, has brought only misery to whomsoever has possessed it, so never beg me to go into the library and fetch it down from the shelf for you, for you will surely regret it. I shall never vouchsafe its name to you, lest you seek it out for yourself in the Taboo Texts section of the library under E for *Encyclopaedia Culinaria*.'

Encyclopaedia Culinaria! E'en now the name sends a shiver of incomprehensible magnitude through my vitals, yet how my mind thrilled to the dark whispers and implications that it first conveyed. Alas, the curse of the civilised man is to thirst after forbidden knowledge.

'Here it is,' said Mrs Slugworthy, laying the book before me on the kitchen table. *Encyclopaedia Culinaria*. I ran nerveless fingers over the book's binding, tracing the letters of the title embossed in gold, digging for which countless miners must surely have perished. Hesitantly I opened the cover, flicked through and almost immediately found the engraving of a ghastly apparition glaring balefully up at me. It was possessed of a beak-like maw, two evilly glittering eyes and legs scaly like a lizard's, with feathers protruding all over it at fantastic angles in a manner reminiscent of the garb of an Aztec priest. I was transfixed with horror at the drawing.

'What can it be, Mrs Slugworthy?' I gasped.

She replied, in measured tones, 'Why, a chicken.'

'Yes, but surely it is a demon chicken.'

'Then the Manor is overrun with demons, for we have fifty such beasts in the back yard.'

'But most certainly, then, it is used for heinous, heretical sacrifices committed in the dead of night by depraved and demented Satanists!'

'It is used, Master Mortimer, for its flesh and its eggs.'

Mrs Slugworthy's words failed to reassure my seething mind, and I continued to inspect the book with mounting apprehension, leafing through page after page of pictures of more and yet more of the hideous creatures. Though they masqueraded under innocent names such as Rabbit and Pig and Lamb, I sensed that this was a mere ruse and that the so-called 'recipes' that accompanied the illustrations were nothing less than thinly disguised necromantic rituals. What could 'cooking' be but an arcane term for summoning up? What could one make of the repeated use of the words 'flame' and 'fire' but as references to the hellish regions where malicious entities dwell? Why else was there a whole chapter devoted to 'Use of Spirits' if the book was not intended as a guide for one who would have truck with beings from the Other Side?

I was trembling when I closed the volume, sweat on my palms, my hairs erect.

'What you need is a good rub down,' Mrs Slugworthy told me, and promptly gave me one.

The next passage is obscure and largely illegible, although the mention of 'visiting the nether regions' would suggest that my great-grandfather commenced straight away upon his ill-advised attempts to make contact with the spirit plane. The manuscript continues:

I was ejected from my slumber in the depths of the night by a sound that made my skin crawl. At first I thought it must be the wheezing of some hideous, suppurating creature from beyond the Veil that squatted unseen in a corner of the room, but after some moments of abject dread it occurred to me that the source of the sounds was in fact lying beside me. Mrs Slugworthy's nasal cavity, and the stentorian vibrations made by the breaths passing in and out of those mighty passages, were the agent of my anxiety.

Solicitous that I should not disturb Mrs Slugworthy's rest, for the good lady was plainly exhausted after her exertions, I lit a candle and crept from the bedchamber. As I passed along the corridor the candle guttered in the chilly draughts that blew through the Manor but fortunately remained alight, sparing me from being plunged into utter darkness. I headed downstairs, prompted by an instinctive urge that would not let up until I had found a privy wherein to relieve myself. Then I felt something – I dare not guess what, some terrible hunger – that drew me to the kitchen with a remorseless, inexorable power and was not sated until I had finished the rest of the ham and the last of the wine.

My eye then alighted upon the book which had lain on the table undisturbed since Mrs Slugworthy and I had departed hence in some haste a few hours earlier. I sat before it, set down the candle, and opened the heavy tome once more, breathless with anticipation, my heart pounding with fear. Again I pored over that mystic, runic text and those symbolic, cabalistic illustrations. Some showed the lines along which one should cut the sacrificial beast, others depicted the utensils necessary for this unspeakable practice.

At one point I started, startled by a stark sound. It was a tapping on the window such as of dry, scaly claws, although the demonic owner of those talons would have had me believe that the sound was caused by the tips of the branches of the old oak tree directly outside the kitchen rattling against the glass in the wind. I knew better, and warily resumed my reading.

So struck was I by the spells in the *Encyclopaedia Culinaria* that I set about incanting them over and over to myself. What follies does madness inflict upon the deranged mind of an insane man! As I reiterated those phrases intended for no human tongue, I sensed a strangeness in the kitchen. It seemed that myriad tiny scarlet eyes were peering at me from the darkened crevices and corners beyond the range of the feeble light of the candle. I peered round in the hope that I might catch a glimpse of my observers. It may have been an illusion, a trick of the light brought about by the flickering of the candle flame, but the shadows seemed to move to form horrible shapes. They lurked close to the floor, and flowed over one another in a dark tide, as tiny and as quiet as . . .

Could it be . . . ?

The Many-Sided Ones!

I had on my travels heard numerous rumours concerning these ancient gods who were old when Atlantis sank beneath the waves. Beings of awesome power, I had learned that they had many sides.

I fear these old gods were manifesting themselves in the kitchen in the superficially innocuous form of mice, the book acting as the portal that granted them access from their nameless native dimension to this earthly plane. Their goal was nothing less than the conquest and submission of all men. I vowed, however, that they would gain no foothold in our world, and with the utmost force of will slammed the book shut, simultaneously extinguishing the candle and depriving the Many-Sided Ones of light. For, as the great Chinese philosopher Mou Shu says, 'Where no light is cast, no shadows may form.'

I stumbled madly up to the bedchamber. It seemed the very Manor itself resented me for having come so dangerously close to unleashing such absolute evil in my impetuous lust for knowledge, for the stairs tripped me again and again, causing me often to bark my shins, and the walls flung themselves violently at my forehead. Bruised and shaken, I slipped beneath the bedcovers and cowered against the vast form of the loyal Mrs Slugworthy, who awoke and

Here, again, the text is indecipherable. One is to assume that Mrs Slugworthy successfully comforted my great-grandfather in his extremity, for he shortly thereafter fell asleep.

I dreamed the rest of that night of chanting – monotonous, rhythmic, sibilant murmurings whose source seemed to be catacombs deep in the earth beneath the Manor. I heard what sounded like a thousand voices joining in unholy unison to proclaim the very words I had read in the *Encyclopaedia Culinaria*, sending their hideous paean echoing down to the Stygian mists where demons and the nether-gods dwell. I awoke at daybreak, the dream reverberating in my brain. I had no doubt that the vision I had had in my sleep was a prophetic one, and immediately roused Mrs Slugworthy to enquire feverishly what lay beneath the foundations of Peculiar Manor. Her enigmatic reply disturbed me.

'Soil, I should suppose. Soil and rock. Why do you ask, my poppet?'

'There is nothing else? Nothing such as a dungeon, perhaps?'

'Well, not as such. There is a cellar.'

'A cellar!' I cried.

'Of course. Where else do you think I keep the food and wine? I don't know what the matter is with you, Master Mortimer, but if you are to lay your head just here, I shall do my best to soothe your troubled brow.'

I had no desire to inflict my apprehensions upon the dear lady any further, so I excused my interest on the grounds of geological curiosity and we turned our attention to an altogether different mode of intercourse.

I have omitted an exchange of no possible interest to the reader.

The sun rose bright and warm that morning, almost evaporating my gloomy spirits and my memory of the terrors of the night before – almost, but not quite, for a lingering sense of foreboding remained – and in my somewhat more wholesome frame of mind I elected, contrary to Mrs Slugworthy's recommendations, to pay a visit on the good townsfolk of Surgeon Mills, so that they might have the opportunity to view for themselves the new owner of Peculiar Manor.

Strolling along Main Street, I received several looks askance, and many of the townsfolk turned to one another and whispered behind their hands as I passed. No doubt my uncanny resemblance to my third cousin once removed gave rise to their intrigue, or perhaps it was my spanking-new pair of stout walking shoes, but I had the suspicion that the knowledge of arcane secrets I had attained at the Manor was what these superstitious men and women sensed most strongly of all. This is the only reason I can account for the manner in which several of them spat at my feet, unless, of course, it was my spanking-new pair of stout walking shoes.

I entered a grocer's store, which was run by a plump,

balding fellow and his similarly endowed wife. I greeted them civilly. 'Good morning, poor but honest people. I am the new owner of Peculiar Manor.'

'We know who you are,' growled the man, whose name was Rudderbilge.

'Then all is well.' I handed him a list of the provisions I required and allowed him and his wife to fill my basket, which they did in silence. They included an abnormal quantity of cabbage, far more than I had requested (I had not, in fact, requested any), but I took it that this was the manner in which they were wont to welcome newcomers.

Rudderbilge returned the basket to me laden with cabbages and said, 'You must be the new owner of Peculiar Manor.'

'That is quite correct,' I replied, not wishing to remind him that I had already drawn attention to this fact.

'Ah, it's a bad place, sir. A bad, bad place.'

'Really? In what respect is it bad?'

Mrs Rudderbilge made a curious sound like a sneeze, covered her face and turned her back to me.

'There have been wicked doings up there, sir. You don't want to be having anything to do with the Manor.' His eyes transfixed me with an hypnotic intensity and I noticed that he had suddenly developed a nervous tic, for the corners of his mouth had begun to twitch.

'Has it something to do with my distant relative?' I ventured. I will not deny that my most fundamental responses had been aroused.

'Aye, well, it might, and there again, it might not.'

Mrs Rudderbilge's shoulders were shaking now, as though her body were racked with sobs.

'Tell me more.'

'Sir, I cannot. I wouldn't wish to scare you away, so I shall keep mum. I can only warn you to remain on your guard at all times.' I understood the conversation to be terminated with these words, for Rudderbilge then named a price for the purchases I had made. Tentatively I hinted that the sum was not a little excessive.

'Have you been round these parts long, sir?'

I replied in the negative, that I had not.

'Then these are the prices folk pay round here.'

They say that a fool and his money are soon parted, but nevertheless I handed over the sum in full. I had hoped to establish an easy-going rapport with these characters, but that hope was not to be fulfilled in so short a space of time. A close-knit community of this ilk must take unkindly to strangers.

Perhaps the most peculiar aspect of this whole episode was my discovery, upon returning to the Manor, that my basket contained cabbages and nothing else. Mrs Slugworthy enlightened me to the fact that neither Rudderbilge nor his wife was able to read, and I laughed self-deprecatingly at my failure to anticipate such a likelihood.

But this was a brief respite of happiness, and in the ensuing weeks my overriding sense of gloom did not lessen, while the conviction grew within me that I had unwittingly allowed some monstrous evil access to our material realm and that this thing, which I could only bring myself to call the Unmentionable, had taken up residence beneath the Manor and now lurked in the cellar, biding its time, awaiting the moment when it would rise forth and wreak havoc. Mrs Slugworthy did not share my belief. Her customary response whenever I voiced my thoughts on the matter was to reprimand me with a cry of 'Stuff and nonsense!' followed by a mild application of corporal punishment – for which reason I would sometimes initiate just such a discussion deliberately.

On many an occasion I would pass by the cellar door and fancy I heard strange, inexplicable noises coming from within. My hand was often tempted to try the handle, but was stayed by a shapeless, numinous dread.

Finally, one evening, as a particularly vicious thunderstorm raged outside, weather in which no sane man would be mad enough to go out, I decided I could stand it no longer. I rushed indoors and demanded of Mrs Slugworthy the key to the cellar. My fears had reached such a fever pitch that only by seeking out the evil I had summoned and banishing it whence it came would those fears be quelled. I resolved to defeat the Unmentionable or die in the attempt.

'More cabbage soufflé?' she said by way of a reply.

Over the growling of my belly I shrieked uncontrollably, 'I must have that key, woman!'

'My, we're a bit touchy tonight, aren't we, Master Mortimer? Well, I know what to do about *that*.'

She made to deliver upon my person a hefty smack, but I was too quick for her and, evading her blow, seized her by the neck, drew her eye to eye with me and hissed, 'Give me the key, you idiot woman, or I shall cleave your head in twain with this dessert knife!' I admit now that such behaviour might be seen in some quarters as unduly excessive, even unwarranted, and I can only excuse myself on the grounds that I was a man possessed, my extremity of emotion overcoming my usual manners.

'Temper, temper. Just you wait till bedtime, you little devil.'

Devil! I jumped. Did she know?

'The key!' I cried. 'Give me the key before it's too late!'

'If you must know, the cellar's never locked. Why don't you try the handle?'

'What?' I gasped, astonished. 'You mean that that . . . *thing* has been free to roam all this time? Good heavens! I must hurry! I pray I am not too late. If I am, the Lord help us all.' So saying, I sprinted from the kitchen, leaving Mrs Slugworthy to help herself to some cabbage sorbet. In no time at all I found myself at the door to the cellar.

I can scarce bring myself to relate the events that followed. They have taken on in my mind the air of a phantasmagorical nightmare – if, indeed, they ever happened at all and were not some figment of my tormented brain. I remember pulling the door open and stepping into the obsidian darkness beyond, but after that my only recollection is of falling and suffering an appalling battering as I fell, as though unseen malignant hands were hitting me one after another with wooden planks not unlike the steps of a staircase. When consciousness returned, I found myself lying on damp stone, my body a mass of contusions. All around me was darkness and abysmal silence, such silence as must have existed before the universe was born, a primordial absence of sound. Ah God, how great then was my terror for my immortal soul! What foul things gibbered and drooled in that loathsome, perpetual night? What tentacled, gelatinous creatures were at that very moment sucking themselves up out of bottomless pits, bent on cramming me screaming into their savage, bloody maws? What multiple-limbed, yellow-fanged, slime-scaled, stagnant, repellent monstrosities were hunched steaming in that filthy, cess-black, vile place? How my heart hammered! How my skin sweated! How my bowels quaked!

Then it was that I beheld it. Lord, blind these eyes that they might never see such a sight again. The Unmentionable itself! It floated towards me, glimmering with the pallid, sickly luminescence of a flame that burned from its very hand! I could not tear my eyes from its repugnant features. Its head – if head it was – was bloated and swollen, adorned with cankerous growths, with a single eye that glistened wetly as it searched for me. Its body was inflated to horrid proportions, misshapen and lumpen, as though fatted on human meat and gorged on human blood, and it moved with a remorseless rolling gait. But far worse than all of this was the smell of the thing, a noxious stench that had its origins in the deepest, foulest charnel pits of Hades.

The thing's mouth formed a word. My name! It uttered my name!

Fear lent wings to my heels. I do not know how I managed to escape that walking nightmare. I have no memory of my flight from the Manor. All I know is that I made it to the town and here I am, in lodgings. The door is locked and bolted and I am scribbling these lines in the few moments left to me before time runs out. There is a frantic banging at the door and a voice much like that of Mrs Slugworthy assures me that everything is all right and that a doctor and two constables accompany her, but this is a demon trick to get me to open the door.

I know my life is at an end. I pray to Him that grants mercy to all men to take pity on my folly and redeem my poor soul.

Wait! What is that sound? Like wood splintering under hammer blows. They are coming. My God, they are coming for me. They are co

The text ends abruptly, tantalisingly, with this unfinished sentence, scribbled by my great-grandfather – with impressive presence of mind – even as Nemesis pounded at the door. History relates that my great-grandfather spent the remaining thirty-one years of his life in a succession of nursing homes, walking around with a pillow strapped to his head in order to protect his brain from 'electrostatic etheric transmissions', and turning out a seemingly endless flow of short stories which – on account of the disturbing nature of their content and not, as many have suggested, owing to a complete lack of literary merit – no editor has yet deemed fit for publication.

Thanatophile Seeks Similar

The Dark Man of Your Dreams. Slender, morbid, pallid, prefers black clothing. Would you be willing to meet me?

There were four of them in the waiting room, three old women and Alice. All four sat apart, with at least one empty plastic chair between each of them, but the old women shared a bond that physical separation could neither disguise nor diminish. Every now and then their gazes would meet and looks of implicit understanding would pass across the room. They were in on a secret – the secret that came with false teeth and cloud-cotton hair, with joints that sang arias in the morning, with husbands buried and children mourned. All three had heard the whisper of their own mortality for longer than they could remember, so long that they had learned to ignore its hissing, wheedling voice. In twisted bodies they skipped and danced ahead of the inevitable, encroaching end, and no one could tell them they had outlived their usefulness, for while they remained alive they were reminders to all of the feebleness of death, object lessons in the capacity of the human body to survive.

And Alice? Alice, for once in her life, was not acutely conscious of being excluded from a group. Her attention was entirely focused on the newspaper in her hands, the *Argus and Recorder*, and on the advert in the back pages of that newspaper which had seized her attention and suddenly transformed the game of reading the Lonely Hearts columns into something much more serious.

The Dark Man of Your Dreams.

Usually Alice perused the Lonely Hearts with an idle, ironic eye, wondering why, if half the things these people said about themselves were true, they had to advertise for love at all. Love, surely, was hammering down the doors of Attractive, Outgoing Blondes and Genuine, Sincere Guys. How could anyone blessed with a Bubbly Personality and a Good Sense of Humour walk down the street without being mobbed by love?

Alice had always believed that, no matter how bad things got, she would never stoop to taking out or responding to a Lonely Hearts advert. If nothing else, she was by nature too fatalistic for that. Unless her ideal companion happened along in the natural course of events, she had resolved to be content to do without. Like all closet romantics, Alice was waiting for the thunderbolt, and until that came – if it ever came – she wouldn't accept anything less.

But sometimes lightning can strike with a sound no louder than the dry rustle of newsprint.

Slender, morbid, pallid, prefers black clothing.

What kind of man would list those characteristics as his best points? One, she thought, with few illusions about himself. One who demanded honesty from himself and from others. That was attractive. Lies had teeth, and Alice bore the psychic bitemarks of a lifetime of disappointments and deceptions and mortifications.

The three old women sat in silence, nodding to themselves and one another. Their whiskered lips were parted in pearly-grey half-smiles, and their eyes, yellowed from decades of seeing, glistered with the knowledge they had accumulated.

Would you be willing to meet me?

Willing, maybe. Curious, certainly. But was she brave enough? Did she dare? It would take every ounce of courage she had to write to him. What if he didn't reply? Worse – what if he did?

Alice shook her head at the stupidity of it all. She knew what she was really going to do. She was going to put the newspaper back on the waiting room table among the stacks of magazines and comics and forget all about the advert. It had been fun for a moment to pretend that she had been about to get a grip on her life and seize an opportunity, but that moment was over now and everything was back to normal.

But when Dr Muirhead poked her head out from her surgery and asked Alice to come in, Alice calmly folded the *Argus and Recorder* up as though it was her own copy and stuffed it into her shoulder-bag before standing up and going through.

And the three old women nodded along in rhythmic unison, confirming the secret they shared. It would be Alice's secret, too, in time.

'Six and a half stone is not a healthy weight,' Dr Muirhead had said, but Alice had heard it all before and felt that the doctor, who erred on the side of plumpness, could have no way of understanding what it was like to be stuck in a body you loathed. Dr Muirhead's sheath of subcutaneous fat, which seemed to be distributed evenly over every square inch of her, even the tips of her fingers, was a sign of contentment. Dr Muirhead was comfortable with who she was. Alice was not, and her protruding bones proved it. She was on the rack of her own ribs. Outwardly was how she felt inwardly: ungainly, unattractive, angular.

'I can't stress how important it is that you discipline yourself to a proper diet,' Dr Muirhead had said, but what did she know? She probably kept éclairs in a drawer of her desk. 'Otherwise, if you don't stop punishing yourself in this way, we may have to consider the possibility of having you admitted to a clinic.'

On the bus rumbling home, Alice took out the newspaper again and reread the advert. Well, what harm could it do? He never had to see her. It could be a purely postal relationship. Penpals. And if, after the exchange of several letters, she thought she knew him well enough to trust him, then she might – only might, mind – propose that they meet.

She would ask Monica's advice when Monica came home.

But by the time Monica came home, Alice had already written the letter.

She had gone through three drafts and thought she had it perfect.

Dear 'Dark Man of My Dreams',
If I start by saying that I'm not the sort of person who normally does this sort of thing, would you believe me or would you think I was protesting too much? I just don't want you to think I'm someone who regularly turns to the Lonely Hearts columns in a constant, desperate search for affection. I'm not, and on the strength of your advert I don't think you are either.

My name is Alice, and I am not slender (at least, I don't think I am), but I am morbid, I am pallid, and I do prefer black clothing. So when I first saw your advert, as you can imagine I thought I must have placed it myself. From somewhere on high I heard a voice say, 'Snap!' That was how it felt, and that's why I'm replying. From what I know of you – and I know almost nothing, and yet I feel that I know you very well – I think we have a lot in common. Not just interests in common, but a similar, for want of a better phrase, spiritual outlook. I could be jumping the gun here, and I don't want to presume to tell you who or what you are, so instead I will tell you about myself, and if any of it strikes a chord then perhaps you will consider writing back.

I am 22. I don't have a job. I was taking a degree in Social Sciences but dropped out in the second year for medical reasons. I live with a friend called Monica, who is much older than me and a health visitor. I like rock music, the darker the better. I adore The Cure. I prefer winter to summer and autumn to spring, and I am at my happiest sitting alone in a curtained room listening to the sound of my own heartbeat.

Of course I may be wrong about you and you may find all of the above a complete turn-off in which case I'd be obliged if you didn't go to the trouble of replying. Your silence will be your answer. If, on

226

the other hand, you're interested in continuing this correspondence,
then I'd be very happy if you did so.

sincerely,
Alice

And not wanting Monica's opinion on the letter, because if Monica was anything less than wholeheartedly enthusiastic then all that work would have been for nothing, Alice sealed it in an envelope, checked she had addressed the envelope to the correct box number, and went down to the postbox and mailed it.

She spent the next three days in an agony of uncertainty and regret. Not one minute went by when she didn't wish she could turn back the clock and pluck the envelope out of the postbox the instant before it disappeared. She even contemplated telephoning the sorting depot to ask if the letter could be stopped. What had she done? What had she done?

It was only on the fourth day that a sense of resignation set in, moving across the country of her mind like a cold front on a TV weatherman's map, and when a fifth day passed without a reply, and then a sixth, she accepted that she had made a fool of herself. Somewhere, someone was laughing at her. It was nothing new. It was no less than she deserved for taking matters into her own hands. Her life was so much easier when she left the running of it to other people, and she had been mad to hope otherwise.

A week after she answered the advert, the reply came. Monica handed the envelope across the breakfast table without a word. Alice knew Monica expected to be told whom it was from and what it contained, and surprised her by not opening it there and then. Instead, with a coolness that astonished even herself, Alice sat and drank her tea (no milk, no sugar) and read the newspaper and studiously ignored the scrambled eggs Monica had made for her and even more studiously ignored Monica's searching glances. She did not know for sure that the letter was from the Dark Man of Her

227

Dreams, but then when was the last time she had received a handwritten envelope? Besides, the envelope was addressed simply to 'Alice'. (She had deliberately not given her surname, fearing – as demons do – that names have power.) Who else could it be from?

Monica had to go to work and was angry that Alice was keeping something from her. She slammed the front door. When the clacking of her heels on the pavement had faded away, Alice took a table knife to the flap of the envelope. Inside were two sheets of feint-ruled A4, folded into quarters.

The Gatehouse
Riverwood Cemetery

Dear Alice,

You know me. You have always known me. There is no other explanation. If you did not know me, you would not have known how to sell yourself so well to me. I do not mean that to sound pejorative, but what else do we do to each other all the time but sell ourselves? Our clothes, our habits, our mannerisms – these are the methods we use to advertise our souls. Most people window-dress to a ludicrous degree, gift-wrapping their true selves in tawdry tinsel lies. They are terrified that, if they don't, the merchandise will seem bland and dull. You, Alice, are smart enough to realise that the only way to avoid the inevitable disappointment we cause to others when our true ordinariness becomes clear to them is by not heightening their expectations in the first place. That is good. You have saved both of us the effort of tearing down one another's artifices. Honesty begets honesty, and so I shall give you nothing but the unadorned, unvarnished truth about myself.

My name is David, I am 25, I live alone and work alone. I have no friends. There are some acquaintances from school I see every so often. We drink in a pub and they reminisce about the only time they were happy, when they were children living under the wing of their parents, the real world a place far beyond the walls of school and home. They are sad and bitter now because nothing they have

228

encountered since matches up to the blissful security of that time. I, on the other hand, was blessed from an early age with the knowledge that life is cruel and pointless and hard. For no reason that I can pinpoint, other than that perhaps I was simply born old, I entered adulthood with my eyes fully open. Nothing could surprise me. I knew – and nothing I have seen yet has altered my opinion – that every day of my life is no more than a tick on a calendar marking my progress towards death. Why deny that fact? Why not embrace it? To think otherwise, to treat life as a journey towards some worthwhile goal, some great reward, is to delude oneself. We are born to degenerate and die. Accepting this liberates.

Alice, I have to say that your letter has excited me. I feel that I may have unearthed a kindred spirit, a fellow bearer of the Cross of understanding, and that my lonely vigil may be at an end.

Yours,
David

Alice went for a walk in the park, taking the letter with her, and after ten minutes of strolling beneath the black-leafed trees sat down on a bench to rest her aching legs. There, she took out David's letter and read and reread his words until she knew them by heart. What a mind he had! He had taken the raw stuff of thoughts that were only just forming in her mind and spun from it a single coherent strand, making sudden sense of almost everything that had confused and perplexed her these past couple of years.

And she felt justified, she felt *vindicated*, and the feeling thrilled her. The courage it had taken to reply to the advert was now a permanent part of her. She would never need to screw herself up to that pitch of bravery again.

Fizzing with new-found confidence, she wrote back to David.

Dear David,
I can hardly believe I am about to do this, but then we are not strangers, not now. Somehow we have skipped that awkward phase.

Will you meet me?

The time and the place can be of your choosing. I am flexible. Lunchtime, evening, whenever I am always free. At least, there aren't any appointments I can't cancel.

Perhaps at your home address? The gatehouse?

Yours,
Alice

Over the next few days Alice was a different person. Though she still only picked at the meals Monica cooked for her, eating perhaps one floret of broccoli or a few forkfuls of green salad and pushing the rest around her plate, in every other respect she showed, and felt, a relish for life which, when she thought about it, made her habitual state of despair and self-loathing seem absurdly, pointlessly blinkered.

Monica couldn't help but notice the change, though she commented on it only obliquely, when she heard Alice singing 'The Lovecats' to herself one morning: 'Been at the happy pills again, have we?' She was still sore at Alice for not confiding in her about the letter, and Alice felt guilty about that and promised herself that when the time was right she would tell Monica about David. But that time was still some way off, if it ever came at all, and anyway she could see Monica was secretly pleased that she was not moping around as usual, and this, undoubtedly, was a bonus for both of them.

'Your anonymous correspondent,' Monica said dryly as she handed Alice David's next letter.

Alice took it to her room to read.

Dear Alice,
Next Friday, the 17th, 1 pm. Come to the gatehouse. I'll supply the lunch.

Yours,
David

She was going to meet the Dark Man of Her Dreams.

The face in the bathroom mirror that Friday morning startled her. She almost didn't recognise herself. Her eyes were hollow in their sockets, her forehead was unnaturally large and domed, her cheekbones loomed like angels' wings, and she could see the ridged outline of her teeth beneath her thin skin – their roots seemed to reach all the way up to her nose and all the way down to the bottom of her jaw. When had this happened, this transformation from girl to living skeleton?

She hid it as best she could with make-up, which she hadn't worn in ages, but the crimson of her lipstick only served to draw attention to her outsized teeth and the shadows cast by her blusher only accentuated the cavernousness of her cheeks. By the light of the small strip-bulb above the mirror she looked ghastly, haglike. If she repelled herself, God knew what David would think of her.

She decided not to go.

At midday she cleaned up the smeared mascara around her eyes, wiped her nose and decided she would go after all.

In her best black velvet dress she walked to the bus stop and boarded a bus that took her through the heart of the city and out the other side to the Riverwood Cemetery.

This was not the first time Alice had visited the Riverwood Cemetery. During her first year at university she had spent many an afternoon there wandering alone, undisturbed, untroubled, uninhibited. Among the gently curving pathways and white headstones, with all the quiet dead beneath her feet, safe under two yards of soil, she had felt utterly at peace. The crosses, tombs, small mausoleums and penitent marble angels held no threat for her. Rather, they promised release. *Soon,* they whispered, *it will all be over*. It was the only guarantee she had had at the time, and she had clung to it as though nothing else on earth mattered.

Stationed between two long stretches of spiked iron railings, the gatehouse arched over the southern entrance to the cemetery, rising to red-brick crenellations. Its windows were leaded in a diamond pattern, and ivy crawled across one flank like broken veins in an old man's face. It had never occurred to Alice that anyone might live there – the purpose of the gatehouse had always seemed symbolic rather than functional – but now that she thought about it, as a home for one person it wouldn't be at all unpleasant, assuming you didn't have a problem with graveyards. It was the sort of place where she herself could quite happily have stayed.

The bus dropped her off right outside. She hesitated only briefly before pressing the ceramic bellpush set into the brickwork beside the bolt-studded wooden door.

Footsteps descended a spiral staircase, and the door opened.

'Alice.'

She looked at his eyes first. The eyes could tell you so much. His were hazel, with stars of jade-green about the pupils, and stared at her as though her face was a computer screen filled with mesmerising information. They were set in heavy lids, with faint purplish crescents beneath them that suggested pain and sensitivity. The rest of his face was pale and tapered to a chin that was more pointed than squared. He had full lips, maroon like a Slav's, and a long fine neck in which the jugular veins lay proud against the lean muscle. He was wearing black jeans and a black T-shirt which hung loosely on a frame that was, as he had promised, slender. His hair, too, was black and, if the uneven fringe was anything to go by, self-cut. But it was his eyes Alice returned to and met with a steady gaze of her own, not only because she didn't want to appear to be avoiding them but because they fascinated her and were, in turn, fascinated by her.

'You're everything I thought you'd be,' David said. He was carrying a rolled-up blanket and a lightly laden supermarket carrier-bag. 'I've got the picnic things. Shall we go for a walk?'

He led her through the cemetery gates and along the narrow streets of the necropolis, choosing his turns confidently, until they came to a spot Alice knew well, where a semicircle of silver birches cast their skeletal shadows over two raised tombs that sat side by side like solid stone tables, their surfaces encrusted with saffron lichen. Autumn rooks croaked overhead. David made a cushion of the blanket on one tomb and beckoned Alice to sit on one of the tombs, then settled himself down on the other, facing her. Their legs dangled, knees not quite touching, toes not quite reaching the lawn.

'I don't eat much,' he said, offering her a thinly cut tuna and salad sandwich, which she nibbled politely. They drank bottled water, and the sun, a cold yellow pebble, rolled across the sky.

David told her that he was writing a work of philosophy that was going to unite all the philosophies of the world, a massive undertaking which had so far consumed three years of his life and looked set to take up another seven or eight. Alice hoped he was going to discuss the work in progress with her, sound out her opinions, but instead he moved almost immediately on to another subject, explaining how he earned a living as a caretaker for the cemetery, one of a team of five who mowed the grass and pruned the trees and clipped the hedgerows and swept the pathways of leaves and generally saw to it that the homes of the dead weren't neglected even after the bereaved had long since ceased coming to pay their respects. He did not dig graves because Riverwood had reached capacity several years ago and new land had been found elsewhere for the newly deceased. One of his other duties was to make sure that the cemetery wasn't vandalised or despoiled, and at dusk each evening he patrolled the grounds to check there was no one loitering inside before he locked the gates.

This prompted Alice to ask, 'Do you walk around in here at night? Just you and the moon and the wind?'

'Sometimes. When there's enough light to see without a torch. Then I can sneak up on couples without being spotted.'

'Couples?'

'They come here to fornicate. Even though the gates are

locked, there are still ways to get in, if you're desperate enough.'

She could barely bring herself to ask the next question. 'Do you watch them? I mean, everything they do?'

'Sometimes.' He shrugged and smiled. 'The unvarnished truth. Wouldn't you?'

'I don't know. Yes, I might, I suppose.'

'Here.' He tapped her knee. 'Come on. I've got something to show you.'

They gathered up the unfinished picnic and set off across the grass between the parades of headstones, David running at a gentle lope, Alice doing her best to keep up. Normally this kind of exertion would have been beyond her, but David's sudden burst of energy was infectious, and her legs and lungs did what was demanded of them. She found herself laughing as she ran, and she didn't know why.

David came to a halt beside a mausoleum of pale, weathered stone, with a sloping roof, gables, eaves and a low chain fence surrounding it. When Alice caught up, the first thing she said was, 'A home.'

'It is a home,' David said. 'A little one-room house. And look.' On the iron door there was a bolt secured by a rusty padlock. He undid the padlock with a key from his pocket, shot back the bolt, put both hands to the door and shoved. The door scraped inwards a few inches. 'Want to go in?'

She hated herself for hesitating. 'I don't know. Is it . . . right?' She peered into the gap between door and frame and could see nothing within but blackness.

'They're dead. They're beyond caring.' Using his shoulder David shunted the door slightly further open, creating a space through which a thin person could easily slip. 'There's nothing in there but dust, cobwebs and bones.'

'All right.' Alice swelled with bravado. 'All right. Who cares?'

She eased herself through the gap. Pure and perfect darkness engulfed her, a darkness that smelled of damp and earth and age. Ahead she could make out a stone ledge of some sort and what looked like a brass handle, tarnished but glinting. Turning round, she saw David following her in, squeezing himself through a sliver of daylight that was weaker than she expected, as though to be contained by the interior of a tomb diminished it. Then David grunted and the daylight narrowed to a thin line and disappeared.

'David . . .'

'Don't worry,' he said. Alice couldn't tell where his voice was coming from until a hand softly took her hand. 'It's only darkness. It can't hurt you.'

A part of her ached with fear; another part was quietly thrilled, and this part seemed to have the upper hand and made the fear its passive consort. She marvelled that her eyes could be wide open and yet useless, showing her nothing except the gibbous green afterimage of David's silhouette in the doorway.

I am in a tomb, she thought. *So this is what it's like.*

'Why don't we lie down?' David suggested.

'Lie down?'

'Here, on the ground. To see how it feels. How *they* feel.'

She didn't need to ask who 'they' were. They were all around her. The very air she was inhaling was infused with their decay. Close by, an arm's reach away, they were pinned in their narrow beds, dressed in their rotting best, hands clasped over their breastbones – a family, generations, a dynasty, reduced to dust and ashes. If she wanted to join them, they would not reject her. They were nothing if not accepting.

She lowered herself to the ground, David providing gentlemanly assistance.

'Lie back,' he said. She heard him settling down beside her. A small voice cried out in the back of her head, *What are you doing, girl? This man could be a rapist! A sex fiend!* But she believed – no, she *trusted* – that David was not like that at all. He was above such things.

235

The cold of the packed earth beneath her penetrated the fabric of her dress and chilled her skin, but in every other respect she felt comfortable. For a while there was only the sound of their breathing. Then David said, 'Hear that? Perfect silence. Perfect darkness. Perfect peace. This is what it's like to be dead.'

'It's beautiful,' Alice sighed.

'Here.'

She heard a scratching, and a moment later felt David's fingertips at her lips.

'Try this.'

'What is it?'

'You want to know what it feels like to be dead?'

'Yes.'

'Then open your mouth.'

She parted her lips, and a sift of soil dribbled into her mouth.

'Best get used to it,' David said. 'You'll be eating nothing else for eternity.'

Fighting back the gag reflex, Alice rolled the soil around her tongue and found to her surprise that the taste, though acrid, could have been a lot worse. It reminded her of the smell of forests on damp afternoons, of lakes and rabbit holes, of falling over as a child face-first into dirt, of carrots raw from the ground. With a gulp she swallowed down the gritty paste and cleaned a few lingering granules from her teeth with her tongue.

'I've coined a word for people like you and me, Alice,' David said. ' "Thanatophile". I thought the term already existed, but I looked in *Chambers* and the *OED* and it wasn't in either. Perhaps there are some concepts society just can't bring itself to name.'

'What does it mean?'

'It means "a lover of death". Not somebody who likes to fuck corpses. There've been no problems about naming *that* state of mind. It means someone for whom death and dying hold no fear, someone who actively welcomes the concept of death into their life. I'm not talking about martyrs or people with terminal illnesses. I'm talking about sane, healthy people who make a conscious decision to befriend the Reaper – people who feel calmer within themselves because they're looking forward to one day hearing the swish of his scythe.'

'I do,' she said, but David didn't seem to hear. 'Sometimes.'

'You see, what Plato and Wittgenstein and Nietzsche and Sartre and all the great thinkers throughout history were flailing about looking for was the answer to the problem of how to live a pure and honest life, a life free from fear. They didn't find it because they were approaching the problem from the wrong end, examining life itself, seeing life as the be all and end all, not seeing it as a preliminary to the ultimate purpose of being, which is to die. The Tibetans almost got it right, but they insisted on introducing reincarnation into the equation, a get-out clause, a second chance. We don't come back. When life stops, it stops for good.'

'And beyond that, there's only peace.'

'Only peace,' he echoed approvingly. 'I know that's what *you* want, Alice. I know that's what you've wanted ever since you were old enough to formulate an independent thought. I can tell just by looking at you. You've begun the process already. Gradually wasting away. Feeling your body getting lighter on you every day, becoming less burdensome. Letting your flesh erode and your joints atrophy. Letting your bones show through your skin. Letting the truth emerge from beneath all the trash.'

'It's true,' she said, like a sigh. And it *was* true, and she wondered why she had never realised it before. She wasn't punishing herself at all. She was *shaping* herself, making herself into what she most desired to be. 'And what do *you* want, David? Don't you want it too?'

'I want you to be happy, Alice. I want you to be free.'

She heard his shoes grating on the soil as he pulled himself

237

up to a kneeling position, and she braced herself for the coming kiss. He grasped her shoulders and laid one leg over her thighs, but the kiss did not come.

'I can free you, Alice,' he said. 'The question is, do you want to be freed?'

Freed from what? From uncertainty? From feelings of rejection? From loneliness? Oh yes, she wanted to be free from all of those.

'I do,' she said.

His hands moved to her neck in a dry caress.

'Then let me free you,' he said.

She felt his fingers squeeze an instant before they actually did so. It was as though she detected the electrical impulse travelling down his arms before it reached the nerve endings and delivered its message to the poised muscles. It was not much of a warning but it gave her time to twist her head away and at the same time bring her legs up in a foetal reflex.

She did not mean to knee David in the testicles and incapacitate him, but that was what she did, far more effectively than if she had actually been trying to. The air whooshed out of her lungs and he rolled away from her, gargling and wheezing. Next thing she knew, she was on her feet and stumbling gropingly backwards.

'Alice?' David croaked through the pain. 'Alice what did you – Christ, what did you do that for?'

Alice backed up against something hard that scraped her calves. Her fingers found a ridge of smooth, dust-coated wood and followed it until they were sufficiently convinced that it was, as she had thought, the rim of the lid of a coffin which rested on the stone ledge she had glimpsed earlier.

'I thought we . . . understood each other,' David went on in a voice filled with such agony that it almost brought tears to Alice's eyes.

Which way was the door? Her sense of direction had been completely thrown. She thought it must lie somewhere to her right, and keeping her calves in contact with the ledge she

238

shuffled sideways in that direction. At any moment she expected a hand to come out of nowhere and grab her ankle. Wherever David was lying in the pure and perfect darkness of the mausoleum, he could only be less than half a dozen short paces away. She might even be passing within inches of him now and not know it. She struggled to keep her breathing under control and continued to move crablike alongside the ledge.

Her right shoulder butted a wall, and she reached out to the side and a little to the front, and to her relief felt the rough flaky texture of rusted iron. Her fingers danced as delicately as a spider over the surface of the door but could find no handle. Of course not. Why would anyone put a handle on the *inside* of the door to a tomb? But there had to be some other way of opening it. David wouldn't have shut both of them in there if there wasn't a way of letting them out again, would he? Would he?

'Talk to me, Alice. Where are you?'

The door was not solid iron but a sheet of iron moulded around a frame, overlapping at the edges to leave an even, inch-wide strip of spare metal. Alice inserted her fingers and braced herself.

'Alice?'

She heard David behind her getting unsteadily to his feet, and she put everything she had into the heave, knowing that if she didn't make a gap large enough on the first attempt she probably wouldn't get a second chance. The door wrenched stubbornly inwards, juddering against stone and soil. The sudden glare of daylight screwed her pupils painfully tight, and the edge of the iron overlap dug into the joints between the pads of her fingers, but she kept pulling, jamming her knee into the aperture to speed the process.

'Alice!'

A hand grabbed the shoulder of her dress. With a shriek Alice let go of the door and squirmed through the opening she had made, praying feverishly that it would be wide enough.

The edge of the door ground against her ribs and hips, the stone frame scraped her spine, and then she was through and diving free with a rend of tearing fabric.

She fell headlong on to the grass and immediately struggled to her knees, only to discover that the hem of her dress had snagged on the inside of the door. Turning to tug it loose, she looked up to see David worming through the gap, a scrap of black velvet clutched in his outstretched fist. His face, whiter than ever, was wedged between the door and the frame, and his hazel-and-jade eyes stared at her with a mixture of pain and incomprehension.

'What's wrong?' he said. 'You wanted to be free, didn't you?'

Giving vent to something that was both a grunt and a scream, Alice jerked her dress free from the door and set off across the grass, stumbling between the headstones. She went about ten yards before realising that David was not chasing her, and glancing back she saw that he was stuck in the doorway and trying to extricate himself in reverse so that he could haul the door further open.

After that, she did not look back again until she had reached the gates of the cemetery.

Monica came home to find Alice bathed, in her pyjamas and in bed. Alice said she was feeling a bit under the weather, you know, time of the month due and all that. She lied with a fluency that surprised and mildly ashamed her. Monica heated up some chicken broth and sat by her bedside and spooned it into her mouth. Alice drank half the bowlful, which pleased them both. Then she dozed for a while, waking up at around ten p.m. to find Monica sitting in the armchair in the corner, examining some sheets of A4 paper. It didn't take Alice long to recognise David's letters.

'What are you doing with those?' Alice asked, softly but with an undertone of unmistakable menace.

'Who is this David?' Monica turned one of the sheets over

and frowned. 'Whoever he is, he doesn't sound like a very nice person to me.'

Alice shunted the bedclothes aside and said, in a venomous whisper, 'Give them back.'

'In fact, he sounds a bit sick.'

'You have no right to be reading them.'

Monica looked up then, and her eyes were righteously wide. 'I have every right, Alice. The last thing someone in your condition needs is some *boy* playing games with your mind.'

'It's private correspondence.' Alice lowered her bare feet to the carpet, testing her left ankle, which she had twisted during her flight across the cemetery. There was a faint corona of bruising around the joint, but it didn't appear to have been sprained badly.

'As long as you're living under my roof at my expense, Alice, nothing of yours is private. Did you go and see him this afternoon?'

'Nothing happened.'

'That's not what I asked,' said Monica, though it more than adequately answered her question.

Alice took a few short limping steps across the room. 'Give them here.'

' "We are born to degenerate and die," ' Monica read out. 'If you ask me, this fellow sounds deeply disturbed.'

'He might be, but at least he's not an interfering old *dyke*,' Alice snarled, and made a grab for the letters, but Monica was quicker. She leapt from the chair, holding the pieces of paper defensively behind her head, out of Alice's reach. Her expression was sad, not angry; cold, not hot.

'How dare you talk to me like that, Alice Beckett!' she hissed. 'How *dare* you! Aren't I the one who's looked after you for going on two years now? I took you in when no one else would, when even your parents had given up on you. If it wasn't for me, you'd probably be lying in some mental hospital right now with a drip-feed in your arm. I've been mother, sister and nurse to you, and this is the thanks I get?'

241

'You're evil,' Alice hissed back. 'Poking around in other people's belongings. That's what evil people do.'

'I will not be spoken to like that in my home.'

'Your home, your home! You keep shoving that down my throat, don't you?'

'I have to shove things down your throat, Alice, because that's the only way you'll take anything in!'

'That was a cheap shot, Monica, even for you.'

Monica tried to appear wholly reasonable. 'You're not well, Alice. How many times do you have to be told that?'

'I am the way I am because that's the way I want to be,' Alice replied. 'Because it's about the only thing in my life I can still control. The only thing you or my parents or the doctor can't have any say in. And if you can't accept that, well then, *fuck you*.'

They glared at each other for several moments, chins jutting, nostrils flared, eyes as big as boiled eggs. For a time it seemed that they might even come to blows. Then, abruptly, Alice turned away.

'Go on then,' she said. 'Take them and burn them. I don't care.'

Monica peered lamely at the pieces of paper in her hands. 'I never said anything about burning them.'

'Well, do whatever you want with them. I don't care.' Alice crawled back into bed. 'I'm too tired to care.' She pulled the bedclothes up over her head. 'I'm too tired to care about anything any more.'

They had had arguments before, of course. It was only natural. Two people sharing a flat together were bound to disagree now and then. This time, however, Alice had felt something break between them. The slender bridge that had connected them – constructed from her vulnerability and Monica's need to protect – had collapsed, and she knew that it was gone for ever and could not be rebuilt. She knew she had no choice now but to leave. But where would she go?

*

242

After the television had gone off in the living room and the light had gone out in Monica's room, Alice waited a further hour until she was certain that Monica was fast asleep, then stole a five-pound note from her handbag, phoned for a cab, and went downstairs to meet it outside the front door.

'Where to, love?' said the cabbie.

'The Riverwood Cemetery.'

'At this time of night?' The cabbie bounced his eyebrows up and down a couple of times. 'S'pose you want to reach your grave before dawn, eh?'

'Shut up and drive.'

'I knew you'd come back.'

Alice stood shivering on the gatehouse doorstep. David was wearing just a T-shirt and black briefs, and his legs were stippled with gooseflesh. He moved aside to allow her to enter. She climbed the spiral staircase and found herself in a long vaulted room equipped with basic second-hand furniture and a small kitchen unit. A door at the end led off to what she presumed was a bedroom, another to a bathroom. There was a raw cosiness about the place. A twin-bar electric fire glowed on the floor beside a desk on which books, files and sheaves of paper were loosely stacked. A desk lamp provided the only other illumination.

'You were working?' she asked.

'I always write at night. Sunlight shrivels my inspiration. About this afternoon . . .'

'It was a misunderstanding,' she said. 'You thought you knew what I wanted, and you were nearly right, but things have changed. Would you – would you like to go for a walk?'

'Right now?'

'Right now.'

Armed with the same blanket as before, they stole through the night-bound necropolis. The brown sky offered them a handful of stars and a singed moon to see by. Headstones,

243

crucifixes and angels loomed around them, white as ghosts. The stillness in the cemetery was deeper than the background rumble of a city usually permits: it seemed to come from the ground itself, an exhalation of silence, a communal open-mouthed sigh from the airless, earth-choked windpipes of the thousands buried beneath the damp grass, those for whom the suffering was over, for whom all disappointments were past.

In the mausoleum David laid the blanket out on the ground and Alice lay down, hoisted her skirt up around her waist and see-sawed her knickers down her legs. They made love without much in the way of prelude or preamble, David forcing himself into her in the same manner that he had forced his way into the mausoleum, with one brutal shove. Somewhere in the back of Alice's mind, somewhere away from the pain, a warning clanged like an old school bell: shouldn't they be taking precautions? But she reasoned that, surrounded by so much death, no life could possibly take root. And if David's jism happened to be carrying a fatal disease, well, what else would he be doing then but granting her deepest, darkest wish?

It was over quickly. A squirting shudder from David, and then he was clambering off her, pulling up his jeans, buttoning up.

'Alice?'

She nodded, but then, realising he couldn't see her in the dark, croaked, 'Yes?'

'Will you stay with me?'

'For ever, David. For ever and ever.'

His living space, though small, was large enough for the two of them – a kind of private mausoleum of their own which Alice had all to herself during the day while David was out caretaking. To occupy her mind she bought a very cheap second-hand typewriter and set to work typing up the two hundred or so longhand pages of David's magnum opus, to which David added nightly, gradually unfurling his unifying philosophy, his grand plan for the mind of Man. And after dark, when he wasn't writing, he and Alice would slip out into the cemetery and flit between the memorials to the dead, two thin figures with skin so white it was almost luminescent. Sometimes they would make love in the open air or in their secret second home with the rusty iron door, or else they would sneak up on other amorous couples and observe their antics with the quiet, rapt air of unseen elves or sprites. They frightened drunken tramps, too, whispering in their ears to wake them up from their methylated slumbers. The tramps took one bleary look at the pair of skeletal faces hovering over them and scuttled away, vowing never to sleep off their hangovers in the Riverwood Cemetery again. And slowly the cemetery gathered a reputation. Tales of ghosts and ghouls in the graveyard spread through the local schools and the housing estates nearby. Even David's fellow caretakers began to get a little anxious around the place towards dusk.

The *Argus and Recorder* ran an article on the rumours, and three old women in the waiting room at Dr Muirhead's surgery nodded knowingly over that particular edition of the newspaper – not the same three old women as before, another three, any three. They were all alike, these white-haired sibyls. They all looked and thought and spoke the same, and they all smiled the same shop-bought smiles: gleaming plastic grins that would remain, like the Cheshire Cat's, long after the rest of them had faded away to dust and nothingness.

Rosemary for Remembrance

At nine o'clock every morning, in scorching sunshine, in freezing rain, in sickness and in health, Rosemary would go down to the old brick bus shelter.

In the sixteen years since the routes had changed no buses had plied this street, but still Rosemary walked down to the shelter every day and sat or stood peering out along the long straight stretch of road, waiting for a certain green bus to draw up and a certain man to disembark. In winter she would be there in her overcoat and the peculiar woollen hat she had knitted for herself (it resembled nothing so much as a tea-cosy), stamping her felt boots and clapping her mittened hands. In summer, wearing sandals and a plain cotton dress, she would sit where the sunlight reached in through the doorway, inching herself in one direction along the bench as the sun rolled in the other direction across the sky. She never brought a book or newspaper with her, occupying herself solely with the act of waiting. And after a day of waiting she would go home again. And every day for fifty-two years she had done this – even after the buses stopped coming, the buses she had never once climbed aboard.

People called her mad, and Rosemary would have been the first to admit that this wasn't exactly *normal* behaviour. But she was not mad. Oh no. She knew that the bus she was waiting for would come eventually, and on that bus would be the man she loved. She was perfectly clear about that. She had been perfectly clear about that for fifty-two years. And when children streaking by on their bicycles caught sight of her lurking in the shelter and screamed, 'Mad Rosemary! Mad Rosemary!', she would grimly shake her head (her heart was too callused to be wounded by the words of babies). No, not mad. Not unless believing a promise was a form of madness.

There had once been a line of shops on the opposite side of the road from the shelter – an ironmonger's, a greengrocer's, a bakery – but when the first big supermarket opened in the city centre the shops had died, one by one. Rosemary had watched as the Closing Down signs were replaced by For Sale signs and then by broken glass and then boards, to which children had quickly added signatures and obscene slogans. Finally, in a long deafening month of demolition, the shops had been erased altogether, and now there was just a patch of hummocky wasteland littered with oil drums and tin cans and rotting lengths of two-by-four and broken chunks of brick and breeze-blocks and nettles and foxgloves and the occasional poppy. From this minor apocalypse Rosemary's bus shelter had for some reason been spared. Perhaps it was too small, too insignificant. Beneath the demolishers' notice.

The loss of the row of shops had brought with it a gain, for it had revealed a view of the city beyond – rooftops and factories, railyards and copper-green steeples – a view which had entranced Rosemary and which had not staled with familiarity but had over the years become a part of her inner landscape, so deeply ingrained in her imagination that she could lie in bed at night and conjure it up, perfect down to the smallest detail. Rosemary had witnessed the rise and fall of tower blocks and the rise again of shopping centres and multistorey car parks and eight-screen cinemas. Over the years she had watched the skyline fluctuate like a sea in motion. The city was never still. It was restless and ever-changing – something that could only be perceived by the eyes of a constant, faithful observer.

And each day at dusk, when the bus had not come, Rosemary would sigh and brush the dust from her skirt and say, 'Maybe tomorrow.' And home she would go to the small, neat, scrupulously clean flat the council had appointed her, and there she would peck at a bird-sized meal before turning in for the night. And the last thing she said before she fell asleep every night, her private prayer, was: 'Maybe tomorrow.'

And so it was for fifty-two years, until the day tomorrow came.

It was a gusty November afternoon. Tramps had used the shelter the night before, and Rosemary had to huddle in the doorway, her face out to the wind, to keep the smells of urine and cider from her nose. Black-bellied clouds flowed overhead and there was the taste of rain in the air. Grit swirled along the pavement and sheets of newspaper turned cartwheels in the roadway. Rosemary had endured colder weather than this, but still the wind reached fingers through her flesh and twanged her bones like harp strings. She had never yet missed a day at the bus stop through illness, although there had been many mornings when she would rather have stayed indoors and in bed, when opening the door to her flat and walking down the stairs had been a mental as well as a physical effort. One of these bitter days might see her sicken for something serious. Sometimes she could feel an ache deep within her, like iron, like knives. What if she should be laid up in bed the day the bus came? What if she failed to keep her half of the bargain? Please God, no.

As she shivered painfully, over in the wasteland on the other side of the road a flutter of black caught her eye.

It was a magpie, resplendent in piebald livery. Perched on an outcrop of rubble, it was cocking its head this way and that, the blue glints in its plumage sparkling with each twist and turn.

Rosemary watched the magpie, waiting, listening. The bird did nothing, merely stood and eyed the unpromising sky. Then a second magpie arrived, swirling down on splayed, gust-buffeted wings, to land beside the first. The two birds ignored one another for a while on their rubble island, with just a contemptuous flicking of tails to show that either acknowledged the other's existence at all. Then one opened its beak and let out a cry – *ak-ak-ak-ak-ak*! – to which the other replied in kind, and their chatter whooped and skirled in the wind. All at once, as if on a prearranged cue, both birds took flight, allowing the wind to lift them and carry them away and away until they were no more than dots on the horizon, twin specks circling one another into oblivion.

Rosemary smiled gently to herself. Smiled knowingly. Perhaps today, after all . . .

Now another sound drew her attention.

It came from the west, and at first it seemed to be the noise of an aeroplane swooping in low to the airport that lay a mile or so out of town, beyond the ring road. Sometimes the prevailing wind blew sudden demented bursts of reverse jet-thrust clean across the city, the distant brays of gargantuan beasts.

But this wasn't an aeroplane. The sound was too precise, too near.

She had been fooled before, had let her heart leap with hope only to plummet when what she could have sworn was the diesel engine of a bus turned out to be that of a lorry or a taxi or a goods van. Nevertheless, bearing the magpies in mind, Rosemary listened intently, canting her head and squinting. And hoping. Dear God, hoping.

There was nothing.

Then there was something that shimmered into existence at the end of the road as though from a desert heat-haze: a green rectangle, growing larger, coming closer, gaining size and solidity.

Suddenly trembling from head to foot, from scalp to bunions, Rosemary clutched the wooden frame of the shelter doorway. Yellow teeth crawled out to bite her lower lip. Straining old eyes, she made out smaller darker rectangles inset within the green rectangle; now what looked like a

252

downturned drooping chrome-plated mouth; now two white eyes. It took her a moment to identify these as the windows, the radiator grille and the headlights of an old green bus. Now she could read the number on the front of the bus, although it wasn't any number she recognised. It looked like an eight on its side. The destination board below was blank.

And she could hardly bear to believe it, and yet there it was, plain as day, trundling towards her. The bus she had waited fifty-two years to meet. Fifty-two years! Here it was. At last. Good Lord, shouldn't she be happy? Delighted? Delirious? After all this time? Instead, she was only apprehensive.

The bus approached at a furious pace, racing the clouds. When it was less than fifty yards away and showed no sign of slowing, Rosemary was gripped by a sudden panic. What if it didn't stop? What if she had waited all these years only to have the reason for that wait whoosh past, leaving her waving and begging vainly in its wake?

She stuck out her hand.

The bus loomed.

She gesticulated.

The bus drew level with her.

She yelled, 'STOP!'

And with a momentous groan the bus jammed on its brakes and, wheels locking, tyres screaming on the tarmac, white smoke billowing out from under its wheel arches, shuddered to a halt, lurching forwards on its suspension so violently its body seemed in danger of breaking free from its chassis and skidding on down the road.

Rocking back on its axles, the bus came to rest. The tyre smoke drifted on.

Ten seconds ticked by, ten seconds in which Rosemary had time to note the long narrow poster advertising Craven 'A' cigarettes and the fine film of dirt that coated the bus's bodywork like a second skin. Then, dimly through the smeary windows, she saw in silhouette a man rise to his feet and make his way down the aisle. He seemed to be the bus's only

253

passenger. He exchanged a word with the driver, whom Rosemary could not make out at all, and then with a pneumatic hiss the doors of the bus concertinaed open. The man stepped out. The doors closed behind him.

He stood before her.

'Hello, love,' he said.

Rosemary hesitated, then said, 'George,' breathlessly, like a schoolgirl, like a giddy little schoolgirl.

George braved a smile. 'How are you?'

'I'm . . .'

Whatever she might have been going to say was lost – mercifully, perhaps – in the growl and churn of the bus's engine starting up.

Exhaust pipe spouting black fumes, the bus lumbered off, and Rosemary looked worriedly at George, who was still struggling to make that awkward smile fit.

'Don't panic,' he said. 'It'll be back.'

When it occurred to her to look for the bus again, it had disappeared from view, the sound of its engine mingling with the wind and fading.

The wind dragged a strand of George's hair across his face, and Rosemary reached up to push it back into place. Her hand, brushing against his skin, felt its coolness.

She said, 'I hoped . . . I mean, I *thought* you'd look older. I don't know why. I thought you might at least have aged along with me.'

'You look fine,' he said. Irrelevantly, she thought.

'No, that's not it at all. It just doesn't seem fair that I should have dried up and wrinkled and my fingers have grown gnarled – I've even sprouted a moustache, for heaven's sake! – and you've stayed, well . . . Perfect.'

He touched *his* moustache self-consciously, as if by wearing it he had inadvertently insulted her. 'There are certain rules . . .'

'I'm not blaming you,' she said. 'I'm happy to see you, George, honestly I am. It's been quite a wait.' And with that, and a light laugh, she dismissed fifty-two patient, seemingly interminable years.

'You didn't have to wait.'

'Yes, I did. What else was I supposed to do? Marry?'

'I wouldn't have minded.'

'And who was I to have married?'

'There was that Blakeney chap, what was his first name? Christopher?'

'Charlie. Charlie Blakeney.'

'That's the one. He was sweet on you, I seem to recall. And he had money. He'd have made a good husband.'

'I didn't want a good husband, George, I wanted you.'

George raised an eyebrow in an immaculate arch and the smile settled more comfortably on his face. 'Oh, you're a one, Rosemary. How I've missed your sense of humour. You wouldn't believe how boring it is where—'

'No,' she interrupted, cupping her hands over her ears. 'I don't want to hear about it. I don't want to hear anything about it.'

'I'm sorry. How about we just kiss?'

'I don't want you to kiss me either. It'd be revolting for you.'

'I've so missed kissing you.'

'You're looking at me. Don't you *see* me? Don't you see what I am? I'm an old woman, George! I'm old enough to be your grandmother!'

'That's not what I see. Are you cold?'

'No.'

'You shivered. Shall we take cover?' He gestured at the shelter, taking her arm to guide her in. She stood her ground.

'No, not there.'

'Is there somewhere else we could go?'

'How long have we got?'

'A while. Enough time.'

'Oh well, in that case – there's a café at the end of the road.'

'May I?' George crooked an elbow, and Rosemary slotted her hand through it, and like that, like a grandmother and her grown-up grandson out for an evening stroll, they set off down the road.

She was eighteen and a shop girl when George waltzed into her life at a tea-dance at the Hotel Grand; he was twenty and a bank teller. When he first asked her if he might have the honour of the next dance, she refused, bending down and pretending to adjust the seam of her best (her only) nylons. He insisted, she refused again, at which point Maureen nudged her in the ribs, hard, and whispered in her ear that she would have to be doolally to let *this* fish slip through the net. He was devilishly handsome, Maureen added. And so he was, and that was what worried Rosemary. Why should so handsome a man pick on so plain a girl as her, not least when there were a dozen prettier among those lined up along the wall? Might he be doing it for a bet?

Nevertheless, she accepted George's third request. It meant something, that he had asked three times. She let him take her hand and lead her out on to the floor, and as the band warbled through a glutinously slow version of 'My Blue Heaven', a muted tenor saxophone carrying the melody, she let him draw her around the ballroom until they were directly under the large crystal chandelier. There, beneath that glittering man-made constellation, he asked her name and told her his, and then they moved off again into the slowly spiralling flow of dancing couples.

He danced well, but that was only to be expected for a man of his polish and sophistication. He led confidently and Rosemary was content to follow, fitting her slingback steps around those of his brogues. She found she was liking the feel of his dry hands and the rasp of his serge trousers against the front of her legs, and just when she was on the verge of enjoying herself, the dance ended, there was applause, and the whole band rose to their feet to hipsway through a faster, jazzier number. George broke contact, stepped back and said, 'Only slow dances for me.'

'Oh?'

'You can lose yourself in a slow dance,' he explained. 'You can drift out of time and it seems that the dance will never end. The fast ones just make time pass more quickly, and we're given so little time, so few years to live, it seems a shame to hurry things along.'

A few moments later Rosemary was worming her way through the cavorting crowd back to Maureen, who grabbed her and said, 'Well?'

'Well what?'

Maureen rolled her eyes. 'Am I talking to a simpleton? Did he ask you out, Rosie? Are you going to see him again?'

'Yes,' said Rosemary vaguely. 'Yes, we're going to the pictures. Tomorrow evening.'

It was a good year for the pictures. Rosemary was especially looking forward to *The Wizard of Oz*, about which she had heard so much, but as it hadn't yet reached this corner of the world she was quite happy to settle for *Wuthering Heights*.

George was late arriving at the cinema, and it occurred to Rosemary as she waited outside that she was being stood up, and just as she was steeling herself to go home, nonchalantly around the corner sauntered George. Catching sight of her, he took the Capstan from his lips, ground it out beneath his heel, then pecked her on the cheek. 'Shall we go in?'

Now that he was here, she was glad that he had been late. She had been hoping to miss the newsreel. He wasn't quite late enough, however, and the few minutes of Pathé they did catch left Rosemary feeling sick and dizzy as the knowledge of what was coming tightened its coils inside her. Not even the Porky Pig short could completely dispel her sense of dread. George smoked his Capstans all the way through the main feature, adding to the wreaths of cigarette mist that floated above the audience's heads, into which the projector shed ghost images – phantoms of Laurence Olivier and Merle Oberon flitting across a spectral moor – before the true images finally reached the screen. Towards the tragic dénouement of the film George took Rosemary's hand in his, enclosing her fingers in smooth dryness. She couldn't be sure through the blur of her own tears, but she had a pretty good idea that he was crying, too.

He was an unusual man, she thought. He looked like a dashing gay blade – and she had met enough of *those* to know what a waste of time they were, mentioning no names, Charlie Blakeney – but he had an intelligence and a subtlety, an intrinsic wryness, an inner smile, that you couldn't help but love. Love? Had she just thought the word 'love'? Silly thing! Warm to. That was what she had meant to think. Or like. You couldn't help but like. Yes.

They walked out into the August evening. The entire western sky from zenith to horizon was filled with milky orange light, as though reflecting the glare of a vast furnace burning over the edge of the world.

'I must be getting home,' she said. 'My parents . . .'

'I understand. May I see you again?'

She laughed in surprise. 'Of course.'

'This weekend?' he said. 'What are you doing this weekend?'

There was not much life in the café. An indolent chef tended chips in a bubbling fat-fryer, every so often giving the basket handle a good shake, the peak of his culinary expertise. A sleepy waitress lounged on the counter watching a studio discussion programme on a portable TV set. The only other patrons apart from Rosemary and George were a pair of grey-headed old men stirring their tea and studying the sports pages. Even the flies circling around the ultraviolet light on the wall seemed in no hurry to close in and meet their deaths on the electrified grille that stood between them and the mesmerising white-purple glow.

'Yes?' the waitress called over to the two new customers as they settled down at a table.

'Nothing for me,' George told Rosemary.

'Just coffee for me,' Rosemary told the waitress, who

repeated the order sardonically (it was hardly stretching her service skills to fetch a cup of coffee). 'I shouldn't,' Rosemary confided to George, 'what with my bladder and all, but then this is a special occasion.'

George was carefully laying the salt and pepper cruets, the sugar cellar and the plastic tomato-shaped ketchup dispenser to one side of the table so that there was nothing except a couple of feet of checked, chipped Formica between him and Rosemary. She in turn removed her tea-cosy hat and her mittens.

'It's no Joe Lyons,' he remarked.

'There aren't any of those any more.' She lowered her voice. 'This is the best we can do.'

'I know. I have been keeping up with current events.'

'Can you do that?'

'I thought you didn't want to know anything about it,' he said with a teasing grin. 'I distinctly heard you say—'

'Yes, sorry, you're right. But you can't blame me for being curious. I'll find out soon enough, won't I?'

He nodded somewhat sadly. 'Don't get your hopes up.'

'We'll be together, though, won't we?'

'Yes,' he said.

'That's all I've ever wanted.'

'It can get frightfully dull.'

'Then we'll liven it up.'

'There are rules.'

'You make it sound so stuffy. That's not like you.'

'I'm simply preparing you. I don't want you to be disappointed.'

The waitress slapped Rosemary's coffee down on the table and looked at George. He shrugged. 'Sorry, I've no money on me.'

Rosemary fumbled for her purse.

The arrangement was that they should meet near her house that Sunday, not actually *at* her house, because she didn't

259

think she was ready for him to meet her parents quite yet, but by the railings of the church a couple of streets away, and then they would take the bus out into the countryside. She was to prepare a picnic, he would bring something to drink. Her mother was wise to the game, but for her father's sake they pretended that Rosemary was going on a jaunt with Maureen, and Maureen helped cement the alibi by coming round the evening before on the pretext of making plans. Maureen giggled a lot and dropped the unsubtlest hints, but Rosemary's father did not cotton on; at least, he gave no indication of cottoning on. He merely told the girls to enjoy themselves, be careful and watch out for strange men. This sent Maureen into gales of laughter. Rosemary was not amused.

George was late, naturally. He didn't seem to be aware that he had no sense of time. He wore a watch and wound it regularly but it was no more than a sartorial adornment, like a tie or a collar stud. Rosemary didn't criticise. It was one of those faults that could only be corrected with constant dedicated attention, in months, not minutes. And she didn't want him to think her a nag. She merely said, 'We've missed one bus already.'

'Then we shall catch the next one,' he replied.

They walked to the bus shelter and waited for the noon bus. The weather was hectic but warm, and Rosemary regretted her decision to wear a tweed skirt. They talked idly, and Rosemary made George laugh with a story about a difficult customer she had had to assist yesterday, a woman who was clearly a size fourteen but who insisted on trying out nothing larger than a ten and then complaining that it was too tight around the bust and waist. When Rosemary had had the temerity to suggest a garment with a little more room in it perhaps, the woman had rounded on her and given her a good ear-bashing. *Are you calling me fat?* she had roared. *Are you implying I'm blooming well fat?* Rosemary could laugh about it now but at the time she had been quite upset.

'The perils of honesty,' said George.

The bus came and George bought two day-return tickets to a small village ten miles west of the city. Half an hour later they alighted on the village green and stood there swaying slightly beneath the oppressive weight of the sun. Ducks preened themselves beside a standing pond and from somewhere there came the sound of a hammer striking an anvil, tolling like a bell.

George spent a moment or two in consultation of his map, then shouldered the knapsack that contained the picnic and two bottles of stout, pointed to the hills, said, 'This way,' and set off at a brisk pace. Rosemary followed.

They soon left the village behind, taking a bridlepath until it met a chalk track that curved upwards into the flank of a hill, then following this. Blackberry bushes sprung about on either side, their fruit mellow red and tightly budded. Trees drooped their branches in the young couple's hair, and in cool recesses of shade flies and gnats swarmed. A dragonfly kept pace with them for a while, supporting itself with a blur of air, until some urgent errand called it away in a wink of electric blue. George took a clinical delight in each and every manifestation of nature, even a spongy cluster of horse droppings; it made a welcome change from the vicissitudes of life behind the teller's window, he claimed. Rosemary agreed. She loved the smell of fresh air.

She didn't want to appear weak and she kept pace with him as best she could, but eventually, when they were about halfway up the hill, she had to beg for a rest. George glanced around and decided this was as good a place as any to stop for lunch, and they sat down on a sloping patch of grass beside the track and ate potted beef and tomato sandwiches and apples and shared a bar of softening chocolate with the entire valley spread out at their feet. George uncapped the beer bottles with a rock and Rosemary drank just enough of hers so that she wouldn't get tipsy and, when George wasn't looking, poured the rest away.

Gazing across to the next ridge of hills, pale with distance, lilac in the haze, she suddenly said, 'Do you think we're really going to war?'

'I think there's a pretty good chance,' said George after a moment's thought, 'now that Mr Hitler and Uncle Joe have joined hands. It all depends. You can't predict these things. We've sworn to protect Poland, and that's good. It's important we show that we're prepared to fight. If we don't do that, we might as well let them walk in and hoist the swastika over Buckingham Palace tomorrow.'

'Can't we talk with them? Bargain? Negotiate?'

'We can. We have. We should keep on doing so, and we should hope for the best but prepare for the worst.'

'But so many people will die.'

'Come on, old girl,' said George, leaping lithely to his feet and extending a hand. 'Let's not think about that. Not today. Let's think about it when it happens.'

They gathered up their things and began the slow steady climb to the top.

For the next four weeks, and then even after war was declared, they spent their Sundays this way, taking the bus to some remote unpopulated area and losing themselves in the vastness of the land. They would find trails and byways not marked on the map and follow them to their conclusion, which was more often than not a dead end or a gate leading to farmland and signposted KEEP OUT. They had a none-too-perilous encounter with an angry bull, and passed the whole of one afternoon lying in long grass watching a ploughman and team convert a fallow field to a corded rectangle of dark brown earth. Conversation as they walked was unforced and easy, and when they were out of breath or had run out of things to say they carried on in companionable silence, the subtle background sigh of the countryside filling in the vacancies. It never rained on their Sundays.

The inevitable meeting with Rosemary's parents went well. George and her father discovered a mutual love of Will Hay, and one whole course of the meal was taken up with improvised quickfire music-hall repartee which left the men red-faced and helpless with laughter and Rosemary and her mother nonplussed but quietly smiling. After George went home, her father's seal of approval was characteristically terse: 'Nice fellow. You can bring him round again.'

George's parents lived in London, so the obligation did not have to be reciprocated, at least not yet, and Rosemary was relieved. She doubted she would have made as good an impression on George's parents as he had on hers, for she behaved awkwardly in the company of strangers, and she was hardly the sort of girl she imagined George's mother had in mind for her son. She had few illusions about that. Looking in the mirror at her little nose and drab brown eyes and narrow lips, Rosemary wondered again what George had first seen in her at the tea-dance, what had drawn him – heart in mouth, or so he claimed – all the way across the ballroom floor. What *was* it? What quality did she possess that was invisible to everyone except him? Was he playing some sort of game with her? She knew there was a certain kind of man who liked to string a dull plain girl along while romancing a whole chorus line of glittering beauties behind her back, returning to the dull plain girl whenever one of the glittering beauties rejected him because the dull plain girl was always there, the dull plain girl would inevitably be waiting for him; but they were a vicious breed, such men, a terrier breed. Charlie Blakeney was one. Although he had taken Rosemary out on a number of occasions, and had once asked her to marry him, Maureen had told her that he kept a gaggle of dolly-birds on the go, flitting from one to the next. Besides, he was flash with his money, and flash men only wanted one thing from a girl.

George was not like that at all. He would never betray her like that.

She picked up the coffee and sipped at it loudly. George stared at her, just curiously, with a slight flicker of amusement in his eyes. There were argumentative shouts from the portable television. She set the coffee down again, not sure she had even tasted it.

At last she said, 'Does it hurt?'

'Does it still hurt?'

'No, I mean in general. When it happens. Does it hurt everyone?'

George sighed. 'To be honest, love, I wouldn't know. I know it hurt *me*, but that's because it took about a day, after the wound, a day lying in a cot in the field hospital with this heaviness in my chest, this feeling of wrongness, and blood filling my throat, and—'

She held up her hands, wincing. 'Please. I can't bear it.'

'I thought you wanted to know.'

'In general. No details.'

'It varies from person to person, that's all I can tell you. Some slip peacefully away, no struggle. Others linger.'

'I'm prepared for it to hurt. I don't mind a bit of pain. Especially if I know there's an end to it and something beyond.'

'There's an end,' George assured her.

Night had drifted down outside, and Rosemary caught sight of herself in the window, and the other diners and the waitress and the chef, all pale ghosts in the darkened glass. Of George in that black mirror-café there was no sign, yet there he was sitting right in front of her. She wondered if anyone else would notice that her companion cast no reflection.

There were all kinds of pain.

There was pain the day George volunteered. He came round to her house as soon as the bank closed, and even as she stood at the top of the stairs while her mother opened the front door, Rosemary knew what he had done, because his face was calm, the self-control more in evidence than ever before, and because a recruiting office had opened up on the high street yesterday afternoon. Before he could even say, 'Hello, Mrs Thomas,' to her mother, Rosemary turned and fled to her room.

His knock was quiet and polite. He had never been in her bedroom before. 'Love? Love?' He opened the door softly. He looked for her on the bed but she wasn't there; she was standing at the window with her arms folded and her head held high, gazing out at the rows of roofs that rolled away and grew fainter in the thick autumnal twilight. He came to her and took her waist in his hands and turned her gently around to face him. He was surprised to see tears. He simply had not prepared himself for tears. He reached for his handkerchief, this being the appropriate thing to do, and she let him dab it around her eyes. If it made him feel better.

'I can't explain it,' he said, leading her to the bed and sitting her down and sitting himself down beside her. 'I can't expect you to understand.'

'Why? Am I stupid or something?'

'It had to be done.' Not *I had to do it*. It had to be done. 'I saw that poster in the window, and it was as if it was calling out to me.'

'But I thought you said we should negotiate.'

'But it's too late for that now. It's been tried and it's failed. I said we should hope for the best but prepare for the worst, and the worst has happened. I can't simply ignore it now. I have to show how I feel.'

'So much of being a man is about show,' she said, half to herself. She thought she hated him then, but that hate was just a darker love.

'It would have happened anyway,' he said, as if this was some compensation. 'This war isn't going to be won overnight, and sooner or later they're going to have to start calling people up. I'm young, I'm healthy, and being a bank teller is hardly vital to the national interest. It would only have been a matter of time.'

'So when do you leave?'

'A fortnight tomorrow.'

'Where are you going?'

'A camp down on the coast. After that, who knows? But

I'll write to you. I'll write every day. If that's what you want.'

It wasn't what she wanted but, all things being equal, it was the best she could hope for.

And there was pain that final fortnight: a long drawn-out ache of loss that tainted everything Rosemary did, made her dreary work days drearier, fragmented her sleep into short naps that lengthened the night, and, on evenings out with George, required her to wear a brittle mask of jollity from beginning to end. He for his part gamely struggled to be himself and keep her amused at all times, and she smiled whenever possible, and both of them avoided the subject that they had to avoid, but the anticipation of their parting lurked behind their laughter, dogged them along the gas-lit streets, trailed them into restaurants and clubs, and squatted at their feet sighing quietly throughout their goodnight kisses on the front doorstep to her parents' house. It was as if the sadness to come had cast its shadow back through time, and the closer they came to the day George had to leave, the deeper, broader and thicker that shadow grew.

And there was a special kind of pain the very last Sunday they shared together.

As usual – even after only a couple of months the habit had worn itself comfortably smooth into their lives – they packed up a picnic and took the bus out into the countryside, to walk and lose and find themselves. It was the first day that really felt like autumn. The air smelled of brown leaves and bonfires and had that cold tang that would not really disappear now until spring. Trees slumped (the effort of summer having finally taken its toll) and, with the harvest in, the fields were turned and empty and expectant. Rooks like priests and inland gulls like white-coated doctors ministered to the broken earth, dragging out worms and grubs. In two days' time, George would be on the train to the coast.

They picked their way through the raw landscape until they found a spot to eat their picnic on the wrinkled slope of a hill.

Rosemary drank all of her bottle of stout, pouring none away, and then said, 'You will be careful, won't you? When you get out there?'

'Careful? As in dodge bullets? As in hold back while everyone else is charging forwards? I can't be careful, old girl, I can only be lucky.'

'You sound brave.'

'I'm scared silly. I don't want to die any more than you do.'

'Then don't die!' It was a ridiculous thing to say but, through a mist of sorrow and anger and beer, it made perfect sense to her. You could choose not to die in the same way that you could choose not to live. It wasn't a question of bullets or grenades or shells or gas. It was a question of belief.

'I'll try,' George said, taking her hand and patting it. 'I'll do my level best. When it's over, I'll come back for you, and we'll . . .'

'Yes?'

That was when he should have asked her to marry him, on that cool green hillside on that brisk afternoon. Why didn't he? What stopped him? What thought came to him holding a grim finger to its lips? A foreboding? Fear of tempting providence? Or was it merely the fear of making a promise that he did not know for certain that he would be able to keep? That was most likely it. And when he turned away, Rosemary could tell what he was thinking. She had seen it in his face. He was thinking, *Well, there'll be time enough for that later, when I come back and there's a future again. There'll be time for plans and schemes and dreams. There'll always be time.*

'We'll see,' is what he said eventually.

It was then that a magpie swooped down, landing with uncharacteristic boldness less than five yards away from them. It stood for a while, gazing at them both with eyes that were filled with deep, dark, glittering avian understanding, and then it seemed to come to a decision and it opened its beak and it cried: *ak-ak-ak-ak-ak! ak-ak! ak-ak-ak-ak-ak!*

And Rosemary, remembering something her mother used to say when she was little, that the chattering of magpies signified a death, felt a coldness steal over her.

And there was a unique pain in the bus shelter that night.

The city was silent and dark, and inside the bus shelter was darker still, and on the slats of the wooden bench, awkwardly, Rosemary gave herself to George.

During the clumsy overtures, as they shuffled into position, clothing rustling about them, he asked her in a choked whisper if it was safe, wasn't there some risk if he . . . ? And she hushed him and said it was safe, she had seen to it that it was safe, perfectly safe.

It was only the whitest shade of a lie. Maureen, being better versed in such matters than she, had given Rosemary sound advice on choosing her moment, striking when the iron was, so to speak, cooling, and Rosemary had listened carefully because she wanted nothing more to come from this moment than a memory.

And the memory was made of this: of George's quickening gasps, of his fingernails digging through her jersey into the flesh of her back, of the terror of being caught, of his final cry, of her relief as he climbed off her that no one had chanced along. But above all the memory was of the initial exquisite lancing between her legs. That pain fixed the memory into place like a pin through a butterfly.

And there was more pain when it came to accompanying George on the bus down to the railway station and saying goodbye to him there, but this pain was mitigated by the fact that she had been preparing herself for it for over a fortnight. It was like the pain of an injection, worse in the anticipation than the execution. Surrounded by clouds of steam and other couples parting, it was also a pain shared and therefore lessened. The two of them simply clutched one another, just as the other couples were clutching, and their kisses were no different from anyone else's kisses, just a pair of lips pressing a pair of lips, and then the train's whistle screeched impatiently and George clambered up into the carriage and had to go. He waved to her all the way down the platform. He waved until he dissolved in steam.

'We're closing now,' the waitress informed them without a hint of apology. 'You'd better be off.' The two old men with the sports pages, being regulars here, knowing the form, had left a few minutes ago.

'It's all right,' said Rosemary. 'We were just going anyway. We've got a bus to catch.'

George rose to help her to her feet. She did not refuse his hand. Her hip bones were a little stiff.

'Come on,' said the waitress, holding open the door. 'I haven't got all bloody evening.'

'You're frightfully rude,' George said, and the waitress puckered her mouth as though she had just swallowed a sour grape.

'Out,' she said.

They went out into the night, and just as the waitress was about to close the door behind them George turned and said, 'January, eleven years from now.'

The waitress scowled. 'You what?'

'Ovarian cancer.'

The waitress's expression brightened and she returned a contemptuous grin. 'Wrong. Pisces, *actually*.'

George just smiled, and it was only after he and Rosemary had walked well out of earshot that she asked him what all that had been about.

'She won't even think about it until the time comes, and then she'll remember,' he said, looking satisfied.

'Oh,' said Rosemary, understanding. 'Wasn't that a bit mean? I must say I don't recall you ever being cruel like that. Not even to be kind.'

'I can't help having changed, love. Just the waiting itself wore me down. The boredom was enough to turn the sweetest nature bitter. From time to time, I screamed for release.'

'And isn't there release?'

'Only for those allowed to take it.'

'And weren't you?'

George halted to look at her. 'Don't you see?'

She shook her head.

'I made a promise.' He said it as if it were the most obvious thing in the world. 'I made a promise to you. And you held me to it by waiting.'

'Oh my God.' Her hand flew to her whiskery mouth.

'By waiting, all day, every day,' he said with a confirming nod.

'Oh my good God, I never thought . . . It never occurred . . . I never realised . . .'

'Of course you didn't, old girl.'

'Fifty-two years,' she said with a sigh, a wisp of breath in the wind. 'If I'd known . . .'

'I don't hold it against you. If I hold it against anyone, it's whoever made up the rules of the game and then refused to explain them to us.'

'How can I say I'm sorry?'

'Don't.'

'All that time . . .'

'It wasn't so bad,' he said, in the same airy dismissive tone that she had said, *It's been quite a wait*, just after he stepped off the bus. 'For either of us. Was it?'

'But at least I had a life.'

'Did you?' he asked matter-of-factly. 'Did you really? How different was your existence from mine? Not much. You weren't living, you were just going through the motions, that's all. At least I didn't have to pretend that.'

'I never realised,' she said again.

'That's the tragedy of it,' he said. 'Neither of us did.'

His letters from camp were filled with amusing little episodes that happened during training, jokes at the expense of the RSM, thumbnail sketches of his comrades and cheerfully blithe descriptions of the privations and hardships of military life – cleaning the latrines on a frosty morning, the greasy food doled out in the mess, being shouted at from dawn till dusk, and the sheer daily fatigue that, come bedtime, made a camp bed seem as soft and welcoming as a king-sized feather divan. He always signed off on an optimistic note. 'Everyone keeps telling us to keep our chins up,' one letter ended, 'but I know you'll be doing that anyway, old girl, so all I can say is keep yours higher than the rest of them. I remain, yours affectionately, G.'

She tried, for his sake, and her mother and Maureen rallied round. Her mother kept her busy around the house. She had taken on piecework, and enlisted Rosemary to spend a couple of hours with her each evening mending trousers and reattaching buttons, their needles darting while her father read the paper by the sighing grate. Maureen, meanwhile, became a surrogate George, dragging Rosemary out to the pictures and tea-dances. Her father, for his part, was not unaware of the situation and did his best to keep his daughter entertained at mealtimes with solo Will Hay routines, although these, being closely associated in her mind with George, caused her as much pain as they did pleasure. And she wrote to George almost daily, matching him anecdote for anecdote, keeping him informed about funny and finicky customers, giving small critiques of films she had seen because there were no cinemas near the camp, and trying to show him that she was getting on with her life as normal, as he wanted, while still making it clear that things were not the same. The closest she came to saying she missed him was mentioning their Sunday day trips, which was the one role of George's that Maureen could not and would not fill. 'When you come back,' she wrote, 'we shall each buy a bicycle or perhaps even a tandem (!) and pedal our way further and further out of town. We shall form our very own cycling club and we shall go when we like and where we like.'

In George's last letter from camp the levity was still there, but between the lines there was agony and, as the letter progressed, the agony seeped out.

Basic training is complete (he wrote), and I am now a full-fledged Private in the King's army, or so I am told, although I don't feel any different, I just feel like a bank teller in a uniform with big boots and a gun. Nothing else here has changed, either. The food is still awful and the weather is still rotten and the Sergeant Major is still both. The wind from the sea smells foul, like bad fish. I long for the still sweet air of home. (Ho ho!)

But here's the bad news, old girl. (But as you turned nineteen last week, perhaps I ought to be calling you 'young woman' instead!) We've been given our marching orders. It's time to up sticks and go. Britannia calls, England expects and all that. We'll be shipping out in four days' time. What do you know? Action! So soon! As for where we're going, I'm not at liberty to say, malheureusement, but rest assured that I will be keeping an eye out for myself. I won't forget what you said about not dying. Why would I be so stupid as to get myself killed when there's so much to live for?

In the past I haven't promised you anything, Rosemary. This is not because I had no promises to make but because I did not want to make a promise I couldn't keep. I realise now that this was a mistake, now when it is almost – but still not! – too late to rectify the error. I realise that my notion of honesty was misguided. I believed that if I said anything to you that contained the smallest hint of a lie, it would somehow hurt you, damage you in some way, that you were a tender fragile creature to whom it was better to say nothing than say something untrue. But little lies are necessary, useful things, as necessary and useful as – if you will pardon a slightly crude analogy – manure is to a rose.

It doesn't matter if a promise is made that cannot be kept as long as it is made with every intention of being kept. I particularly regret not promising that I would come home safe and well, and I make that promise now, here, on paper, in black ink. Lacking the witness of your own eyes, I will call on God instead.

I promise that I will come home. I promise that I will come home to you, Rosemary. Come what may, I will be back. One day, when the fighting's done, I will take the bus from the station and you will meet me at the shelter where you gave me my first glimpse of the truth about necessary lies, and there I will make another promise to you, the promise I should have made on that hillside on that cold Sunday afternoon, that we will be together. Always.

I don't know when you will get another letter from me, love. I will write, but I can't vouch for the postal system. It's bad enough here. Imagine what it's going to be like abroad!

My fondest regards to your parents and to Maureen – and to you, old girl, the promise.

Yours affectionately, G.

The next letter she received, three months later, was not from George but from his mother. It began:

'Dear Rosemary Thomas,

'As a precaution, my son gave me your address before he left, and although we have not met, I am not ignorant of the regard in which he held you, and so I feel that it is only right and fair that you, after his close relatives, should be the first to be informed . . .'

They were near the bus shelter now. From a distance, with its tiled roof and sturdy walls, it looked like a tiny house, a single tiny house at the side of an uncommonly wide road.

The wind pounded at their backs, urging them on, but George was in no hurry and Rosemary was certainly in no hurry. These were her last few steps on this earth. She savoured them. She savoured the taste of the city air in her mouth, the sight of the city's grey-sea skyline, the sound of the wind batting at her ears, the slap of her coat-tails around her legs, the pressure of George's hand on her arm, the sensation of her body still working, her muscles still propelling her, her bones still obliging, her heart still thumping, the blood still rolling through her veins and the breath still heaving in and out of her lungs. She cherished the little life left to her, her last possession of any value, even as she prepared herself to surrender it up.

At the entrance they stopped.

'What do we do?' she asked.

'We just sit.'

'Will it be long?'

'Not long.'

The tramp reek inside wasn't bad, once she had resigned herself to it. George seemed not to notice. Used, discarded containers of one kind or another littered the floor: crisp packets, condoms, fish-and-chip newspaper. Crudely scrawled messages of love and hate on the walls, with their numerals and misspellings, were so many incomprehensible hieroglyphs.

George heard the bus first, when the rumble of its engine was still beyond the threshold of normal human hearing. He put his cool dry hand on Rosemary's.

'Here it comes,' he said. 'Don't be scared.'

'I'm not scared.'

'Good girl.'

At that moment she felt a slight discomfort, a little like a twinge of trapped wind in her innards, but it quickly passed, and then she could hear it too: the distant grind of cogs meshing, teeth gnashing, gears and gear-shafts, wheels turning, coming closer, combustion, a thousand tiny fiery detonations per second, approaching, the low steady thrum of rubber tread on tarmac, the wheeze of exhaust, getting nearer now and nearer and nearer still, the churning engine, the thunderous engine, growing in size and might until the noise drowned all others and was the only noise in the whole world, an immense, engulfing roar of motion and travel and revolution and repetition, and at last the bus appeared in the entrance to the shelter, sliding across the doorway and filling the aperture with dusty green and rectangles of glass, and came to a halt with a hiss of hydraulics and a sigh of pneumatics.

'Now,' said George kindly. 'Are you ready?'

'Of course.'

They stood up and stepped out.

Clouds of fumes purled around the bus and great shudders passed through it, the pulsing vibrations of the idling motor rattling its windows.

The doors concertinaed open. Rosemary peered up at the dark driver within. He was smiling whitely, brightly.

'All aboard,' he said.

She turned to George. 'There's no pain,' she said. This was almost a revelation. 'There's no pain at all.'

'The Landlady's Dog' first appeared in *Narrow Houses* (Little, Brown, 1992); 'Wings' in *Heaven Sent* (Creed, 1995); 'Satisfaction Guaranteed' in *FEAR* (October 1990); 'Britworld™' in *Interzone* (December 1992); 'The House of Lazarus' in *Destination Unknown* (Borealis, 1997); 'The Driftling' in *Interzone* (July 1997); 'Dead Letters' in *Scaremongers* (Tanjen, 1997); 'A Taste of Heaven' in *Dante's Disciples* (Borealis, 1995); 'The Gift' in *Interzone* (February 1996, under the title 'Giving and Taking'); 'Thanatophile Seeks Similar' in *The Third Alternative* #16 (1998); and 'Rosemary for Remembrance' in *Blue Motel: Narrow Houses 3* (Little, Brown, 1994). A big thank you to all the editors of the above – Andy Cox, Peter Crowther, John Gilbert, Andrew Haigh, Ed Kramer, David Pringle – for commissioning the stories and/or accepting them for publication.

'Nana' and 'The Unmentionable' appear for the first time in this collection.